CATRIONA'S SECRET

MADELINE MARTIN

Copyright 2019 © Madeline Martin

CATRIONA'S SECRET © 2019 Madeline Martin. ALL RIGHTS RESERVED. No part or the whole of this book may be reproduced, distributed, transmitted or utilized (other than for reading by the intended reader) in ANY form (now known or hereafter invented) without prior written permission by the author. The unauthorized reproduction or distribution of this copyrighted work is illegal, and punishable by law.

CATRIONA'S SECRET is a work of fiction. The characters and events portrayed in this book are fictional and or are used fictitiously and solely the product of the author's imagination. Any similarity to real persons, living or dead, places, businesses, events or locales is purely coincidental.

Cover Design by Teresa Sprecklemeyer @ The Midnight Muse Designs.

To John

Thank you for being the hero of my story and for our own happily ever after. I love you.

1

May 1341
Brampton, England

Lady Catriona Barrington awoke to a familiar clenching of her stomach. She squeezed her eyes shut against the discomfort in the hopes it would pass. It did sometimes.

She hated this queasiness. It reminded her of the sensation of being drunk, of having too much wine. Of that regrettable night with too many bad decisions. She hadn't had a sip of wine since.

That had been nearly two months ago, and still the memory was so strong in her mind. The wine, the poor decisions, Sir Gawain, that resonating hollowness within her.

She shuddered under a fresh wave of nausea. Sweat prickled at her brow. She was losing her battle with the strange illness that had plagued her since her return to Werrick Castle.

Isla thought it might be the switch from English fare to the more rustic food of the border. Cat had accepted the explanation and hadn't bothered to seek further counsel, even though she continued to be ill. Eventually, she would readjust to the food at home. Wouldn't she?

Cat's mouth filled with a flood of saliva. She clenched her hands into the sheets, inundated by thoughts of Sir Gawain's whispered promises and flattery.

All of court had been thus: promises and flattery. Resplendent with costly fabric and sparkling gems that lay like a fine veneer over all the cultured courtiers.

Her older sister, Ella, had always been the one to sway toward romance, but even Cat had fallen prey to the seduction of court. There she was not merely a younger sister, but a woman in the prime of her life, ripe for wooing. She had felt beautiful, special.

She did not feel either such thing on the last night of her time at court, when she'd accompanied Sir Gawain into the rose-laden alcove. What had followed had been over quickly enough to send her reeling, leaving her with a sticky mess and regret.

He had not mentioned marriage, but she could not help but think of it. She ought to marry him after what they had done.

Cat lurched upright, yanked crudely from her unpleasant thoughts. Her attempt to put off her illness had left her with scarcely enough time to reach the ewer before her stomach divested itself of any remaining food in her stomach from the night before.

When she'd first returned to Werrick Castle and found her effects moved to her mother's former room, Cat's reaction had been a blend of emotions. Disappointment to no longer share a room with her youngest sister, Leila, after eighteen years of having done so. But there was also an appreciation for her own maturity in now occupying her mother's room, as all her older sisters had before her. Now, Cat was simply grateful.

She was able to keep everyone from worrying unnecessarily over her while she readjusted to food on the border.

After she'd cleaned herself, she made her way down to the

great hall. A familiar voice among the conversations floated toward her.

Marin.

The realization that Cat's eldest sister was visiting sent her speeding through the stone archway and into the wide expanse of the great hall. She'd always loved this room best in all the castle. It was where life happened, dances and weddings and feasts. Troubadours' voices echoed in the great space as they spun their tales and added their own spice of magic to the room already filled with colorful tapestries.

And now this room brought her a reunion with Marin, whom she had not seen in more than a year. Marin got to her feet as soon as her gaze landed on Catriona.

Women as tall as Marin often wore their height like an ill-fitting mantle. But not Marin. Nay, she rose like a queen, her slender frame regal and beautiful.

"My precious Cat." She opened her arms and drew Cat into her embrace.

Cat remained cradled against Marin for a long moment. Perhaps too long, but Cat didn't care. She could stay forever hugged against Marin, breathing in the comforting scent of lavender that always surrounded her sister. Cat had been only six when their mother had died, thus Marin had been more mother to her than their own.

"I hear you've been unwell." Marin released Cat and examined her with a concerned eye.

Cat waved her off and smiled as brilliantly as she could muster. "'Tis naught to concern yourself with. I simply need to get accustomed to border food again after all the rich fare at court."

"I hear you had a lovely time at court." Marin tilted her head in suspicion. "You attracted the attention of quite a few eligible nobles."

She simply shrugged as the heat blazed in her cheeks. Sir

Gawain would likely propose marriage soon and they would all know exactly which noble's attention she had caught.

Marin laughed. "If you are being quiet, then what I heard must be true." She withdrew a missive from her bag. "I was visiting with Ella and she asked me to give you this."

"That was so kind of you to bring it all the way here to me." It was all Cat could do to remain calm as she took the note. It was even more difficult to keep from tearing it open to read what Ella had written. No doubt it contained the requested information on Sir Gawain, exactly as Cat had asked.

"Of course, I was already planning to visit." Marin peered at the entrance of the hall. Not once, but several times. Cat turned to regard the empty corridor behind her to see what pulled at Marin's attention.

"Forgive me." Marin flushed. "I confess, I'm also here to see Isla, in the hopes she might offer some advice on what I can do to encourage my ability to conceive."

"Oh, Marin." Cat's heart flinched for her sister's barrenness. It was so unfair that the one who had been mother to them all for the last eighteen years would now be without her own children.

"I'm not unhappy with my life," Marin said quickly. Her face softened. "I'm incredibly happy at Kendal with Bran. It is quiet and peaceful. Mayhap a little too peaceful now that his sister and her family have moved to their own home." The familiar, wistful smile tugged at the corners of her lips, the same as it always did when she spoke of her Bran. He'd been an unlikely husband when he'd threatened to kill Cat in order to breach Werrick Castle's walls seven years prior.

She'd forgiven him almost immediately when she realized he'd managed to take the castle with only one single death. Eversham. The brave soldier's name would forever be emblazoned on her heart. He had fought valiantly to keep Cat from being used as bait to force open the castle gates.

Cat fingered her letter, prodding her fingertips with the

corners as she listened to Marin, who always took the time to give everyone her full attention.

"Regardless of what I try, of how much I pray, I continue to get my courses." Marin glanced at the hall again. "Ella suggested I see Isla."

Something tickled at Cat's mind. She hadn't had her courses since just before going to court and hadn't had them again since she'd returned. Cold prickled all over her.

"Ah, there she is." Marin reached for Cat's hand. "Say a prayer for me."

Cat simply nodded, mute with the force of the sudden realization. How could she still be sensitive to food she'd spent a lifetime eating? Especially when Nan was such an exceptional cook.

Cat had heard women with child were often ill. One of her sisters, Anice, had mentioned as much before. Typically, the illness occurred in the morning. Cat's pulse thundered in her ears with the very real possibility that had not dawned on her until that very moment.

She could be with child.

With shaking hands, she wrenched open the letter from Ella, tearing through the Countess of Calville's carefully stamped seal without ceremony. In desperation. Had Sir Gawain asked after her? Sought to see her again? Asked for her hand in marriage?

They would have to be wed soon, of course. Immediately. The thought sent a shudder racing down her spine. But she could not think now on if she wanted to wed him or not.

She unfolded her sister's missive with haste and skimmed over the carefully curling letters looping across the parchment. There were several noblemen asking about Catriona after she'd left; one in particular, Lord Loughton, wanted to see her again so that she might meet his son who would be a wonderful match. Ella strongly encouraged the introduction. Cat drew her brows at that and read on. Why was Ella not mentioning Sir Gawain?

More details on men who had showed interest, then a bit of information on Ella's daughter, Blanche.

Nearly panting in her frenzy for any news about Gawain, Cat flipped to the back of the page where one short paragraph was written. One awful, damning paragraph.

You asked after Sir Gawain, and I tell you that you need not waste another breath on him. I learned that not only has he been married for some time, but that his wife is soon to bear their first child.

Whatever strength had been holding Cat upright drained from her. She put her hand to the table to brace herself and carefully lowered herself to the bench.

She touched her hand to her stomach as another wave of nausea rolled through her.

Cat's gaze went to the empty hall where Marin had departed with such hope, so desperate for what Cat did not want and irony's cruel twist had most likely delivered upon her.

For there was a very strong possibility that Cat was carrying a married man's child.

FOUR YEARS HAD PASSED SINCE GEORDIE STRAFFORD LEFT Werrick Castle. Now it rose before him, larger and far grander than even he remembered. The king's coffers ran low from the war campaign and he'd sent the vast majority of his force home, including Geordie, who had no real home.

With parents who had abandoned him, leaving him to be slain for their sins, and no wife, Geordie returned to the closest thing to a home he had: Werrick Castle. To Cat.

His heart pounded in a collision of excitement, anticipation and nerves. He hadn't seen Cat in four years, though they had exchanged missives when he was somewhere long enough to receive one. His gaze skimmed the top of the castle wall, seeking out a woman with ribbons of gold hair dancing in the sunlight, her bow drawn back to track his approach.

But there were only Werrick guards. And no white-fledged arrow sank into the ground when he got within an archer's range. She was still at Werrick Castle, was she not?

But then, he had not received a letter in several months. Had she been married off, as Lady Ella had? The thought churned his stomach. If Cat was not at Werrick castle, was it still home?

He did not ask after Cat when a soldier called down for him to announce himself, nor did he see her in the bailey. Lord Werrick emerged from the keep and gave him a hearty embrace as soon as Geordie disembarked from his steed.

"My boy," the older man said fondly. "Has the campaign finally run its course?"

"For now," Geordie confirmed. "Until the king can secure more coin, from what I understand."

"And you, a knight." The Earl of Werrick nodded in approval.

Geordie's chest swelled with the praise. Lord Werrick was as close to a father as he'd ever had, and Geordie had spent his entire life in the pursuit of the honor of becoming a knight. A profession of the most noble, to compensate for his true father's notorious perfidy. It was an accomplishment Geordie was proud of. One he could not wait to share with Cat.

He glanced about the courtyard but did not see her.

Lady Leila, the youngest of the Earl of Werrick's five daughters, welcomed him next. The little girl had grown into a lovely young woman. His fellow knights would have tripped over themselves to bestow her with trite endearments of affection and nonsensical sonnets. She gave him a huge smile and embraced him. The scent of dried herbs told him she was still dabbling in the art of healing.

"It's good to have you back." Lady Leila released him and stepped back. "Cat will be overjoyed to see you again."

"Is she—"

Before he could finish the question, Drake, Werrick Castle's Captain of the Guard, clasped arms with him in greeting. "Sir Georgie." He flashed a wide grin at him and emphasized the word "Sir."

"You'll be in these ranks soon," Geordie promised. If it weren't for the constant training from Drake, Geordie might never have succeeded in becoming a knight at all. Or lived through battle, for that matter.

"Being half-Scottish doesna recommend me." Drake spoke stoically, as though it didn't matter, but Geordie knew it did. They had always shared their hopes of becoming knights.

A howl of delight turned Geordie's head. A large woman with gray hair peeking beneath a floppy mob cap bustled toward him and stopped abruptly. "Surely, this isn't my Geordie." Nan, the castle cook, cast a playfully shrewd look up at him. "He was a stick of a lad, as tall as he was thin."

Geordie offered a helpless shrug.

"Always the quiet one." She leaned close and offered a saucy wink. "You just wait 'til Cat sets her eyes on you."

Geordie's pulse spiked. "Is she here?"

Nan's kindly face split into a wide smile. "That she is, but she's only been home for a bit of time since her jaunt at court. You've got excellent timing."

"How is she?" Geordie asked the simple question, rather than the storm of the ones assaulting his mind. Was she healthy? Was she happy? Had she missed him? Had she become betrothed?

It was the last question that left a gnawing at his gut.

Nans lips pulled downward. "She's been ill since returning from court. The food there might have been too much for her. Aside from that, she's been as bright as the sun, the same as she's always been." Nan winked at him. "And always eager to get a letter from you."

Warmth touched his cheeks at Nan's last comment. "She is well now?"

Geordie had only been to court once for a sennight, but he knew how rich the food could be, and how vastly different than the fare Nan dished out.

"I've not heard of any more complaints of her illness, and she looks bonny as ever." Nan clasped her hands to her chest. "I'm so delighted to have you home. I'll make some roast pheasant in honor of your arrival." She hesitated. "If you still care for pheasant..."

It was all too easy to recall Nan's roasted pheasant, baked within a wall of bread and rising from a sea of roasted vegetables. After nothing but cold cheese, murky ale and the tough bit of grain they called bread at taverns, the idea of getting such a meal was nearly more than he could bear.

"Oh, aye," he confirmed. "I very much like pheasant still, especially if you already have some on hand. You needn't go out of your way on my behalf."

"I don't." Nan swept at a dusting of flour on her apron. "But, I'm on fine terms with the butcher." A flush colored her cheeks.

Geordie stared at Nan with curious assessment. Was she actually blushing? "You mean the butcher you hated when he first bought old Betsy's business?"

Nan gave a girlish giggle. "Edmund is not so bad once you get to know him."

Any other questions Geordie might have asked died away on his tongue as the slender figure of a young woman filled the entrance to the keep. She strode outside, into a beam of sunlight that lit her hair like rare gold and made the deep sapphire blue of her eyes glow. If Cat had been ill, she did not look it now. She radiated with good health, her cheeks and lips a becoming shade of pink.

She stopped abruptly, then gave a squeal of delight and rushed toward him, not stopping until she had thrown herself into his arms. He embraced her gently despite her firm grip around him and breathed in her delicate floral scent. She still smelled the same, like summer roses fresh in bloom on a sunny day.

"Geordie." She eased back and looked up at him, no longer a girl, but very much a woman.

The most beautiful woman in all the world.

High cheekbones showed where once her cheeks had been apple round, and he noticed for the first time how full her lips were, how supple. But it was more than just her face, it was her body as well. Her waist nipped in at the middle, then flared out with a swell of womanly hips, and her narrow chest had blossomed into firm, rounded breasts. He was staring. He knew it and yet he could not stop himself.

But he was not the only one.

She gazed at him, lost in her own observation. Her mouth parted. "Geordie," she said his name again.

Even her voice had lost its childish softness and was now stronger, with confidence and sensual femininity.

All at once, those four years of separation, the hollow loneliness, the letters having to make do for her absence, they all faded away. Catriona. Cat. *His* Cat.

She was all that mattered. And with her, he was finally, truly home.

2

Cat knew she was staring. She ought to say something more than his name. But her tongue remained rooted in her mouth, stuck in a tangle of emotions. Geordie was home. Finally.

She wanted to throw her arms around him again and hold tight to his tall, strong body. And he was strong. Far more than he'd been when she'd seen him last. He'd been a skinny youth with a lanky gait. He certainly was not that boy anymore, and his embrace had been everything her soul needed.

Only, she could not allow herself to give in to another hug, or the fragile dam holding back her emotions might break. If that happened, the tears might never stop flowing as the whirlwind of the day claimed her. She was with child, made so by a man who was already married. And now Geordie was home. Of all days.

It was so much. Too much. The worst and the best and completely overwhelming.

"Ach, go on, the both of you, say something." Nan nudged at Catriona's shoulder.

Geordie gazed down at Cat with eyes she knew well, tender and brown with an edge of pain that never abated. Sad eyes, she'd once thought of them. Eyes to the soul, she now knew.

At that moment, his mouth lifted in a smile, an expression as familiar as his eyes.

His embrace, however, had been different. Where once he'd had a thin chest and arms, now his body was a solid wall against her cheek, and his strong arms protective in the most wonderful ways.

There was so much she had wanted to say. How badly she'd missed him. How Werrick Castle had been different without him. How she'd thought of him every day. How in her darkest moments, she feared to never see him again.

This man in front of her had taken her aback at how very masculine he had become. No longer a boy, but a warrior. And what must he think of her?

In the time since he left Werrick Castle, she had grown breasts, and the fit of her gown cradled the outline of a woman's curves. It made her suddenly reticent to think on how much her own body had changed. He'd noticed it, she knew. His eyes had swept over her when she'd first released him from her embrace. Quick. Assessing. More polite than her own ogling.

"Come, then," Nan said, ever one to come to the rescue. "Let's get some food into you. I'm sure the journey was a long one and without a fine, solid meal."

Geordie's eyes met Cat's before shifting back to the cook. "None as good as yours, to be sure."

"Flattery works on me every time, and you well know it, Sir Geordie." Nan winked at him and ordered one of the servants to take his effects to Geordie's room, then led them to the kitchen. She nudged them toward a small table. "Sit there while I go fetch you some pastries that I made earlier. Your favorite—honey. I'm so pleased I decided to make them, as the timing was perfect."

With that, she bustled away to fetch the pastries. Cat sat down in the hard-backed wooden chair opposite Geordie. For the first time in four years, Cat and Geordie were alone. He offered a shy smile and her heart immediately went warm.

"Sir Geordie," Cat breathed in admiration for her friend. "You did exactly what you said you were going to."

He flushed. "I never would have had the chance if you hadn't recommended me as a squire. If you hadn't saved my life."

His humility was as familiar, and just as endearing, as it had always been. "Papa would never have killed you," Cat said.

It was an exchange they'd debated for years, stretching back to the time when Geordie was a boy of only seven. His father, Lord Strafford, had given him as collateral in an agreement with the Earl of Werrick, and then reneged. Doubtless the baron had never intended to make good on his agreement and was willing to sacrifice his spare heir.

"If you hadn't made your way to the dungeon when you did, I might be dead now." His face was more solemn than usual, reverent, and caught at something deep in her chest.

"In that case, you're welcome." It was her usual reply at this point of the conversation.

Except that he'd been serious when he'd spoken, and her own emotions were roiling just under the surface. And it had been so, so terribly long since she last seen him. Tears stung at her eyes. "Oh, Geordie, I'm so glad to have you home."

The tears did come then, slow at first and then harder. Geordie was up in a flash, at her side and pulling her into his strong, comforting arms that were as much foreign as they were familiar.

She was ruined, and Geordie was home.

"Come now, there's no need to cry." Nan set a plate of pastries in the center of the small table. "He's home now, sweet girl. And these honey pastries will set the both of you to rights."

Geordie backed away reluctantly as Cat wiped at her eyes. The platter on the small table held pastries with a sheen of honey glistening on flaky crusts.

"You always enjoy these." Cat gave a little laugh at her own foolish tears. "Or at least you did."

"I still do." Geordie cast an anxious glance at Cat before taking his seat opposite her once more. "Thank you, Nan."

Cat nodded to Geordie to silently let him know she had recovered from her bout of tears. In fact, she'd recovered enough for her mouth to water at the delicious pastries. After her daily illness passed each morning, she was always left ravenous, especially for treats like Nan's honeyed pastries.

Generally, Nan kept them under tight control, only allowing one per person. Today though, the plate was heaped with them. A celebration indeed.

Cat and Geordie both reached for one at the same time, then met each other's gaze and grinned. They were thinking alike, together again already.

He quickly released the pastry and winked at her as he snatched up a fresh one for himself. Cat bit into the sweet dough. It melted on her tongue and helped allay some of her pressing sadness.

Nan wiped her hands on her apron. "How long will you be staying with us, Sir Geordie?"

Geordie cast a hesitant glance in Cat's direction and swallowed before replying. "Until the king summons me again."

Cat's heart plummeted into her stomach. He had only just arrived. She did not want to anticipate him leaving again. Her heart staggered under the idea of having to resort back to letters that came with less and less frequency; the absence of the companionship they'd shared since they were children.

He was the foundation of her strength and never had she needed him more than she did now.

GEORDIE COULD NOT HELP BUT NOTICE THE SHADOW THAT FELL over Cat's face at his statement about returning back to the king's side.

"I do not expect it to be soon," he offered reassuringly.

She smiled at him, but the expression was tense at the corners, stretching unnaturally at her pretty lips. It was perhaps the most forced smile he'd ever seen Cat give.

As if understanding the utter failure of her ruse, she dropped the pretense of happiness. "Forgive me. It's only that...I do not want you to go to battle again, Geordie."

"Sometimes we are summoned to court instead." He bit into his pastry, uncertain what else he might say by reassurance. He knew her well enough to know what concerned her. Men who went into battle did not always return.

Geordie had been lucky in battle thus far and his skills learned on the border had worked well in his favor. There had been much combat in those four years and there had been many wounds, but Geordie had always survived.

He'd always won.

She tucked her rosy lower lip into her mouth and nodded.

"Cat enjoyed court," Nan offered. "I hear she attracted the attention of nearly every man there when she went two months ago."

Something hot twisted in Geordie's chest. He could see it too easily: Catriona at court, innocent from her life on the border, blissfully ignorant to the ways of courtly debauchery. A fresh young face, beautiful and alight with optimism. Aye, he did not doubt she was the newest sweet offered at court.

For her part, Cat flushed.

Nan gazed between them and wiped her hands on her apron in an old habit, no doubt realizing what she'd said had not gone over well. "I've got some pies to get into the oven." Following her murmured excuse, she quickly fled farther into the kitchen.

Geordie curled his hand into a fist under the table. The honey pastry in his stomach became thick and heavy, its sweetness in his mouth suddenly cloying.

Of course, Cat had attracted the attention of the men at

court. Undoubtedly, every man had noticed her. Even he had been taken aback by her beauty when he saw her today.

Now that his shock had worn off, however, he was intrigued by it. How the light played over her hair and turned strands to glinting gold, how the thickness of her dark lashes hid and revealed the beautiful blue of her eyes, the way her full lips pulled back when she laughed to reveal her perfect white teeth.

She'd always had lovely teeth. Even when they were children. While most of the population was plagued with unflattering gaps and spaces, hers had been even and white. As a result, she had never covered her laughter with her hands. Her joy had been unfettered and free. It was one of the many things that spurred his affection for her.

"Tell me of everything I've missed in the years you've been gone." Cat stretched her hand across the table and grasped his fingers, pulling him from his thoughts.

He gazed down at their joined fingers, his large and calloused, hers small and warm. The way they fit with one another's felt perfect.

"I wrote about the last several years in the letters," he answered. "There's little to tell aside from all that."

"I do not believe that," Cat said with a grin. "You've become a knight."

"The ceremony is not to be discussed." He winked. In truth, if he were ever to break the vow of silence and divulge the details of his knighting, it would be to Cat. Not that he would, of course, but for the first time since the ceremony, he found himself sorely tempted.

"You've been all over England and even to parts of France," she pressed.

He didn't want to think of the last four years, especially of France, and of battle, and of some of the more horrendous deeds he'd seen done there. "All detailed in my letters."

She lifted her brow in that way she'd done as a girl when she knew he was being obdurate. He laughed at that and her grin took on a more natural curve.

"What of you?" he asked. "What have I missed?"

Aside from her. Her smile, her laughing blue eyes, the way she ran through the forest with the grace of a deer, and how she tilted her head back when she twirled in an open meadow.

He'd thought often of her carefree freedom in his many days at camp before and after fighting. Even when his world was cold and gray, bloodstained with battle and he was exhausted to the marrow of his bones, his memories had been lit by Cat and sunshine . He'd fallen asleep to thoughts of her and it filled his heart with a warmth no amount of war or chaos could touch.

She tilted her head coyly. "I wrote it all down in my letters."

Oh, he knew. Every one of those missives had been carefully folded and saved in his bags. On a journey that allowed little space for personal effects, he had always managed to make a place to keep them all.

"I enjoyed them." He reached for another pastry.

Cat's cheeks flushed. "I enjoyed yours as well. I have all of them still. I confess, I've read them over and over again, as though doing so might make up for your absence." Her brows flinched. "They did not."

"I'm here now." He leaned forward in his seat, closer to her.

It was bittersweet, this time at Werrick Castle. For he wanted to be with Catriona, to spend their days with one another as they had always done. And yet, he knew he needed the summons from the king if he was to receive a commission from a lord wealthy enough to support him.

It was what Geordie had spent these four years working toward: a knighthood to establish himself, a commission to build his own fortune, and a home with which to raise a family.

Only then, when he had secured all of those aspects necessary for life, would he finally be worthy to ask Lady Catriona Barrington to be his wife.

Cat leaned closer to him, as though drawn by the trail of his thoughts. "I'm glad you're here now." She reached out and took his other hand with hers. The connection was instantaneous. Instantaneous and sticky.

Cat realized she'd taken the hand he'd eaten a honey pastry with and laughed her sweet, tinkling laugh. She pulled away and licked the honey from her fingers.

Desire slammed into him, hard and without mercy. He'd had many nights where he'd thought of her: kissing her, touching his tongue to hers, slowly undressing her until she lay naked beneath him, her head tilted in supplication. On those nights, he had used his fist to quell the rising need within him. Now, there was no reprieve. He was grateful for the table between them and the length of his tunic covering his very rigid cock.

"Geordie," a voice called from the doorway. Cat's eldest sister, Marin, strode in. "I was told you had returned." She rushed to him. "Welcome home."

Geordie shot Cat a glance, but Cat shook her head. "Bran is not here," she whispered.

Marin's husband had once used Cat to get into the castle by holding a blade to her throat. It was an offense Geordie could never remove from his mind or his heart, no matter how happy the man made Marin.

"That explains why Bixby hasn't come out of the shadows." Geordie winked at her.

Cat covered her mouth with her hand and gave a little laugh. Bixby was Werrick Castle's most notorious cat and was best known for finding rats. It had been a joke around the castle how much Bixby had been drawn to Bran upon first meeting him.

Marin cast them a chastising glance when she approached, having no doubt heard some of their quiet conversation. However humorous it might have been, the jest was not enough to quell the hardening of Geordie's arousal. So, when Marin opened her arms to embrace him, clearly well-meaning, he practically shrank away. The last thing he needed was his hardness pressing against Cat's sister as she hugged him in greeting.

Fortunately, Marin bent over him and embraced him as he sat, saving him from the humiliating event. As disciplined as he'd been with his training and weaponry, he needed to learn to be just as disciplined with his lust. If not, his stay at Werrick Castle in the constant companionship of Cat would prove most difficult.

3

Cat's gaze wandered repeatedly over Geordie's face. With him distracted by Marin, Cat now took the time to explore his appearance. Some things were very different, like the scar at the edge of his eyebrow, or the slight bump in his nose where it had obviously been broken. And some things were exactly the same. Like how easily he blushed, and how his eyes held all of his emotion.

She'd waited years to see him again. Not only to catch up on the friendship they'd missed in all that time, but also to celebrate his knighthood. He had succeeded on the path he'd first set foot upon as a small boy, and the incredible feat that made her proud enough to pop.

And yet, her joy was shadowed by her own fears, ones she had not been able to shake free of since that morning. Was she indeed with child?

She had the signs, between the illness and the cessation of her courses.

Marin's conversation with Geordie fell to the background as Cat tried to remember when last she'd bled. It should have happened since her arrival home. But nay, it had been just before they'd arrived at court and had not occurred since. It was especially disconcerting as prior to this, her cycle had always been predictable, coming at nearly the same time each month.

And when exactly had the feeling of sickness in the morning begun? Mayhap she had experienced it before. But as she dragged through her memory, she knew the truth of it. The illness was indeed after court, but not until after her arrival back at Werrick. Would a child in her womb have taken so long to make her ill?

Could it mean anything else?

Nay, nothing she was aware of. Nothing save the presence of a babe in one's womb.

Her stomach rolled with nausea, churning the honey pastry she'd kept down. She hadn't been able to eat any more than the one. Not when her mind was so full and her heart so heavy.

"Don't you agree, Cat?" Geordie was looking at her with happiness crinkling his eyes.

"Of course," Cat replied with feigned joy. Geordie would only be at Werrick Castle for a short period of time. She had to savor every moment of time with him she could get.

"Father is waiting for you in the solar," Marin said to Geordie.

"One more first." He grabbed a honey pastry and bit into it. Marin took one herself and ate it where she stood. Cat, however, did not partake, as the first one continued to roil in her stomach, sloshing about on the changing currents of her emotions.

When he was done, he slid from his seat, adjusted his tunic and bowed low, giving them the courtesy of a chivalrous knight. "I bid you ladies good day and anticipate seeing you later at the feast tonight."

Though he spoke to them both, it was Cat he watched with his tender brown eyes. She swallowed down her disappointment at losing him so quickly after having finally gotten him back. Doubtless, Papa would want to discuss political affairs, and matters concerning the king, with Geordie. Such things were of great import, of course.

None of it could be helped by Geordie, and she would not make him feel guilty for doing what he should. Swallowing down her disappointment, she got to her feet and grinned at him. "I look forward to the feast, Sir Geordie."

An endearing flush colored his cheeks and then he was gone.

"I know you must be elated to have Geordie home once more," Marin said to Cat.

"If only Papa wasn't stealing him away so quickly." Cat regretted the selfish words as soon as she'd said them. In the chaotic swirl of her thoughts, Geordie had seemed like a rock, the same as he'd always been when life was difficult. And now he was being pulled from her.

"You know Father has been eager to see Geordie too." Marin placed a length of linen over the honey pastries. After a word to Nan of their departure, she led Cat from the kitchen.

It was true. Papa had missed Geordie as well. He'd listened to the letters Geordie sent with an expression of pride crinkling the corners of his blue eyes.

"What did Isla say?" Cat asked.

Marin was silent and Cat bit the inside of her cheek. Mayhap she shouldn't have asked. She was opening her mouth to apologize when Marin finally spoke, "She said she does not feel as though I am with child currently."

Cat reached for her sister's hand. "Oh, Marin—"

Marin waved off Cat's disappointment. "I did not expect I was. And yet…" She stopped and gently squeezed Cat's fingers. "And yet, hearing her say those words plunged a dagger into my heart."

Cat stared at her eldest sister, praying to God to take the child from her womb and place it into her sister's. Where it belonged. Where it would be welcome.

"How will you know when you are with child when it happens?" Cat asked. Her pulse quickened. Was it too obvious a question? Would Marin wonder at her asking?

Marin sighed, oblivious, and they continued walking. "My courses would stop, of course. There could be some sickness some time after conception, primarily in the morning, as well as tenderness to my breasts and a feeling of exhaustion. If I want confirmation, however, Isla swears by placing a needle in a cup of urine to see if it rusts. That, or..." She settled a hand to her stomach.

Tenderness of the breasts? Cat nearly winced at the suggestion. Her nipples had been highly sensitive to the point of pain and her breasts had felt swollen of late. And the very mention of exhaustion made her want to curl up on her bed to rest, even though it was only mid-day.

"Or?" Cat hated herself for pressing Marin, for trying to glean information to know for certain of her own predicament and using her sister's misfortune to achieve it. And yet if she asked on her own...

"Or I will feel it." Marin pulled in a soft breath. "It's called the quickening. I was told it's like little bumps against the backside of your stomach as the babe moves."

Cat relaxed slightly. At least she had not felt the babe move as yet.

"That happens much later, though." Marin's hand dropped away from her stomach and clenched into a fist. "Isla gave me something to help." But Marin did not look hopeful. She gave a dramatic grimace.

"Is it steeped in urine?" Cat asked.

They shared a smile. The old healer tended to add urine to many of her curatives.

"I believe it may be worse this time than even urine." Marin pulled a small pouch from her pocket and handed it to Cat.

Curious, Cat opened the pouch. A chalky odor escaped and stuck like dust in her nose. As she peered in, she gave a choke of displeasure and covered her nose with her hand. Several round-shaped items smaller than eggs were nestled at the bottom. "What is this?"

"It's..." Marin hesitated. "Pig...bollocks."

Cat nearly dropped the pouch. "What are you supposed to do with them?"

"They are to be ground up and put into wine to drink." Marin took the pouch from her, closed it and replaced it in her pocket.

Nausea rolled over Cat at the very mention of wine. "How will you drink such an awful thing?"

Marin shook her head. "It's for Bran."

Cat wrinkled her nose. The musty smell remained in her nostrils even after the offensive "cure" had been tucked away. "Will he actually agree to drink it?"

"If I asked him to, he would." Marin stopped in front of Cat's door. "But I will not subject him to such a thing. If it is God's will that I conceive, it will be."

"Then I pray you get the child you so deserve." Cat hugged Marin, regretful of her own full womb, even as Marin's remained empty.

"I am going to the chapel, if you would like to join me," Marin offered.

Cat hesitated, knowing her own transgressions had not yet been confessed to the priest, Bernard. Except she could still not bring herself to say what she'd done aloud. Not when her shame burned so deeply. And if she entered the chapel with such sin rotting inside her, it might prevent Marin's prayers from being heard.

Exhaustion weighed down on Cat suddenly, like a large stone coming to rest over her body.

"I will go by later today," Cat promised. "For now, I believe I shall rest."

"I hear you have been resting often." Marin's brow pinched with concern. "Are you still unwell?"

Cat's heart caught in her chest. Was Marin suspicious? Cat shrugged and gave a wide smile. "'Tis just a bit of exhaustion."

"Rest then, Sister." Marin wrapped her in a tender embrace. "I will see you this evening at the feast."

And rest Cat did. Through the entire day. She'd been so weary that she had forgotten to place a needle in her chamber pot to see if it rusted. Not that she needed the needle to tell her what she already knew in her heart. Between her missed courses, the illness, her sore breasts and the fatigue, there was no longer a shadow of a doubt in Cat's mind.

She knew herself to be with child.

A knock at the door startled Cat from her slumber. She bade the person to enter in a groggy voice and Leila entered.

Her youngest sister had grown to be lovely, her long hair like black silk, especially when set against her creamy skin. Her eyes were what captivated one the most: a striking blue, solemn and casting a mysterious air even Cat and her sisters had never quite managed to unravel.

She was incredibly beautiful. Not so much as Anice. No woman in all the world could compare to Anice. But of all four other sisters, she came the closest. And of all the sisters, Leila cared the least.

"You aren't preparing yet for the feast." Leila closed the door gently behind her. "I came to assist you in dressing. You are coming, are you not?"

Leila wore a lovely blue gown that made her dark hair gleam like a raven's wing. It was a pity she refused to leave Werrick Castle. She would have captured the attention of every man at court if she had decided to pursue a husband.

The awareness of Cat's own predicament crushed in on her. Mayhap it was better for Leila to have refrained from going to court. But then, Leila would never have been so gullible and made such poor decisions. Not like Cat, who had always trusted too readily, forgiven too quickly and as a result was a terrible judge of character.

It was her tender heart, as Marin called it. Though Cat wouldn't call it tender now; she'd call it what it was: foolish.

"Of course, I intend to go." Cat drew herself into a sitting position. She'd meant to say more, about how it was so good of Nan to prepare a feast on such short notice, how the woman truly was a wonder, how marvelous it was to have Geordie home.

Then, the room spun about as though it were unhinged. The words died in Cat's throat while her world tried to center once more. For a brief, fearful moment, Cat worried she might purge the meager contents of her stomach.

"Are you well, Cat?" Leila came to her side and pressed her hand to Cat's brow. Her hands were cool and smelled of meadowsweet and chamomile. They were heavenly.

Cat sagged against the comfort and felt her eyes begin to slip closed.

"You've no fever." Leila pulled at Cat's shoulders to keep her upright. "Up with you. Geordie is no doubt excited to see you at the feast more than any one of us."

Geordie. Cat's eyes snapped open. Leila was correct. Geordie was waiting on her.

"Are you still getting ill in the mornings?" The skin around Leila's eyes tightened.

"I've been fine." Cat pulled herself from the bed, suddenly more alert.

Leila did not reply and instead knelt at the trunk at the base of the bed. She drew a scarlet gown from the depths. "I remember when you had this one made that you said you wished Geordie was there to see you in it."

It was true. It had been two years prior when it had been sewn for her, when she'd simply been a girl missing her childhood friend. She still wished Geordie would see her in it, but now as a woman, knowing how it called to attention the slenderness of her waist, the swell of her hips. Her cheeks flushed to think of parading so in front of Geordie. Her sweet Geordie.

And yet, he had been over the whole of England for the last four years, no doubt sampling every woman Christendom had to offer. The flush of her cheeks grew hotter still, spiced by a dash of impetuous jealousy. It was ludicrous an emotion to give way to, especially as she was carrying another man's child.

He was simply Geordie, nothing more. And certainly not interested in her as anything more than simply Cat. Why, then, did that tug at a deep thread of disappointment within her?

GEORDIE TRIED TO KEEP HIS GAZE FROM DRIFTING TO THE empty seats where Cat and Leila were to sit between the Earl of Werrick and himself. He'd spent the greater part of his day with the earl and Drake, learning of everything he'd missed in his absence. All this was followed by a much-needed bath prior to the feast.

Now he sat in a clean doublet and hose, his hair still damp with the effects of bathing, and he was desperate to see Cat once more. He had nearly told Lord Werrick of his decision to seek Cat's hand once he had earned it, and yet pragmatism had stayed his tongue.

The Earl of Werrick had always been Geordie's greatest champion. Mayhap it had been brought on by Lord Strafford giving Geordie up as sacrifice for his own transgressions, or how protective Geordie had been of Cat as they'd grown up. Regardless, he'd always been cast in favorable light with the earl.

It would not be outside Lord Werrick's generosity to offer a position to Geordie, as well as land and a considerable income, to encourage his marriage with Cat. Except Geordie did not want it handed to him. Cat was not the kind of woman whose favor should be given with donated honor. Nay, Cat was a woman whose affections, whose right to wed, were *earned*. And he would do it.

Leila walked in suddenly, wearing a simple blue kirtle. It was the figure behind her, though, that made Geordie sit upright in his seat.

Cat.

If she'd been beautiful by late morning, she was radiant now. The crimson gown she wore caught the light and drew it toward her until she was practically glowing. Her hair flowed down her back, smooth and glossy, no doubt still as soft as it had always been in their youth. His fingers twitched at the memory, with a keen longing to stroke her silken tresses once more.

Her sparkling eyes found his and locked there with such intensity, it nearly took his breath away.

"Geordie." She said his name on a breathy exhale that preceded a brilliant smile. The flush of her cheeks matched the vivid color of her gown.

She might have said more, but Geordie's ears were consumed with the hammering of his heartbeat, to the point he could hear nothing else. And aside from his name on her lips, did he need to hear anything more?

Geordie's own cheeks went warm, a pleasant sensation like what followed after a glass of wine. "You are brighter than any candle in any room, Cat."

His flattery left a lovely smile on her face. "Have you become a charmer?" Cat asked, her tone flirtatious. New. Unfamiliar to him, and yet welcome.

Geordie's cheeks heated further still. "Mayhap I'll let you discover as much for yourself." He stood back and indicated her seat.

She gave a pleasant laugh and sank into the proffered chair. Throughout supper, her conversation was light and airy, revitalizing.

In this way she had not changed at all, and for that he was grateful. He drank from a goblet that did not go empty and ate Nan's richly spiced fare of meat that was far fresher and more tender than anything he'd had in the last several years.

Any awkwardness that had settled between him and Cat cleared like mist, and the casual comfort of their childhood resumed. Eventually, the tables were cleared away to make room for those who wished to dance, and the thrum of music became livelier. Cat bounced her leg under the table to the beat. No doubt she would be up and twirling by the next song.

But she didn't get to her feet right away, as Geordie had expected. Instead, she propped her elbow on the table and cradled her chin with her palm as she gazed up at him. "I missed you, Geordie."

Such wonderful words. The wine running hot in his veins, and the sheer happiness at being in Catriona's company, pulled a smile to his lips. "As I missed you, Lady Catriona."

She laughed. "Lady Catriona." She leaned over and bumped his shoulder with hers. "Save your chivalry for wooing ladies, Sir Geordie. I'm simply 'Cat' to you."

He gazed down at her, a seriousness descending over him with the sincerity of his words. "You'll never be 'simply Cat' to me."

She chuckled and tilted her head coyly. It was a way she often looked at him when they were children, when she wanted something. Except now, she was a woman, one whose long-lashed blue eyes held the power of seduction and whose lips were lush and begging to be kissed.

The swell of her breasts rose round and high over the bodice of her kirtle. He noticed that as well, though he tried not to. It was too easy to wonder at the softness of such skin, to imagine freeing them and cupping them in his palm.

"Do you intend to ask me to dance?" She lifted her brows in expectation.

"Aye." He grinned. "But thought I might make you wait a bit longer." He reached for his goblet of wine, but she caught his hand and tugged him from his seat.

"I'd be honored," she said with a grin.

He didn't bother to resist as she pulled him to the dance floor.

Especially now that he had learned to dance as part of his knighthood training. A knight must excel at life and love, just as he did in battle.

The music gave off a thrumming beat with hearty drums amid the pitched whine of a psaltery, while pipes and a lute tinkled in the background. Of all the instruments he'd tried, it was the lute that Geordie most enjoyed playing. One day he would play for Cat.

Once they were upon the area cleared to be the dance floor, Geordie and Cat began leaping and hopping along with the other dancers. When he'd been a boy, he hadn't noticed the grace of Cat's body as she moved to the music. As a man, he noticed, and was mesmerized. Slender arms, flat stomach, curvy hips, and the jiggle of her bosom as she danced in rhythm to the music.

Geordie's pulse matched that of the drum, pounding lust through his wine-laced veins. After several songs, Cat lifted her brows and clapped. "Your dancing has improved immensely, Sir Geordie."

"Whatever a knight can do for his lady." He bowed humbly.

If Cat had noticed he had called her his lady, she did not comment on it; the slip of his tongue brought on by too much drink.

Part of him had wanted her to notice, to ask. In his less hazy, sober state, he intended not to tell her of his plans to wed her, to have the opportunity to provide a good life for her by his own volition. All the things he anticipated coming sooner than later with the victories he'd won on the battlefield.

And now, with his blood hot from dancing and desire, he longed to tell her. All these years, everything he had done—it had all been for her. He needed her to know that.

"Cat," he said with intent.

She twirled around in a play of red skirts and long blonde hair. Her gaze wandered up to his, where they locked deep into a place in his soul that only she could touch. She grasped his hands and put them on her shoulders. "Dance with me," she said breathlessly.

And dance with her he did, not intending to let her go. Desire roared through his body, desperate for a kiss, a taste of what he had been craving for far too long. He wanted to pull her against him, to tilt that beautiful face of hers back and kiss her until she was flushed and panting with need.

But he was a knight, bound by a code of chivalry. Holding a lady so inappropriately already pressed the boundaries of his conscience, let alone kissing her. Reluctantly, he let his hands fall away. The music resumed a faster pace and once more, he was moving in time with Cat.

"It's far too warm in here," Cat said after the song ended.

Her brow glistened with sweat. Geordie's own body was almost unbearably hot. He caught her hand as he had done when they were children, though now her fingers seemed so small and delicate in his grasp. "Let us go outside for some fresh air."

Cat immediately nodded and allowed him to pull her away.

It wasn't until the door had closed behind them and they were plunged into moonlit darkness and silence that he realized it had not been chivalrous of him to take her outside alone. The line between right and wrong was blurred by what had been normal during their childhood and what was now proper.

Still another thought prevailed, louder and more insistent.

He was here. With her. Alone. He should not squander such an opportunity. And yet, it would not be chivalrous to not say anything.

"We shouldn't be here alone together." His protest was half-hearted, even to his own ears.

She gave a little laugh. Moonlight limned her body, gilding her loveliness with silver. "We were always together, Geordie," she said softly. "It was never wrong before."

"We were children then." His hand reached out of its own volition and delicately traced an invisible line down her jaw.

"We're grown now, me a man, and you a woman. A beautiful woman, at that."

She coquettishly ducked her head. "You think me beautiful?"

It was all he could do to keep his entire confession from tumbling out. "Aye," he whispered. And before he could even realize what he was doing, his face was lowering to hers, anticipating the soft warmth of her lips.

4

Catriona's heart slammed hard against her ribs at Geordie's nearness, at his obvious intention. To kiss her.

Never in all of her youth had she thought of him romantically. But that was before they'd grown into adults, before she'd appreciated how tall he was, how broad his shoulders were, how endearing was the affectionate way he gazed at her. How soft his lips looked. A reciprocating flame ignited within her.

She said his name on an exhale and breathed him in. It had been a mistake to do so. He no longer smelled like the Geordie she had always known, of sweat and mud and mischief. His new scent, of the grease used for polishing armor, of well-worn leather, was the essence of a man. Of a knight.

He found her beautiful.

Her head spun with the dizzying sensation. The way one reacts to flattery from an attractive man. Her stomach clenched. Was she truly considering kissing him? She had allowed Sir Gawain kisses.

Her heart clenched into a knot in her chest.

Was she now considering kissing yet another man? Only two

months later and her womb filled with another man's child, was she truly anticipating Geordie's kiss?

Shame burned within her.

She meant to protest, to pull away, or turn her cheek for his lips to press upon. But she had not acted quickly enough, and his mouth descended upon hers. It was not a greedy kiss with the probing of tongue as Sir Gawain's had been. Nay, Geordie's was gentle and filled with such reverent affection, it made her soul ache.

His lips brushed against hers like a whisper. Chaste, sweet. Thrilling. His reservation made her want more, to open herself to his kiss and taste the spice of wine on his tongue with her own. She, herself, had not drunk the wine that evening, not when it turned her stomach. Tasting it on his lips, however, was suddenly alluring and made her just as intoxicated as if she'd drunk it all herself.

His hand moved to the back of her head, cradling the weight in his large palm with the care one might use when handling spun glass. He pressed his mouth to hers again, savoring with his lips only, delicately kissing her with a restraint that was evident in the slight tremor of his hand.

"Catriona," he murmured against her mouth. "My Cat."

My Cat.

The words simultaneously made her knees go weak, even as they stabbed deep into her, hitting a raw wound that had only recently been torn open and had no chance to begin healing. What was she doing?

Was she really encouraging Geordie's affections? What did she expect? For him to offer marriage and raise another man's bastard?

Geordie would do it, of course. Gladly. And most likely, after having killed Sir Gawain.

Geordie had been the one to save her. He'd helped pull her from the darkness after her mother's death, he'd carried her in his arms when she'd injured her ankle as a girl, and had been there for every fear, every problem. Every difficult step of her life, he had been at her side.

He would do anything for Cat, but he was a knight now with far too much to lose.

She couldn't allow him to risk the future he'd worked so hard to build. It wasn't fair to take away his freedom, to force him to take her and a child on.

Surely, he had attracted many women at court.

Something pulled deep inside her at the thought of it, a visceral and sudden disliking for the women who might have vied for his attention. And even more for the ones who had most likely received it.

She hadn't realized she had stopped kissing Geordie back until he pulled away. His cheeks flushed in a blush she had always loved. At least the hardness of war had not stripped him entirely of his sweetness.

Disappointment crumpled like something useless inside her chest.

She drew in a breath to speak and paused, uncertain what to even say. *I'm with child by a man who is already married? I cannot kiss you because it makes me feel sinful and wanton? I cannot have you ruin your life for me? You cannot save me this time?*

Geordie's brows furrowed and the support of his hand behind her head fell away. "Forgive me, Cat. I should not have taken such liberties."

She almost laughed aloud and would have, were there not a knot firmly lodged in her throat. Sir Gawain had never apologized for "such liberties" as he'd pawed at her and whispered his lies. He'd slid over her like the oily sheen on the surface of a bath, clinging to everything he touched, unapologetic and rapacious.

A flash of anger sparked in Cat. At her own foolishness, aye, but also for the experience Sir Gawain had wielded with her. And even more, how he had ruined this moment, this otherwise wonderful and perfect moment, with Geordie.

"It isn't that," she stammered. "Rather, what I mean was you didn't—"

She hesitated. He'd been her confidante for most of her life. Why should this be any different?

And yet it was. Charming a honey pastry from Nan wouldn't fix her problem; silly faces couldn't heal the depth of her hurt. Nothing could make any of this better.

And she certainly would not allow him to sacrifice everything he'd worked so hard to achieve. Especially not for her.

"I should not have kissed you." He lifted his fingers to gently sweep over the line of her jaw.

She loved how he did that, how the brush of his fingertips sent her skin igniting with a heat she had never experienced before. It made her want to turn into his caress, to welcome it and encourage more.

"I've been taught to respect women," Geordie said with thoughtfulness. "I made a vow of chivalry and have not acted thus."

It was not until he said the last bit that she realized his speech was not just thoughtful, but also laden with guilt.

Not every knight took their vows as seriously. Cat knew better than most women but kept the bitter remark to herself.

"You did not disrespect me." Cat's voice came out breathy and low. "I kissed you back."

He was so fascinating to view this close, to see how much his features had changed. His cheekbones were more pronounced, his jaw harder and darkened with the shadow of a beard, his lips softer. God forgive her for her wantonness, but she wanted to kiss him again.

"Cat..." His fingers on her jaw tilted her chin up.

As though he intended to kiss her again. Her cheeks went hot with yearning and shame and self-loathing. Had she not already experienced passion, if that could be what that was called? Geordie deserved better than this. Better than her.

"I should retire to bed," she said, instead of divulging the truth. Yet she did not pull away from his delicate hold on her chin, and her face remained angled toward him, their mouths only a layer of control apart. "Tomorrow I should like to see you, if time allows it, mayhap to practice."

His eyes crinkled slightly. "I'd like that."

"I can see how much you've learned as a knight." She tried to be playful, but the teasing came out flat.

The tenderness of his expression blossomed into a wide grin regardless. "I doubt I can shoot an arrow as good as you," he said. "I still have yet to find any man who can shoot with your skill. But I may have some new things with a sword to teach you."

"Drake has been teaching me to use the sword as well." She couldn't help the beam of pride. When she'd first learned the bow, it had been to keep her from the fray in battle since she was so young. No one had expected her to excel at it as she did. Now she was plenty old enough and wanted to learn weapons at close range.

"I look forward to seeing what you've learned." His thumb swept over her chin, just grazing the bottom of her lower lip.

A soft sigh escaped her mouth and she found her face lifting higher, encouraging just one more kiss. It was just as gentle, just as restrained and made her burn all the more for him.

"On the morrow," he murmured against her mouth.

"Mmmmmhmmm," she hummed as he broke away from their chaste kiss.

Anticipation and dread twisted together in her stomach. It had been far too easy to kiss him. It would be easier still to let him kiss her again.

Regret burned like an ember in her chest. When she'd been at court, she'd been swept away by flattery, allowing kisses with the shy curiosity of a maiden who was often overlooked. Now though, with Geordie, there was the pull of something deeper, richer.

But she would have to turn her back to it and let it grow cold. She'd had her moment of reckless disobedience and it had cost her everything. Including Geordie.

※

Geordie remained outside long after Cat's figure had disappeared down the hall and he'd heard the door close behind her. He breathed in the spring night air and let the welcomed chill allay the raging heat in his body.

Cat's kisses had been far sweeter than he had imagined. And he had spent a considerable amount of time imagining them over the four years of their separation. His body had reacted instantly to the contact of their mouths, hot and hard and demanding. Not at all the way any knight ought to respond.

He should not have kissed her. He should not have given into the temptation of wanting to have her.

And yet, it had allowed him to sample the extent of her own desires. His affections were requited. Geordie pulled in a deep breath of air that puffed out his chest and slowly, steadily, let it out. He stared up at the bold face of the moon hanging among the heavens. He needed only one good commission, something to grant him land and a home for Cat.

It was all so close that he could nearly taste it.

He had spent so long dreaming of their life together, using those aspirations to get him through the cold, bitter nights on campaign. While others were haunted by the faces of those they'd killed and the perils of battle, he had filled his thoughts with Cat, with the beautiful children they'd have with his dark hair and her laughing blue eyes. When men cried out, he had filled his ears with the sound of her singing lullabies.

They would be parents who loved their children, of that he

was certain. All of them, the naughty ones and well-behaved ones alike. Never, never, *never* would they allow one of them to be sacrificed or lost to any nefarious cause.

Not like his own father. Nay, Geordie's children would have a better life than the one he had been afforded by his own parents.

Anger flashed hot in his chest. Even though he'd risen above his father's lies and treachery, Geordie's rage had never truly been doused. The recollection of his parents singed away the remnants of lust stirring in his loins and finally allowed him to retire to his own room for the evening.

The following morning, after a night of poor sleep, he found Cat waiting for him in the bailey, wearing a pair of snug fitting trews. They stretched up her long, lean legs, revealing finely shaped calves and slender thighs. The plain shirt she wore belted over the trews did nothing to hide the firm roundness of her perfect bottom.

Heaven save his soul, when did Lord Werrick begin to allow his daughters to wear such revealing clothing on the practice field —much less around soldiers.

Cat settled a hand over her lush hip. "Intimidated already?" She touched the hilt at her side, and only then did he see the sword strapped to her waist.

Intimidated wasn't the word he would use. "What happened to the hose and long tunics you used to wear in practice?"

Cat looked down at her clothes without concern. "This is far easier to move about in." She kicked her leg out and stopped her foot in midair, inches from his face. "See?"

Geordie clenched his back teeth. The flexibility of her lithe body called to a deep part of him that made his blood run hot.

"Aye, I see," he replied as casually as he could.

"How did you sleep?" She lowered her leg. "Was it luxurious to finally rest in a bed after so long traveling?"

In truth, he had scarcely slept, despite the fine bedding and the clean comfort around him. He'd been too long on poor beds at best, and filthy stables or hard floors at worst. He almost did not recognize sleep without someone snoring nearby, without the stinging nip of a flea or the itchy welt left behind. Nay, he'd tossed about in his fluffy mattress as he stared at the ceiling and thought about Cat.

"Well enough," he replied. "And you?"

No sooner had the question been asked than he was imagining her in her bed, wearing only a simple chemise. Sweet. Sensual. He could picture himself lifting the hem, drawing it higher over legs he now knew the shape of.

She pulled her sword from its sheath with a hiss. The blade reflected the sun with a flat sheen, the edges dulled for safety. "Do you want to see what I've learned?"

He pulled his own sword free with an element of trepidation. If her kick was indicative of what he would encounter while they sparred, he was in peril from his own imagination.

She flicked her blade against his and grinned. "You needn't look so nervous." She circled him and gave him a teasing look. "I won't hurt you."

"I assure you, that is not my concern." He lifted his drooping blade. He could do this. Cat had sparred with him countless times before. They'd spent the better part of their childhood out in the bailey, firing arrow after arrow at the straw-filled target.

Cat had always been better at it than him, no matter how hard he tried. But his efforts were not in vain. While he had been mediocre next to Cat, he had been exceptional compared to his fellow knights.

But knights were not known for their skill with the bow. They were known for their swordsmanship, for their valiance and bravery.

She launched herself at him without warning, arcing her blade through the air with a dexterity he almost fell prey to. His body acted before his mind could acknowledge the attack. His own sword drew up and knocked hers harmlessly to the side.

He nodded in appreciation. "I see Drake has taught you well."

Cat beamed at the praise. "And I see you've become much faster."

He gave a nonchalant shrug that made her laugh as she settled into a fighting stance. He had missed sparring with her as much as he had their time climbing trees and roaming the land together; the flash of her eyes, the fierce set of determination that quickly gave way to a ready laugh if she misstepped.

Cat could even make battle enjoyable.

He swept his blade at her, and she stepped back. He pursued and circled his weapon around hers, knocking it easily from her grasp. Before he could declare his victory, she crouched low and leapt at him.

As her body slammed into his, she curled one leg around the back of his, so his knee buckled, and they both crashed to the ground. She sat atop him, straddling his waist with her long legs. *Jesu.* Yet another innocent childhood pastime that held so much more awareness as an adult.

She smiled triumphantly down at him. "I win."

5

Geordie wouldn't lose that easily. "Do you really think I would give you such a quick victory?" Careful to keep her from knocking her head on the ground, he flipped her over. "I win."

Her eyes narrowed with that fierce determination he loved. She swept her leg up, impossibly flexible as she'd always been, and attempted to shove him off with her knee. He palmed her thigh and pushed her away. It was hard to ignore how intimate their position was: bodies pressing together, writhing and grunting with effort.

Her body had new curves from the last time they'd battled, and he felt every one of them beneath him now. She panted up at him as they both struggled, the sounds far too similar to that made during intimacy.

Doubtless, this was another act that knights did not engage in. But then, there wasn't protocol for fighting a woman when England had no other female warriors, save the five daughters of the Earl of Werrick. What Geordie did know was that Cat had never wanted to be treated as a delicate lady.

Her long-ago words echoed in his mind: *I'd rather you treat me like a man in training than be in battle and be killed.*

Still, he *was* careful with her. He was no longer a skinny boy, but a man trained to kill.

He managed to shove aside her knee from his chest, then lowered his fist down as he faked punching her in the stomach. Though his hand moved far too slow to be an actual strike, and though he stopped it several inches from ever touching her, she gasped and clasped both hands protectively over her stomach.

He immediately drew away, horrified. "I wasn't actually going to strike you, Cat."

Her cheeks went red. "I know that."

But she would not have blocked herself in such a desperate manner if she truly did. Geordie frowned slightly as he thought through the movements again. Nay, he had truly moved his hand at a glacial pace, so slow, it would have been evident he'd had no intention to strike her.

In the course of their childhood sparring with one another, he'd never struck her. Any weapon, including his fist, had always stopped before connecting with her. Why would she now assume he would actually hit her?

He quickly got to his feet and offered his hand to her to aid her in standing.

She accepted his assistance and allowed him to pull her up. "Forgive me, Geordie, I—" She shook her head.

"I would never hurt you," he said with all the sincerity of his soul.

She looked away. "I know."

"Never," he repeated. "In fact, I would kill any person who ever hurt you."

Her eyes shot back to his and went wide. She quickly covered her expression with the flash of a smile. "Only if I didn't kill them first," she boasted.

"Sir Geordie." Lord Werrick made his way to them at a

clipped pace. He cast an apologetic look toward Cat. "I must speak with him immediately."

"Of course." She held out her hand to clasp forearms with Geordie, departing the way a warrior would. "I'm off to see to Leila. I told her I would assist her with some of her herbs."

Geordie held her arm for a moment longer than necessary, hesitant to let her go. "I'll find you when I'm done."

She nodded and drew away from him. He forced his gaze to Lord Werrick, lest he fixate on the swaying of her well-shaped bottom in those fitted trews as she departed.

"Sir Geordie." The Earl of Werrick held out a sealed letter. "A runner has arrived with a missive for you from the king."

Geordie accepted the sealed parchment with a readiness he did not feel. He'd had almost no time with Cat. He needed a post, aye, but he had not expected to get one so soon, especially since he knew what a king's summon would most likely mean. More war. More fighting. More killing. More turning a blind eye to the terrible things the king ordered his men to do to the innocent people of the villages they attacked.

And, of course, more time away from Cat.

The smile on Lord Werrick's face, however, was one of pride. Like a father watching his son receiving an honor from their sovereign. The affection on the older man's face touched Geordie and left him grateful to have returned to Werrick Castle. It was more of a home than he had realized.

"Go on then, lad." The earl rocked back on his heels. "The message was delivered with such decorum that it could only contain good tidings."

Geordie broke the wax seal and opened the missive. He read it once. Twice. Both times with incredulity.

"What is it?" Lord Werrick tilted his chin to peer at the text.

"The king wishes to hold a feast in honor of me and the men I fought with." Geordie handed the missive to Lord Werrick, wanting the older man to confirm what had been written.

The earl took the letter, skimmed it and shook his head. "Nay, my boy. He doesn't do this to honor the men you fought with. It's all for you and you alone." The older man's brows lifted. "What did you do to earn such an honor from the king?"

Geordie shrugged even as the memory pressed in on him, the swing of his blade, the enemy as they fell one by one, the gilded armor he neared, focusing with every element of his being. *Save the king*.

"What I was trained to do, my lord," Geordie replied.

The earl surprised him with a chuckle. "Your humility was always part of your charm."

Geordie clasped his hands in front, embarrassed at the praise. "Thank you, my lord."

The earl put a hand to Geordie's shoulder and gently squeezed. "I assume you are of a mind to accept this immense honor from the king."

Geordie nodded. He would be a fool to decline. And if the king were indeed willing to honor him in such a way, mayhap an income and land would accompany it. He would have everything he had wanted to be worthy of Cat, even sooner than anticipated.

It was on the tip of his tongue to tell the Earl of Werrick then and there of his desire to wed Cat, in order to obtain permission. But he did not know what honor the king would bestow upon him, apart from the feast. If the king gave him nothing more than a fine toast, Lord Werrick would feel compelled to compensate for Geordie's lack of income.

Nay, Geordie would wait. And hope to God he would be granted everything he needed to make an offer for Cat's hand in marriage.

CAT CURLED HER ARMS OVER HER STOMACH AND STOPPED IN AN

alcove to catch her breath. A feat nearly impossible to do when her heart thundered so hard in her chest.

What had possessed her to have been so protective? In all the years of sparring with Geordie, he had never struck her. He'd never even come close. Yet, when his fist neared her stomach, every nerve in her body shot to high alert and all she could think was to protect the babe in her belly.

It was foolish. She hadn't even felt a quickening yet to confirm she was indeed with child.

But she *was* with child. Wasn't she?

The question buzzed around in her mind like a bee driven into a frenzy with uncertainty. Except that every time she thought she might not be, she felt as though she was trying to convince herself of something she didn't truly believe.

She put her head in her hands and tried to quell the guilt squeezing at her insides. Poor Geordie. His wounded expression had told her exactly how her actions had made him feel. She would apologize to him later.

Bolstered by her decision to make it all right, she forced herself upright. After a quick change in her room into a kirtle, she made her way to Leila's small hut.

With the rest of their sisters married and gone, and Geordie having been on campaign, Cat and Leila had become closer than ever. Though Cat had never had an interest in medicinal herbs or healing, she found herself spending more and more time in the sweet-smelling hut.

She opened the door and found Leila inside, a basket of fresh herbs at her side and a ball of twine on the other. She furrowed her brows in silent question at Cat's early arrival.

"Father wanted to speak with Geordie," Cat said by way of explanation. "Again." She tried to keep the bitterness from her voice.

"I don't think it's anything you need to worry over." Leila

snipped off a bit of twine and drew several similar herbs from the basket.

Cat pursed her lips and considered her sister. One never knew if Leila's words were simply conversational reassurance, or if they were the telling of a vision.

Leila saw things others did not, events that would transpire in the future. However, she was hesitant to share them, as her visions were often difficult to discern. She didn't know when something would happen, only that it would come to pass. And she could not provide specific details, nor could she see all events.

The entirety of it seemed very confusing and rather frightening, if Leila's screaming dreams were any indication. In truth, Cat hated that her sister had such abilities. At times, it made Leila pull away from the family, people who loved her more than life itself. But even while Cat feared it made Leila feel as though she did not belong, she had never been sure how to approach her youngest sister about it, nor how to press her for more information on her visions.

Instead, Cat took her place opposite Leila at the long table and picked through the herbs to pluck out several stalks of basil. The supple plants were still warm from the sun, picked at the perfect time of day when the dew had dried from their tender leaves. Their pleasant scent rose to meet her.

"These are so fragrant," she exclaimed. "All the herbs have held such a stronger smell lately. Have you done something new to the soil?"

Leila regarded her quietly for a moment before binding the bit of twine around the base of the herbs, a leafy variety Cat was unfamiliar with. "Have you still been unwell since your return from court?"

"I am feeling better," Cat replied. It wasn't exactly a lie. She'd only vomited once that morning, whereas the day before she'd purged twice.

Leila cast her a skeptical glance. "You didn't ask for willow's bark this month." She tied the twine into a firm knot.

Cat shook out the basil to ensure no bugs remained and arranged the five sprigs on the wooden tabletop. Any more in the bundle and the herbs might molder as they hung to dry.

Willow bark.

From the first time onwards, Cat suffered terrible pains through her monthly courses. As soon as Leila had learned of the discomfort, she'd set to work creating a tincture made from willow bark with a bit of chamomile. No doubt she'd had it prepared in advance, and Cat had never asked for it.

Cat licked her suddenly dry lips.

"You don't want to bundle those for hanging." Leila nodded toward the basil as she tied a small linen bag over the herbs she had bound together, to keep out the vermin as it dried. "The basil has too much water in it and will rot if it's hung. Best to dry those in the sun." She twisted her lips in thought. "I have seen something of you recently."

The air in the small hut went thin. Cat's head spun. "Have you?"

"Aye, but I do not believe I need the sight for what I already suspect." Leila cast a solemn glance at Cat. "You've been ill, and I do not believe you've gotten your courses. Regardless of having been so ill, your cheeks are rosy with good health and your sense of smell has gotten stronger. I suspect you have also been sensitive."

She glanced to Cat's breasts where they squeezed against the neckline of her gown. Almost none of her gowns fit over her swollen bosom anymore.

Cat's cheeks burned. She abandoned the stalks of basil and crossed her arms over her chest to hide her breasts. Her panic could not be so easily shoved aside. It rushed over her in icy waves of fear.

If anyone found out she was with child, they would tell Marin, and their poor eldest sister would be crushed. How unfair that Cat would have a fertile womb after one brief dalliance, while Marin had been trying for nigh on eight years for a babe without success.

Leila's lashes swept low as she focused on the bundled herbs on the table. "There is life growing inside you, Cat." She lifted her gaze slowly, a haze of pain set in her deep blue eyes. "An unwanted life."

It was the first time Cat's fears had been discussed with any other person. Somehow the terrible truth being vocalized laid bare her shame, open and vulnerable for judgment.

A sob escaped Cat, harsh and unbidden. Leila was there in an instant, wrapping her slender arms around her, shushing gently in a tone that was reminiscent of Marin's, as were the careful circles rubbed against Cat's back.

"You can't tell Marin." Cat pushed away and stared at Leila in desperation. "She wants a child so fiercely that I worry this will destroy her."

Cat didn't have to ask if Leila agreed with her suspicion. The truth of it was written on the youngest sister's face in the painful gleam in her eyes.

Not that Marin would ever allow herself to show it, but Cat's pregnancy, so quickly brought on and so unwanted, would cause Marin great hurt.

"Sir Gawain, I presume," Leila muttered bitterly.

Cat looked away, too ashamed to bring herself to answer.

"What will you do?"

Cat shook her head. "I'm not certain. Ella has invited me back to court to meet Lord Loughton's son, but I could never bring myself to try to pass off another man's babe to a man who wished to marry me."

Leila nodded sagely. "But no one need know that."

Cat regarded her sister curiously.

"Going to court will get you away from Werrick Castle where

Marin would otherwise hear of your delicate state." Leila glanced at the stack of freshly gathered herbs. "Of course, we could also make you a tea..."

"Nay." Cat shook her head vehemently before she even realized what she was doing.

Leila's first suggestion, however, was a strong one. Cat could claim to want to meet Lord Loughton's son and get away without anyone knowing. She could find someone to take her child.

A sudden thought struck her. Mayhap Sir Gawain would want the child, especially if it was a boy. Or perhaps he would know what to do, how to help.

"I think I know what I will need to do," Cat said as the plan began to take form. "I will do as you've suggested: go to court and use meeting Lord Loughton's son as my excuse for wanting to visit."

Geordie's sheepish smile flashed in her mind as soon as she spoke the words. It would hurt him to know she was allowing a man from court to pursue her.

Except that he had just recently vowed to kill any man who hurt her. Cat's stomach roiled as she recalled Sir Gawain and that awful, awful night.

If Geordie knew of it, surely, he would kill Sir Gawain. And be punished for it. He would lose everything he had earned: his knighthood, his honor. And that was if he was lucky. Most likely, he would even lose his life.

Cat clenched her hands into fists, resolute in her decision that he never find out what happened. He had worked too hard to be stripped of everything he had achieved.

Meeting Lord Loughton's son would also discourage Geordie's affections. And while that understanding broke Cat's heart, she knew it to be necessary.

The mistake had been hers and she would have to be the one to make it right. Even if it cost her greatly to do so.

6

Geordie pushed through the door of the solar where he suspected he might find Cat. There she was, sitting on the lushly padded bench by the window with sunlight bathing her in gold. Her gaze was fixed on something on the other side of the window, her expression somber, a slight downcast to her mood.

Aye, she still smiled as readily, laughed as loudly, and yet there had been something under the surface. He'd seen it in flashes when most weren't looking, the sparkle that winked out for little moments at a time as she went somewhere unpleasant in her mind. If he didn't know her so well, he might not have ever seen it.

But he knew Cat better than any person in all of Christendom, and there was definitely something amiss.

She didn't look up as he entered. Instead, she stared out through the distorted glass to the tops of the trees in the small orchard below, lost in thoughts he wished to know.

He approached her slowly to as not to frighten her and stared too out the window to those familiar trees below. They'd played in those very orchards in their youth, finding crisp apples to sink their teeth into and laughing at one another's expressions as the bitter juice crumpled their faces. They'd climbed those sturdy branches and had run about in a silly hiding game they'd both enjoyed.

Cat turned abruptly toward him and her despondent expression came back to life at once, like a burnt-out wick being relit. "What are you grinning about?"

"Thinking about the orchard and all the good times we used to have there." He leaned against the stone wall across from her.

She gave a little laugh. "We did have a jolly time. Remember the time we wanted to start our own orchard so we could sell the apples at market?"

Geordie joined her mirth. "We wanted the seeds but didn't want to waste the fruit and Nan wouldn't let us use the press for making cider. We must have eaten about fifteen apples each."

"They were so sour." Cat's eyes crinkled with mirth. "We had such stomach aches. And Isla gave us something made with heifer's piss that we were too scared to try."

"I think I'd still be too scared to try it."

"I know I am." Cat peered up at him. "Though you don't strike me as being afraid of anything. You've always been brave."

He scoffed. The scrawny boy she'd known had been afraid of the world. He was afraid of the Earl of Werrick changing his mind and killing him; he was afraid that his father might someday find him and drag him away; he was afraid something would happen to Cat and he would be alone forever. Aye, he'd had many fears.

"It's true." She smoothed her hand over the sides of her kirtle, a nervous action he'd not seen before from her. "You never showed fear, even when you thought my father would kill you. Remember when I fell from the rafters when we got it in our heads to climb them once?" Her eyes lifted to the painted ceiling above them. "You caught me, and you didn't even seem frightened."

He remembered that moment all too well. The impact had knocked the breath from him, and he'd nearly fallen with her.

He'd been so weak then, all bones and flesh, that he was surprised he hadn't dropped her. But he'd held tight to her with every thread of determination in his body and by some miracle, he had remained upright with her locked securely in his skinny arms. It'd been worth the effort for the way she'd looked at him then, like he was the greatest hero in all the world.

He sank onto the seat beside her now and met her gaze. "I will always make sure you are safe."

She pressed her lips together and didn't reply.

"What is it?" he asked.

She shook her head. "'Tis nothing."

"Tell me, Cat, please." He gently touched her face, turning her toward him. The night before, it had been so easy to allow himself to be intimately close with her, with wine in his veins and the mask of night shielding them. Now though, in the light of day, the move was bold.

He stroked the pad of his thumb across her chin. "Something has been bothering you since I arrived. What is it?"

She swallowed.

"You used to tell me everything." He let his hand slowly fall away. "I am still the same Geordie. You can still trust me."

"In time." But the slip of her gaze from his told him the light promise was a lie.

He hoped it wasn't though, that she would in time trust him as she had before.

He hadn't wanted to say anything about the king as of yet. But more than wanting to surprise her once he was bestowed his honors from the king, he needed to reassure her. "The king has sent me a missive, summoning me to court for a feast he wishes to have in my honor."

Cat immediately turned toward him, the light back in her eyes. "Geordie, that's astounding."

"I expect him to at least offer a commission, if not give me land." He tried to keep the note of pride from his voice.

"I'm so pleased for you." She clasped his hands in hers. By the light of day, he could make out her nails—all bitten to the quick.

He was right. Something was amiss. He was glad now for telling her about the king's honor. She would know he was a strong warrior, that he was capable.

"Any issue you are facing, I will be in a better position to help you," Geordie said. "I'll always protect you, Cat."

She shook her head.

"Aye." He ran his fingertips over her ragged nails. "Regardless of what you are up against, I'll be there at your side. I'll protect you, no matter the cost."

She stared down at her lap as he made his earnest vow. One he meant to uphold always.

"Mayhap you can allow me to accompany you to London then," she said.

"London?" He tried to keep the hope from showing in his voice. "You are going to London as well?"

She nodded, but still did not look up.

How ideal to have them travel together to London. There would be no one else he'd rather have at his side for the feast than Cat. They would have the entire journey to Westminster Palace to regale each other with what had been missed the prior four years. She would have a maid, of course, and he would do nothing untoward to compromise her reputation.

But once they were married and settled in a house of their own, he would spend hours worshipping her body in every way he'd ever dreamed of. His breath caught.

At last, Cat looked up, but her gaze did not share the anticipation of his own. Nay, there was a deep sadness there that left her bottom lip tucked in her mouth.

"May I inquire about your venture to London?" he asked. "Especially on the heels of having recently returned."

When she did not answer, he tried again, "Cat, why are you going to London?"

This was all so much more difficult than Cat had thought it would be. And already, she'd imagined it to be the most painful thing she'd ever done.

"To go to court..." Cat drew in a deep breath to steady the tremor in her voice.

Geordie touched her face again, as tender as before, his fingertips grazing over her skin. "You can tell me anything." His stare touched her in a deep, intimate place he'd always been able to find within her heart.

She closed her eyes to break that fragile connection, unable to bear what he might see. How she wished she could yield to the emotions churning hot, lustful thoughts in her mind. If she had never met Sir Gawain, if she had never kissed him, never accompanied him into the alcove of the gardens at Westminster, everything would be so very different.

Geordie.

She had been such a fool with Sir Gawain, falling for his smooth words, not giving protest until it was far too late to stop. If she had waited only a mere several months longer, Geordie could have been her prize, with the sweetness in his pain-filled eyes, with the gentle care he'd always given her.

It had always been Geordie in her heart and now it could never be again.

All because of one terrible night.

Geordie's breath brushed her chin and the spiciness of his breath made her instinctively lift her mouth toward his. She squeezed her eyes more tightly shut. She ought to stop. She needed to.

For him.

His lips closed over hers. Warm. Soft. So, so soft. Divine. He tilted her chin up higher and kissed her again, the silence of the room making the sound of their lips touching, parting, and touching again all the more apparent.

She wanted to fall into his strong arms, and yield to the pleasure of his closeness.

I'll protect you, no matter what the cost.

His words echoed in her mind. The cost of her protection would be high, indeed.

"Nay," she whispered.

He immediately straightened and his warmth drew away from her. She opened her eyes and found him watching her with a worried expression. His affection for her was there in the intensity of that concerned gaze, open and given willingly.

Even if she didn't tell him the father of her babe was Sir Gawain, Geordie need only ask several people at court to learn the truth of it. Knights did not kill their own brethren, but Cat feared he would choose her over his sword oath.

"I am going to the Palace of Westminster..." Cat steeled herself against the clench of pain in her chest. "Because Lord Loughton's son wishes to meet me."

Geordie blinked. "Lord Loughton."

"He is a baron." Cat twisted her fingers in her lap. "Marriage to a baron's son is a far better match than a fourth daughter could ever hope to have." She nearly choked on the words, knowing how Geordie would perceive it, being a knight and not a baron.

Or rather, once having been a baron's son...

"It appears his father thought I might be a good match for him after having seen me at court." Her cheeks went red and her gaze slid away from the press of his stare.

"I see." Geordie removed himself from the bench at her side and rose to lean against the wall once more.

Only then, in the absence of his close proximity, was she able to take a full breath. Restored, or as much as one could be in such a situation, she glanced up. He folded his arms over his chest. His very broad chest. The muscles of his arms strained against the soft wool of his doublet.

There was something about him that seemed to draw the air from her lungs. The width of his shoulders, perhaps, the angry hurt simmering in the depths of his eyes just beyond the ever-present pain.

"It would be a marriage made without love," he said abruptly.

Cat chewed at her lower lip, unsure what to say. In truth, she had no plans to even meet Lord Loughton's son, only to use him as an excuse to get to court so she could confront Sir Gawain. After that, she had not yet worked out what she would do. So much of the future hinged on what Sir Gawain was willing to do in the way of aiding her.

"I will get to know him," she said in a faint voice that didn't even convince herself. "How could I not love the man I will be with?"

"And what if you fall in love before you meet him?"

"Geordie..." She got to her feet and reached for him. He pulled away from her, his expression a blank mask to his feelings in every way, but in his eyes where the wounded hurt practically glowed from the brown depths.

"What if you fall in love first?" he demanded.

Instinctively she curled her hands over her stomach, a reminder to herself. "I cannot," she answered honestly.

He looked away. "And I was the fool kissing you when you had your intentions set on a lofty marriage." The bitterness in his voice sliced deep into her. "Do you think he'll make you happy, Cat? That he'll fix whatever is dimming the light in your eyes and making you chew your nails from fretting?"

She paused at his assessment. He had noticed her anxiousness despite her attempts to mask it. Of course, he had. He knew more about her than anyone else. He *would* notice the slight change in her and the poignancy of her unhappiness.

For the first time since Leila had suggested it, Cat thought of the tea. It would indeed solve all of her problems. To allow her to remove the child in her womb, to be free to accept Geordie's affections and return them in kind.

But the babe was innocent in its predicament, as innocent as Geordie in all of it, and hurting one of them was already bad enough.

"You let me kiss you." He didn't say it as an accusation, though he ought to have.

She *had* let him kiss her. And she'd liked it, far more than the forceful probing of Sir Gawain's tongue.

"Forgive me," she whispered. "I did not know how to tell you to stop."

"And now you have." Geordie's chest rose and fell with his pained breath, one mirrored in searing her own heart. "It will not happen again."

"Will you allow me to travel to London with you?" she pressed.

His jaw clenched and he pushed off the wall. "Ask your father. If he agrees, I will." He strode toward the door with purposeful strides.

"Geordie." She ran several steps after him, not stopping until he finally spun around. "I'm sorry," she said.

He met her gaze, emotion blazing in his eyes. "I am too."

7

Geordie rode across the expanse of Werrick Castle's land as though the devil were at his back. Mayhap if that were the case, he would be less filled with rage. At least he could turn his horse about and slay the bastard.

Cat wanted to wed a baron's son. A baron!

When had she ever cared for status?

No doubt the idea had come from her visit to court. Someone sweet and extraordinary like Cat would have been pursued by the men and mocked by the women—all for the same reasons. It was impossible for most to be subjected to its wicked grasp and not be changed.

But Cat...his Cat... He had never anticipated she, of all people, would fall prey to the lure of a higher station.

Geordie had ridden hard through the countryside, even skirting the edge of the border in anticipation of a fight. None had followed. In fact, he'd never seen the border so damn absent of reivers.

Unspent energy flared through his body and left his muscles tense with a need to fight, even as he rode into Werrick Castle's bailey. Peter, the Master of the Horse, met him and took his horse. The man was incredibly handsome, and it rankled at Geordie's jangled nerves. Was that it? Did Cat want a man far more handsome than he?

If so, there were many women who considered Geordie handsome. They'd thrown themselves at him on campaign, promising him pleasure as they pawed appreciatively at him.

But he knew the truth of it deep down. Looks did not make a man. Wealth did. Power, too. A baron's son would someday be a baron; a man with fortune enough to purchase his own knights. To own men like Geordie.

All of his hard work to become a knight, to have a bit of land and a home, and it had not been enough to win Catriona. It would never be enough.

He would never be enough.

Drake appeared beside him. "I know that look, lad."

Geordie slid him a hard glare.

"Aye, I know that one too." Drake lifted a sheathed sword and shoved it against Geordie's chest. "Just ensure it's the practice blade, aye?"

Geordie ripped the sheath from the dulled weapon as Drake went to stand in front of him and lifted his own blade.

"Are you certain?" Geordie growled.

Drake's eyes sparked with the challenge. "I've been waiting for a solid fight like this for a long time."

Without another word, Geordie lunged at his mentor, striking right, left, right, left, across the chest, followed by a downward blow toward the neck. Drake blocked every one, his grunt indicative of the power of each of Geordie's strikes.

Geordie didn't require any time to recover from the blows, after four years of rigorous training, and slammed his blade down with every ounce of his strength. Drake brought his own weapon up with a powerful cry.

Geordie had always appreciated Drake's tutelage, as much as

he'd admired the man's morality: a man who lived by the code of the knight without the real possibility of ever becoming one.

"Dare I ask what has yer mind?" Drake feinted right and took a jab at Geordie, which he quickly deflected.

Initially, Geordie hadn't intended to answer. But as the silence stretched between them, punctuated only by the clang of swords striking, Geordie finally replied with one simple word, "Women."

Drake tilted his head thoughtfully before arcing his sword in Geordie's direction.

Geordie ducked low to avoid it and jammed his blade upward, only to have his own hit evaded.

"I imagine one in particular," Drake supplied before delivering yet another blow.

Geordie grunted and threw an empty punch at Drake.

Drake knocked his arm aside. "Ye're distracted, lad."

Geordie stopped to let his racing heart calm to a gallop. "If the woman you love wanted an escort to another place with the intention of marrying another, would you go?"

Drake lifted his brows with purpose. "Do ye jest?"

Geordie shrugged, not sure what Drake was referring to.

Drake smirked. "I did do it. And I would do it again."

"And you were fine with letting her go?" Geordie lowered his weapon to give his full attention to their conversation.

Drake followed suit. "She was above my station."

Such a simple answer rankled Geordie. "What of you?"

"She was happy," Drake replied. "I dinna know if I would have made her so. I know I would have tried, but it doesna mean it would work."

"Do you regret losing her?" Geordie asked.

A muscle worked in Drake's jaw. "She's happy," he repeated.

Geordie looked up to find the Earl of Werrick making his way over to them. The two warriors sheathed their blades.

Drake leveled his gaze at Geordie. "Ye're a knight, sworn to protect women and do what is just. That said, ye need to keep one thing forefront in yer mind." He straightened his back as the earl approached and glanced at Geordie out of the corner of his eye. "Do what is best for the lady. Even if it means putting her from yer heart."

Lord Werrick smiled at both as he approached. "Do you mind if I take Geordie away for a moment?"

"I believe Sir Geordie got what he needed." Drake gave a respectful incline of his head before he departed.

Lord Werrick put a hand on Geordie's shoulder. "Cat approached me today to ask if she can return to court. Apparently, she feels there may be the opportunity of marriage to Lord Loughton's son." The skin around the earl's eyes went tight and his gaze became searching. "What say you of this?"

The question put Geordie momentarily off guard. Was this an attempt to lure Geordie into confessing his affection for Cat? His reply of his true intention teetered on the edge of his tongue.

In the end, he fell back on the code of chivalry, being courteous and honorable. Wishing to wed an earl's daughter with no means of supporting her was not what a chivalrous knight would do.

"If it pleases her to do so." Geordie's diplomatic reply pulled the earl's expression downward. His brows lowered and his mouth fell into a thoughtful frown.

"I see." Lord Werrick withdrew his hand from Geordie's shoulder. "Will you see her safely to court and look after her while she is there? She'll have a maid, of course, but I would feel better knowing she was going with a friend at her side."

"It would be my honor to so," Geordie answered earnestly. It would indeed be his honor. And also, his temptation.

For if Cat truly wanted to marry the baron's son, Geordie would step aside and allow her to do as she wished. But he knew Cat. Surely, the person she was within her heart would not change so completely in only four years. She had never been one to covet wealth and power. And he would have just over a fortnight to find out for certain.

※

Cat paced the expanse of her room with restless agitation. As bad as she'd thought telling Geordie about Lord Loughton's son would be, it had been far worse. But it had been necessary. First to get her to court where she could confront Sir Gawain, where she may be able to convince him to keep the babe, or even help her find a new home for it. Also to keep Geordie from ever learning the truth.

It had been a painful, crucial lie.

After he'd left, she'd swallowed down her hurt and approached her father for permission to accompany Geordie to court. Papa had been reluctant to offer his blessing and had asked several times if she truly might be happy with someone she did not know.

At last, her father finally conceded and said he would speak with Geordie that afternoon. Now she had only to wait, alone with her thoughts and the recollection of the pained unhappiness in Geordie's sweet eyes. Every prod at the memory cut her deeply.

A knock sounded at her door, bringing her pacing to an abrupt halt. It couldn't be Geordie, of course. Even in their carefree childhood he hadn't approached her bedchamber to seek her out. Still, the possibility that somehow it was him set her pulse racing.

She opened her door with trembling hands, grateful she had not allowed herself to give into the threat of tears. Her visitor was not Geordie, but Marin, who stood in the hall with her hands patiently folded in front of her. "I hoped to find you here. May I come in?"

"Of course." Cat stood back in invitation. "After all, it was once your room."

Marin entered and let her gaze scan the large bedchamber with the canopied wooden bed and all the same familiar dark furnishings that had been there since their mother had occupied the room. Marin's clean, lavender scent filled the air, stronger and more poignant than ever before.

"Oh, I remember." Marin gave a slight smile. "This is where I tried to kill Bran."

"Which time?" Cat chuckled. Her sister's husband had been their enemy before she'd been forced into offering a marriage to him.

Marin gave a little laugh. "Most of them. I thought he was going to kill you that day. That he would murder us all."

Cat had too, though she didn't say as much. Being held captive by Bran in his ploy to enter Werrick Castle had been one of the most terrible days of her life, one she did not relish recalling. She'd tried to counter it with optimism, the same as she did everything, even though it had felt so hollow at the time. Now, she was glad she had, that it had all worked out so perfectly. Bran made Marin so very happy.

"What brings you to see me?" Cat asked.

Marin sat on the edge of the bed and waved Cat over. "I spoke to Father several moments ago."

Cat joined Marin on the edge of the mattress. "About what?"

Marin stroked a hand down Cat's hair as she'd done when they were children. The way their mother used to do. Cat shifted on the bed to put her back to Marin.

"Father mentioned you intend to return to court." Marin's hand ran through Cat's tresses.

Tingles of pleasure danced over Cat's scalp. "Aye. I enjoyed it when I was there. The music, the dancing, the clothing, the pomp of it all." It was only partially a lie. She had enjoyed it when she'd first arrived. Mayhap she had even enjoyed it throughout, except her memories were soured by that last night, by the consequences she was now left to face on her own.

"You plan to go to court to find a husband, as I understand it?" Marin's tone remained bland as her fingers moved through Cat's locks.

Despite the pleasure of Marin's hands, a needle of unease worked its way into Cat's awareness. "Aye," Cat said again. "Lord Loughton is quite wealthy, and a baron. His son would be a good match for me."

"That's what Father has said," Marin confirmed. "And it's what you want?"

Cat was glad she faced away from Marin, so her older sister would not see through the hurt of her lie. "I do. I'd like a husband who will be at court, so that I may stay there more often as well. Like Ella sometimes does."

"This comes as a surprise to me, I confess." Marin spoke slowly, and with apparent care. "I'd often thought you would one day wed Geordie."

Cat's face crumpled in pain. "Oh, Geordie?" She forced a laugh, something light and airy and detached from the agony clawing inside her chest. "He's only ever been just a friend."

"I see." Marin brushed her fingers through Cat's hair in contemplative silence.

What had once been soothing was now unbearable. Cat wanted to sit forward, to pull herself from Marin's repeated petting. Each pass of her hand over Cat's scalp dug into her skull and made it nearly impossible to think.

"I believe," Marin began before tapering off.

Cat used the pause in Marin's statement to turn around and regard her sister. Marin's mouth pressed together, her expression one of regret.

"What is it?" Cat edged closer to her older sister, closer to the comforting scent of lavender. Everything in her wanted to curl into Marin's lap as she'd done when she was a child, when the ache of their mother's loss had been greater than Cat could bear.

Marin pressed her lips together before taking a deep breath and trying again. "I think Geordie is in love with you."

Her admission was a twist to the dagger already lodged in Cat's heart.

Marin met her gaze solemnly. "I believe he always has been. I would caution you to bear that in mind as you travel with him on your way to seek marriage with another. He is quiet, I know, but I believe there is great sensitivity within him."

Cat knew well of his sensitivities, for he had never been quiet with her. Though he'd made mention of it only several times in their lives, she knew the rejection he'd suffered at his father's abandonment.

Cat clenched her hands so hard, it pained her fingertips where the nails had been bitten down to the tender pink skin beneath. She could only nod for fear her voice would tremble if she tried to speak. His affection for her had always been apparent; after all, they had both always cared for each other. But she had never realized the true depth of his feelings.

She had not even realized the true depth of her own feelings for him. It hit her now, powerful and poignant and altogether too late.

If he saved her, he would lose everything. She could never let him know how very much she loved him. It was far too dangerous.

8

A sennight later, they were ready to depart for the Palace of Westminster. Though to Geordie, the time had flown by so quickly with preparations, it'd seemed like only two days.

As he'd only recently journeyed to Werrick Castle, that made the preparation much more time-consuming. His horse, a black destrier he'd named Bentley, needed to be reshod, as well as receive plenty of rest. Everything else Geordie owned had to be thoroughly scrubbed, with all the iron bits well-oiled.

Their small traveling party would only require two additional soldiers for security as they were going through England. Especially in light of Catriona's ability to protect herself.

Cat.

Though he'd only seen her at meals, and the rest of the time they'd both been preoccupied with their own preparations, she had consumed his thoughts. Mayhap he ought to leave her to the baron's son, but there was a part of him somewhere deep and certain that knew she loved him as well. It was in the way she'd looked at him, how she kissed him, how she held him. She was not indifferent to his affection.

He waited now for her in the bailey with two of Drake's best soldiers at his side. When at last she exited the castle, she captivated him wholly and completely. She wore her hair pulled back in a single braid like a long, golden rope tossed over her shoulder. Her green gown was of soft wool that made her look like something the faeries of Scotland might dream up to tempt a man to his death.

Her new lady's maid followed behind her; a woman who had been recommended by the laundress from her own staff. She would travel with them, more for safeguarding Cat's virtue than anything else. Cat and her sisters had never had much need for the assistance of a lady's maid when they had been there to help one another.

Geordie approached Cat and bowed. "We are fortunate to have pleasant weather to start us on our journey."

She lifted her gaze toward the sky as he straightened and closed her eyes to bask in the sun's warmth. He wanted to kiss her like that, unexpected but tender, gently cradling her jaw with his fingertips while he lowered his mouth to hers. Like before.

"You will both be missed." Marin stepped forward and hugged first Cat, then Geordie. She would be departing soon after them, having finished her assistance with the estate matters Lord Werrick had asked her to stay for.

"Keep her safe at court," Marin said to Geordie as she hugged him. "There is much about this plan I do not trust."

Geordie nodded, of the same mindset but unable to speak further on it, as he found himself clasping arms with Lord Werrick. The older man gave a confident nod, his mouth curled in a half smile. "You'll do very well, Sir Geordie. I look forward to when next we meet."

Lord Werrick cast his gaze to Cat and his face softened with paternal affection.

Geordie shifted away to give them their privacy and made his way to Drake. Of all the soldiers at Werrick Castle, Geordie wished Drake would be the one accompanying them. Not only for the companionship, but for the opportunity for Drake to be presented at court, to have a chance to make an impression outside of prejudice. Drake deserved a knighthood more than anyone, even if his blood was half Scot.

"Remember, lad." Drake lifted his dark gaze toward Geordie. "Ye're a knight. Ye do first and foremost what is best for your lady." A muscle worked in his jaw. "Even if it isna the easiest choice to make, aye?"

Geordie nodded solemnly. "Thank you, Drake."

They said farewell as soldiers often do: with a hard clap on one another's backs.

Leila was the last to bid farewell with a tender embrace. "There is more to Cat than she wishes you to know," she whispered before pulling away.

She watched him in that quiet, knowing way of hers, not divulging anything more than the obscure reference to a premonition that might come to pass. He tried to hide his wary expression and apparently did a poor job, because she gave an apologetic shrug as if to say she understood exactly how frustrating her gift could be.

Geordie aided Cat onto her horse, a brown courser she'd named Star for the patch of white on his flat forehead. She watched Geordie climb atop his own horse and smiled at the beast.

"That is a fine destrier." She reached over to stroke her fingers over Bentley's glossy black neck. The horse remained stoic.

"He was a gift from Sir John Howard, once he saw my skill with the longbow." It had been after the Battle of Cadzand, a decimation of the Flemish by the English, mainly due to their use of longbows. Geordie had led many of the men, instructing them through the battle. Sir John had claimed they won because of Geordie and gifted him the horse. The praise hadn't settled well with Geordie, but to refuse the gift would have caused offense.

"You have always been good with the bow." Cat shifted her gaze from the horse to Geordie.

"Not as good as you."

She waved her hand dismissively. "Do not discount your own skills. You are exceptional." A flush colored her cheeks and she returned her attention to the destrier. "What is his name?"

Geordie couldn't help but grin. The only reason he'd given the beast a name was because he knew she would ask him for it one day. "Bentley."

She repeated the horse's name and nodded approvingly. "It fits him."

As they spoke, Cat's maid, Freya, was helped onto her horse by Peter, who pressed his lips to the back of her hand in a gesture clearly meant to be discreet. The two soldiers who would accompany their party mounted their steeds as well. The taller, more rigid of the two was Eldon, who had been trained with an axe the same time as Geordie and Cat when they were all children. The other was Drake's most trusted soldier, Durham, whose wild dark hair and beard gave him a savage appearance that his friendly blue eyes did not match.

Together, they waved one final farewell to the people of Werrick Castle and departed the bailey. The sun shone brilliantly in the cloudless sky above. If they were fortunate, the weather would hold for the better part of their journey.

"What do you enjoy the most about being on the open road, Geordie?" Cat asked, once they had entered the great stretch of rolling green hills. Her expression was wistful, reminiscent of the days they spent on their backs, gazing up at the clouds drifting in a sea-blue sky.

"Your letters," he answered without pause. Heat crept over his face at his own honesty.

But she did not rebuke him the foolish reply. She did exactly as the Cat from his childhood would have: she fixed her gaze on him with a caring smile.

"Truly?" she asked. "Did they mean so much to you?"

"Aye. I kept them all." He flicked a shy gaze her way and was rewarded with the radiance of her unrestrained joy.

"I tried to make them as detailed as possible for you." She lifted her shoulders in a shrug, but her eyes sparkled.

"I could tell. I liked it." He led the party down the long path departing from Werrick Castle, following a trail he'd traveled many times in his life from battles and leaving on campaign. Either he'd been departing with trepidation, hoping it would not be the last time he saw Cat, or returning with elation to see her once more.

Now, riding together might be the most perilous of all. For he had only weeks to woo Cat before she met Lord Loughton's eldest son. She was not contracted, nor even being courted. It was well within his code of morals to win her heart before another could steal it away.

༺༻

Cat tried to hide her pleasure at Geordie's admission of having enjoyed her missives. She'd described all the events of Werrick Castle, speaking to him through ink. It had been easy as the words flowed in her head, as though he was there with her.

The hardest part had been when the letter was finished, and the flood of loneliness resonated within her. She had her sisters, of course, but they were not the same as Geordie.

They hadn't been able to speak much as they prepared to leave in the past sennight. She'd missed their talks. She'd missed *him*.

"Tell me of your travels," Cat encouraged. "I want to know about the places you went, the visits you had to court, the times you won the battle for the king. Mayhap even the ladies you wooed."

The last question was like ash in her mouth. Color worked up in Geordie's cheeks, even as she wanted to squirm in her saddle.

She'd meant it as a way to seed the suggestion that he might find someone else rather than her. He needed a woman who wouldn't destroy his life, a woman who had not lost her future with one stupid mistake.

Except that the words had felt awkward and forced as they passed her lips.

Why, why, *why* had she gone with Sir Gawain that night?

It was a question she asked herself many times over, and it was one that had many answers.

She hadn't been to court since she was a girl, and she'd been swept away by the grandeur of it, as though she were no longer Lady Catriona Barrington but some faraway princess, like in the books Ella had written. After a lifetime on the English-Scottish border with naught but her sisters and her people around her, it was the only time men had ever flattered her.

Sir Gawain had made her feel important, wanted. His flattery had been blatant and his requests for kisses smooth and enticing. Every protest she'd offered had been met with another form of persuasion until her head spun and she'd felt foolish for declining.

"What is it, Cat?" Geordie asked.

She glanced up, startled from the dark pull of her awful thoughts. He'd edged his horse closer to hers and regarded her with a concerned expression.

"'Tis nothing." She smiled at him and gave a little embarrassed laugh at being caught up in her own thoughts.

"I believe it may be something." He lifted his hand, then stayed it. "You're crying."

She touched her cheek where her fingertips met a tear. "The sun is so very bright today, is it not?" She squinted up at the sky in demonstration, but Geordie did not appear convinced.

"Cat..." He held her gaze for a long moment. "I'm always here for you."

A knot of emotion immediately lodged in her throat, thick and aching. Now she *did* want to cry. To know he was there to talk to, the way she'd always done, except she could not. How could she possibly confess what she had done?

She swallowed down her tears and shook her head, unable to even speak.

"Did I tell you about the first time I saw a man try to shoot an arrow at a target?" Geordie asked abruptly.

Cat grinned in spite of herself, knowing a new story was imminent. Most likely one that had not been in a letter.

"He did well enough." Geordie shrugged and did not appear impressed. "And I told him I knew a woman who could shoot from four times that distance and hit the center of the target every time. He didn't believe me, of course."

Cat laughed, grateful beyond words for Geordie. He'd always done this, switching topics to something distracting when she was upset.

He proceeded to talk through the day, filling her mind with his stories of soldier's camps and rigorous training and the many places he'd visited between battles. As late afternoon descended on them, he sent Durham ahead to act as a harbinger.

As the sun sank, they were securely within their rooms with the smell of a savory stew floating up through the floorboards along with the sounds of conversation and laughter. Her new lady's maid put her attention to Cat once the room was comfortably prepared.

"Are ye certain ye're no' tired, my lady?" Freya's young brow crinkled beneath her dark-haired widow's peak.

Cat shook her head. "Nay, I assure you. You needn't be so overly concerned with me. I am used to caring for myself."

Freya nodded and pressed her lips together, evidently wanting to say more.

"What is it?" Cat asked.

Freya's gaze slid away.

"Please," Cat implored. "You are my maid, aye, but I've never truly had one, with the exception of my recent visit to court and the need for help with the more elaborate hairstyles. I'd prefer you not be cautious with everything you say and do."

The woman nodded slowly, still reserved with apparent trepidation. "I..." She took a deep breath. "I'm merely concerned for yer well-being, my lady."

Her wording took Cat aback. "My well-being?"

"'Twas my job to take the sheets and personal items from the rooms at Werrick Castle, to see them washed and returned." Freya's slender form twisted from one side to the other with obvious discomfort. "I've been doing it for nigh on six months, my lady. I notice things others dinna."

Cat swallowed, understanding now. Personal linens and bedsheets that had been monthly stained with blood would no doubt be apparent in a household with only two ladies. Especially when oftentimes those linens had been used to clean up the sickness each morning.

Freya met her gaze. "I am concerned about ye, my lady," she said in a soft voice that would not travel outside the room. "For I suspect ye're with child."

9

Cat made her way down the stairs of the inn on shaking legs with Freya at her side. The lady's maid had promised she wouldn't share Cat's secret with a soul. Indeed, the young woman had even offered her own confession of being in love with Werrick's Master of the Horse, Peter—a man rumored to have vowed to never give his heart away. And yet, he apparently had shyly admitted to feeling deeper for her than any other woman ever before and she had been left with a hope she did not want shattered.

Not that Cat was truly worried Freya would betray her, though sharing her own heartfelt secret had been considerate. It was the act of Cat confessing her shame to the young woman, admitting aloud her horrible mistake.

But there was more. As Cat had been going through her small bag of close personal effects, some sewing materials, a book Ella had written, and several other various items, Cat had come across an unexpected item wrapped in linen. It was so small; she'd nearly missed where it lay tucked in the bottom corner of her bag.

She'd unwrapped the parcel to reveal a vial filled with liquid. She pulled the stopper free and was hit with a sharp mint odor that she immediately recognized: pennyroyal. Leila had presented her with one final chance to remove the child from her womb.

While Cat did not intend to use the gift, neither could she bring herself to throw the vial out. And so, there it remained, rewrapped in the linen and tucked carefully back into her bag.

She paused at the base of the stairs and searched through the crowd of patrons and servants to find Geordie. She spotted him easily near the hearth with the other two soldiers from Werrick Castle.

"There they are, my lady." Freya took a step to lead Cat through the crowd to where the men gathered.

Cat gently put a hand out to stop her. "A moment, please."

She studied Geordie from across the room. He was of similar height to the many other male patrons, except for his battle-hewn body, which was evident beneath his tunic. The broad shoulders he'd always had in his youth had filled out with masculine strength. Lines of muscle even showed on his throat as he spoke with Eldon and Durham.

Geordie put an arm up on Eldon's shoulder and said something that made the man laugh. It was the first time she'd seen Geordie from afar like this. As a man, confident in his skill and his place in life, a natural leader. The casual ease of his demeanor passed off to those he spoke with. He was both liked and admired by others; that much was apparent in both of Werrick Castle's soldiers.

Pride swelled in her, happy and warm as it expanded nearly too large for her chest. Geordie had worked hard for that admiration. For all of it. And he'd done it through tireless effort and the grit of sheer determination. This was why she could not tell him. She couldn't allow him to sacrifice all those years of dedication, throw them away to settle the score of an offense.

Geordie broke off for a moment to ask a passing serving woman for something. When he was done, his gaze did not skim over her departing backside. Nay, his attention flicked first to the stairs, then to Cat.

His smile widened and he lifted his cup in silent toast toward her. If she hadn't known him, if they hadn't had the lifetime of closeness and bonding, she would still be tempted to approach him following such a welcome invitation. For as handsome as he was, what woman would not?

"Now, Freya." Cat held back a wistful sigh as her heart gave a fluttering beat. "Now we can join them."

"Aye, my lady," Freya replied with a smile in her voice.

Together, they approached the men. Geordie followed Cat's path the entire way, a slight lift to the corner of his mouth in a lazy, appreciative grin. Eddies tickled low in her stomach, a warm, pleasant sensation she enjoyed.

"My lady." Geordie bowed low and kissed her hand.

His lips were soft against her skin and made her recall the gentleness of his kiss the night of his return to Werrick Castle.

How she craved another. How she craved *him*. Even as she knew she shouldn't, even as she knew he would be best without her, she could not stop the thrum of her own true desire.

She inclined her head as he straightened. "Sir Geordie. You appear to be in fine spirits."

"All the finer now." Even as he said the words, and despite the flirtation in his stare, color touched his cheeks.

Ever her sweet Geordie. Her own face flushed warm.

"I hope you're hungry." He glanced to the left as several steaming trenchers of hearty pottage and bread were set upon a nearby table.

"Is all that for us?" Cat asked, incredulous.

"It's for Eldon. Our food will be out shortly." Geordie bumped his arm against the taller soldier.

Eldon rubbed his hands in anticipation. "Finally, someone appreciates my appetite."

Cat laughed and allowed Geordie to lead her to the food-laden table. They had not traveled as long today as she had on the first day of her previous journey to court with Ella. Which meant there would be more days of travel this time than the last.

Cat caught Geordie's shy smile aimed at her and suddenly was grateful for that extra time. It would make her further along in her condition, aye, but it would also give her more time with him.

And more time to figure out what she was going to do if Sir Gawain would not offer his aid.

※

THE FOLLOWING FOUR DAYS WERE BLESSEDLY UNEVENTFUL AS they followed the old road along the river, the remnants of what an ancient city had left behind. In some areas, Geordie noted the brush had not been cut back to two hundred feet as per the king's orders, which meant the likelihood of attacks increased. They kept to the center of the road in those areas, as well as they could over the patches of broken cobbled paving.

Thus far, each inn they stayed at had been clean, proving Durham's ability to pick accommodating lodging. It was one of the reasons the dark-haired Englishman had been sent along with their party. The man had a knack for finding a good place to sleep.

Better than anything, however, was Cat. Over the course of their journey, she had come to life once more. It was as though she was shedding the husk that had become the new Catriona, and revealing a shinier, more exuberant part of herself.

After getting settled into a new inn for the evening, Geordie found himself glancing toward the stairs that led from the private rooms above to the hall. It was a routine they'd fallen comfortably into. Cat and Freya settled into their rented room and refreshed themselves, while the men enjoyed some libation and ordered a round of warm food to be brought down after dumping their belongings unceremoniously into their rooms.

Movement caught Geordie's eye on the stairs. His heart leapt as Cat descended with graceful, airy steps. She made her way toward him, a smile lighting her face. Other men turned to watch in appreciation as she passed, but she paid them no mind, if she even noticed them. Nay, the entirety of her attention was fixed on him alone. As though Geordie was the only man in the room to exist.

That was how it had always been with Cat. Even as his own parents had abandoned him, leaving him to die for their betrayal, Cat had made him feel like he belonged. Like he was wanted. He had a fortnight remaining to enjoy the time with her before she would meet with Lord Loughton and his son. Geordie's stomach twisted.

"Is there to be a feast tonight?" Cat scanned the crowded hall where the musicians were already beginning to play. In the air hung the unmistakable scent of fat crackling over a spit and succulent roasting meat.

"Aye," Geordie grinned, already anticipating a night away from their usual fare of pottage or bread and cheese.

But it was more than that, he wanted to dance with Cat. Mayhap to even kiss her, woo her and keep her from ever thinking of marrying the baron's whelp.

They ate heartily, supping on roasted venison and stewed vegetables, followed by generous helpings of wine and ale. This time, Geordie did not wait for Cat to question if he would ask her to dance. Instead, he simply held out his hand to her.

"Do you anticipate my answer so readily that you do not even ask?" She put her hand into his and allowed him to pull her to standing.

He spun her about and caught her by the waist. "Aye."

She laughed as he led her to where a group of people were already dancing in time to a jaunty tune.

They moved together through the music; their eyes locked on one another. Attraction crackled between them; the air thick with currents of energy like the feeling before lightning strikes.

The closer their bodies got, the more noticeable the sensation, drawing them together as though they'd been made to fit perfectly with one another. They were already nearly touching when a drunkard passed them, his arms and legs flailing in a mockery of the dancers. His lifted leg bumped into Cat's back and sent her sprawling into Geordie.

He caught her in his arms and regarded the man who had hit her. Something in him snapped, that deep part of him trained to be a warrior, a fighter, a protector. Men were to respect women, not hit them and walk by as if nothing had happened.

"Geordie, he's drunk," Cat said softly.

Geordie's muscles went hot with the need to confront the man, to demand an apology on Cat's behalf. The man needed to learn how to respect a woman. "He hit you," Geordie replied tersely.

He hadn't realized he'd taken a step toward the drunkard until Cat put a hand to his chest.

"It was not on purpose," she protested. "And if I were truly offended, I assure you, I could handle it myself."

They both looked down at where her hand rested on his chest at the exact same time. Her cheeks flushed red and she pulled her hand back as if she'd been burned.

"I don't mind your touch." He lifted his gaze to hers. "I never have."

She bit her lip. "Geordie..."

There was trepidation in her voice as she said his name, as though preparing to say something she didn't want to. But something she ought to.

He ran the back of his knuckles down the slope of her smooth cheek. She exhaled a soft breath and it whispered over his skin.

His heart thundered in his chest, his blood pounding—nay, singing—urging him to tilt back her head and claim her luscious mouth. He brushed his thumb over her chin and her lashes swept lower. With a single finger at her jawline, he lifted her face.

A crash sounded nearby. Geordie had just enough time to pull Cat toward him as a tankard went flying past the spot where her head had been. Shouts rang out around and two men launched at one another, their faces red with drink and outrage.

Geordie led Cat away from the men, toward an alcove where no errant drinks might fly at them. Even still, he kept his back to the crowd with her against a wall, blocking anything that might come. "You weren't injured?" It was a statement as much as a question.

Cat chuckled good-naturedly and shook her head. "Even if I'd been struck, I doubt I would have suffered any real harm. Thank you for saving me."

"I told you," he said earnestly. "I'll always protect you."

The laughter in her eyes melted away. "I don't want that. You must leave me to care for myself sometimes."

Geordie pressed closer to her, enough to detect the sweet, familiar scent of her. "But I want to keep you safe."

"Don't say that." Even as she spoke, she lifted her face upward and pulled him toward her. She pressed her mouth to his, not with the lightness of his past kisses, but with a hungry explosion of passion. Her lips closed over his and the tip of her tongue teased into his mouth.

Fire shot through his veins. He wanted to run his fingers over her body, learn with his hands what he saw with his eyes. He wanted to kiss her and kiss her and kiss her until all thoughts of Lord Loughton and court were cleared from her mind.

Abruptly, Cat broke off the kiss and pressed her forehead to his, her eyes squeezed shut.

"Forgive me, Geordie." She leaned back to look at him, her eyes glossy with tears. "I cannot accept your protection."

And with that, she slipped away, darting through the crowd and hastening up the stairs.

10

Cat should never have kissed Geordie. She pushed the door to her room closed and leaned back against it. Her heart raced with such frenzy, she had difficulty catching her breath. Why had she done it?

Her head lowered back with a dull thud against the door.

She knew exactly why she'd done it. Because he was so wonderfully brave; because the concern in his eyes made her insides melt. She wanted to be a girl worthy of his protection, but her secret could destroy him. Nay, it *would* destroy him.

If he'd been ready to confront a drunkard who had bumped into her, what might he do to a man who had plied her with drink and fumbled about under her skirts? A shiver ran down her spine, trailing prickles of goosebumps in its wake.

She was all too aware of what he would do.

That thought weighed on her like a blacksmith's anvil, all through the night and well into the morning. By the time they were on the remnants of the old Roman road once more, exhaustion pulled at her. At mid-day, her eyes were gritty with sleeplessness and her bones felt as though they were sagging in on themselves.

That was when the rain began.

Patters of icy droplets spattered them. At first, the drops were sporadic, but soon became a driving rain as the storm began in earnest. Freya gave a little scream of surprise at the suddenness of it, and Cat pulled her cloak over her head to shield herself from the chilly deluge. Thick clouds blotted out any warmth the sun provided.

Geordie immediately began issuing orders in a calm voice, sending Durham ahead to find lodging and instructing Eldon to aid Freya into the cart so she didn't get wet. Geordie went to Cat himself and helped her from Star.

He caught her with strong arms and guided her to the cart. His arm remained over her as they walked, providing her with warmth, and as much shelter from the rain as he could manage. She was perfectly capable of remaining upright on her own, and yet she reveled in his closeness, in the wonderful comfort of Geordie.

He lifted her into the covered cart as though she weighed nothing and settled her beside Freya. His dark hair hung in wet waves on either side of his face and rain dripped from his strong nose, but he did not appear to notice either. "Stay in here until the rain abates, aye?"

She nodded and scooted closer to her maid so that they might share body warmth. Geordie remained in the rain, seeing to the horses to ensure they were on the firmer parts of the road and out of the sucking puddles of mud.

With that, their small party moved onward once more, moving to meet Durham, who hopefully had found lodging nearby. Their pace was slow, which Cat was grateful for lest the cart rattle her apart.

A swell of pride heated in Cat's breast again, even as icy water seeped through her cloak and wind sent chills prickling over her skin. It was only the rain Geordie was saving them from, aye, but he'd done it with such ease and confidence that she could easily imagine him on a battlefield. She was certain he would make all his decisions as readily, quickly chosen and yet carefully considered with the knowledge of how they would affect the lives of his men.

Durham met them soon after and led them to the inn he'd found. Even then Geordie continued his efforts, first seeing to Cat and Freya, then focusing on the care of the horses. He was the last one to enter the inn and seek shelter for himself. Indeed, his hair was still wet with rain when they sat down for supper.

The following morning when they resumed their journey, she noticed a glassiness to his eyes and a flush to his cheeks. He shrugged off her worry when she asked after it, but she kept her attention on him as they traveled throughout the day. His eyes slipped closed several times as he rode, but each time, he straightened immediately and blinked his eyes open.

Cat's heart gave a little squeeze. He was not well. It was for that reason she went to Durham herself to see if he might find a monastery for them that evening, one with a healing cottage for treating illness. He agreed without complaint, obviously having seen Geordie's condition deteriorate through the day as well.

Geordie protested weakly that he needed no care, but his objections died away after several minutes of riding. Eventually, he fell completely silent, his head dipping forward to his chest multiple times. When they arrived at the monastery, he dismounted on his own, his shoulders squared with determination.

Cat slid from Star before he could approach her to help her from the horse. She would not have him care for her when he needed care himself. He strode toward her, his gait slow, yet purposeful. He staggered slightly, veering to the left and knocking himself off balance.

Cat ran to him and grabbed his arm to steady him. His body blazed with heat, even through his sleeve. She cried out in alarm and put a hand to his brow. His skin was like fire.

"I'm fine," he mumbled.

"You are far from fine," she said in horror. "You must let the monks see to you at once."

He gazed at her through glassy, heavy-lidded eyes and finally acquiesced with a slow, lazy nod. Despite his agreement to receive healing, he insisted on walking himself.

They made their way inside, one slow, stubborn step at a time and were shown to a large room filled with beds. Most were occupied, some neatly made and ready for an occupant.

The aged monk took them to one of these beds. Cat helped pull down the blankets for Geordie, guiding him to the thin mattress. He sagged to the small cot and lay upon it. His eyes fell closed and his breathing became deep and even. He did not wake again for some time.

Cat sat at his side, watching him sleep, grateful for each swell of his chest as he breathed.

She had never been to a monastery for healing. She'd only known of their existence based on conversations she'd overheard at inns. It was not like the little stone room at Werrick Castle, where Isla would have had an herbal concoction at the ready to aid with whatever ailed the person.

Nay, the monks offered the sick several prayers, a bed and a bit of broth thickened with ground almonds and beans.

The heat of Geordie's skin did not abate under such ministrations. In fact, he seemed to grow hotter still as the night dragged on. Panic welled in Cat's chest.

"Is there nothing else to be done?" Cat asked when the monk next appeared.

The man was young, his face unlined. There was something in his wide blue eyes that made her think of their priest at Werrick Castle, Bernard.

This man, however, was not as twitchy and carried himself with an air of authority. "If he is ill, it is doubtless a direct result of a sin committed. Praying will aid with the purging of his fever."

Helpless tears welled in Cat's eyes. She shook her head in angry frustration. "Nay, he is the purest, kindest man there is. Surely, there must be something else."

The monk nodded to where Geordie's sword lay on the ground beneath his bed. "He is a soldier, is he not?"

"Aye, a knight."

Something flashed in the monk's eyes. "Then he is neither kind nor pure."

Cat wanted to protest that the man didn't know Geordie, that whatever he thought of soldiers, Geordie was not like others. But it would do little good. "Is there something we can do for him?"

"A barber will come in two days and will bleed him if his humors are out of balance." The monk lowered his head in reverence. "Until then, he is in God's hands."

The man said nothing more and moved on. Cat clenched her fists in an effort to tamp down her anger at the man's reaction to finding out Geordie was a knight. The monk had not been in battle; he did not know war as Cat did.

And while she knew little of medicine, she knew with certainty Isla did not approve of bleeding. The barbaric practice of educated men, she'd hissed once before.

Cat pressed a hand to Geordie's scalding forehead. He gave a soft humming sound and turned into her touch.

"Cat," he murmured.

"I'm here, Geordie." She pressed her hand lower, to his cheek. It had been years since she'd been sick with fever, but she remembered well how the cool press of a palm felt like heaven.

He muttered her name again and sighed softly. She ground her teeth in frustration, hating that there was nothing more she could do for him than put her hands to his face.

Her thoughts raced, combing through the many herbs she'd helped Leila string together. She'd mainly learned to care for them, which ones ought to be hung up, which were best for drying in the sun, and which were for putting into tinctures or pressing for their oils. But Leila often spoke of their healing properties as well.

Cat closed her eyes and focused on the many she had sorted through, and how very many of them helped to reduce fever. Some of them incredibly common, like...like...

Cat's eyes flew open. *Meadowsweet.* She leapt to her feet to summon Freya. There had been some growing in patches just outside the monastery.

She knew exactly what to do to help Geordie, and she would not leave his side until she made certain it would work.

※

GEORDIE TRIED TO SWALLOW AND FOUND HIS MOUTH impossibly dry. His throat stuck against itself and made him choke into a cough. Cool hands pressed to the back of his neck, lifting his head as a cup was settled against his mouth.

He drank greedily. Ale, sweet and crisp, washing over his tongue and down his parched throat. Gentle hands removed the cup, while Geordie lay his head back down. He opened his eyes and found Cat sitting beside his bed.

He blinked in confusion. What was Cat doing in his room?

"Geordie?" She sat forward. Her fingers moved over his face. "I think your fever is breaking."

Fever. The word conjured heat in his mind. His entire body was hot. He shoved the blanket from his body.

Her eyes were bright with concern. "Geordie, I've been so worried. You've been so ill."

Had he? Geordie frowned. "Where are we?" He looked around, noticing for the first time all the beds around them, some of them filled with people. A monk hovered over a prone form several beds over.

"We're in a monastery," she replied. "We've been here for two days."

Geordie shook his head. "I never get ill." His thoughts were muddy in his mind, too thick.

"Everyone does." She smiled and took his hand. "Even brave knights."

He gazed down at their joined hands. "You stayed by my side."

"I did."

He raised his brows. "For two days and nights."

"I couldn't leave you." She squeezed his fingers with hers.

Geordie wrapped his mind around her confession. She had sat by his bedside for two days tending to him. And yet, she insisted on wanting to marry Lord Loughton's son.

Did she not understand what she meant to him?

He pulled himself to sitting despite her protests. The room spun around in a wild tilt. He focused on Cat while his world settled back into place once more. But then, Cat had always grounded him. When he was lonely. When his heart ached for home. Even in the charge of battle, when excitement melded with the metallic taste of fear.

It had always been Cat, strengthening his heart and focusing his mind.

His thoughts were like gritty sludge churning within his skull. "I don't understand."

"You had a terrible fever," Cat replied. "I believe from the rain—"

Geordie put up a hand to stop her. "I don't understand why you want to wed the baron's son."

She tilted her head, and he knew his statement had been unexpectedly abrupt. He also knew now was not the time to discuss this, but somehow, he could not make himself stop.

"You care about me, Cat." He braced himself on the bed.

"I always have." There was a hesitance to her reply.

"Yet you'll marry another."

Cat drew a deep breath. "Geordie, I—"

"I love you, Cat." The words were out of his mouth before he could stop them. Not that he wanted to. He'd wanted to tell Cat those words since they were children. Since she'd saved his life and his soul all at once.

She was the reason he grew up wanting to be a better man, rather than wanting to give into the hole in his heart that his parents had left.

He knew she cared for him; he always had known. But after the absence of four years and her determination to wed another, his trust in her affection had been shaken. Staying with him the two days of his illness, however, was proof enough to embolden him.

Except now, she was shaking her head. "Don't say that," she whispered.

"But it's true, Cat. I've always loved you. I'd do anything for you."

"Don't say that either." She got to her feet. "You need more ale. I should—"

"Why do you want to wed Lord Loughton's son so badly?" Geordie looked up at her and the room began to tilt again. The dizzying sensation jiggled at his ragged nerves. "Why do you want to be a baron's wife? Is the thought of a title and riches so tempting that you would forgo love?"

"I enjoy life at court," she said in a thin voice. "You know how it is. You said you've been once before."

Geordie gripped the bed. He shouldn't have started this now, but the words had already been said. Once in battle, there was only going forward. Retreat was never an option. "Court is a cesspool of sin and debauchery." Bitterness seeped into his voice. "Filled with gambling, married men and women betraying the sanctity of their vows at every turn. Men mindlessly determined to deflower maidens, and the empty-headed women who foolishly fall prey to their charms. I don't understand why anyone would want to ever return."

The room had stopped spinning somewhat. He gazed up at

her to find her eyes had gone wide, her face pale, and he realized the harshness of what he'd said in his frustration.

He softened his tone. "Especially you. You're too smart, too talented for such a life. The Cat I knew would never have wanted to give up her bow and arrow in place of new gowns and elaborate headwear."

Cat pressed her lips together and looked down at the floor before finally speaking. "Then mayhap you do not know me anymore, Geordie."

With that, she spun from him and strode away, leaving him with only a hollow sensation and the realization of everything he'd said, and how very wrong it had all been.

11

Cat ran from the monastery cottage into the sunshine, where she proceeded to be sick in the grass. She clutched her stomach, her heart slamming in her chest like a drumbeat.

Men mindlessly determined to deflower maidens, and the empty-headed women who foolishly fall prey to their charms.

Was that what she was, then? An empty-headed woman who had foolishly fallen prey to a man's charms? Tears came to her eyes, but she ground them away with the heels of her palms. She wouldn't do this here. Not now, even when she knew the answer to her own question.

She had been an empty-headed woman. She had been so dazzled by court, so overly flattered by the attention. It had all seduced her. It left infatuated with court life...and with Sir Gawain. That night she'd had far too much to drink. She knew that. Even now she could taste the heaviness of the rich wine clinging to the back of her throat, recalled the muddled sensation of having to focus on her words to keep them from slurring.

Even as Cat pushed herself upright and strode to the women's quarters of the monastery, that night at court came rushing back to her. The slurring of her speech from so much wine, allowing Sir Gawain to lead her outside and how her legs had clumsily tripped and staggered through uneven grass in the moonlit garden. Sir Gawain held her upright, his voice like silk in her ears.

There had been a bench beneath an alcove. His mouth fell to hers in an instant. Her head had swum dizzily and even the simple act of closing her eyes made her feel as though she were aboard a small ship in rough seas.

His hand was at her breast first, but she'd pushed him away, only to have it return with relentless intent. He kissed away her protests, murmuring as he did so of her beauty, of his desire for her. She'd been so very tired, wanting only to go to sleep, her mind too weary to keep up with his constant persuasions. By the time his hot hand slid up her thighs under her skirt, she barely had the energy to object, let alone try to push him away.

She'd attempted to tell him to stop, but his kisses had become too amorous, his tongue filling her mouth. Suddenly it wasn't his fingers, but something else pressing against her. In the private, delicate place between her legs that no one but a husband ought to have access.

Even now her pulse ticked too quickly at the helpless memory. The air was suddenly too thin to breathe. She'd tried to stop him, but he'd quieted her with his words with the claim she had played the wanton and couldn't now retract her affections when they had come so far. His statement had so taken her aback, she had gone still with shock.

And then it was too late.

She should have fought him off. She was strong enough. She could have screamed, punched, kicked, whipped out her dagger. But she had been made immobile by pain and confusion and bitter, ugly shame.

Afterward, when she was left hollow and reeling, he'd kissed her and sworn the next time would be more enjoyable. There hadn't been a next time. She made certain she did not see him again before leaving court.

Heavy with the burden of memories, she climbed the stairs to the women's quarters in the monastery. The room was empty within, as it was midday. Cat found the bed Freya had prepared for her and lay upon it without bothering to pull down the covers. The bedding was rough against her skin, uncomfortable enough for any monk.

Not that it mattered. Even if she had the finest sheets in Christendom, she knew she would not be able to rest. Not with such an ache in her breast. Instead, she lay there with her haunted memories and Geordie's words replaying in her mind.

Empty-headed women who foolishly fall prey to their charms.

Tears slipped silent from her eyes and melted into the sheets. She deserved every bit of pain from those words as they slid like splinters into her heart. If only she had not allowed herself to be swayed by Sir Gawain. If only she had stopped him from pouring wine into her goblet. If only she had protested going outside alone at night, and not feared him thinking her unsophisticated.

But time could not make good on "if onlys." And in this case, time would not be enough to heal her mistake.

She settled a hand to her lower stomach where the skin had begun to swell, unmistakable evidence of a life growing within her. They were over a third of the way to London and would arrive in a fortnight. She would have to confront Sir Gawain then.

Her breath quickened with anxiety. What would she say? How would he respond? Would he agree to take the baby?

Her fingers moved over her stomach. Would she care? More tears leaked from her eyes, hot with hurt and shame. Right now, the babe was just a small bump in her lower stomach, but eventually, it would be a baby, a child. Like Ella's Blanche or Anice's Gavin.

Wouldn't she care then?

A harsh sob rose up in her throat and the silent tears gave way to weeping. She was ruining a child's life as well as her own, and Geordie might possibly hate her. All for being an empty-headed fool.

※

GEORDIE HAD MADE A GRAVE MISTAKE. A SENNIGHT HAD PASSED and still Cat was despondent. She did not fill the stretches of time on the road with her cheerful chatter, and the brilliance of her smile had dimmed to nonexistence.

He'd tried to apologize time and again since that terrible day in the monastery. Each time she had shaken her head and told him there was no need. But truly there had been need, or his words would have eased her worries.

Now, he stood by the hearth with a mug of ale for himself and a fine goblet of wine for her. She usually took her ale watered down, but he knew she used to enjoy wine when they were younger and hoped to bring some color to her cheeks again.

Her preparations for supper after their journeys were taking longer and longer, as though it was hard to bring herself downstairs. At last, he saw her on the stairs, her face impassive, revealing nothing of her thoughts. Men still stared as she passed. She would always be the type of woman to turn a man's eye, no matter how muted her spirit.

Her mouth flicked upward in a small smile when she saw him, and his heart lifted a little. He offered her the goblet. "They had a fine Noirien wine in their cellars I thought you might enjoy. That was your favorite, if I recall correctly."

She cast a glance to the wine, opened her mouth, and her forehead crinkled.

Geordie's confidence flagged. "You don't like it anymore." He nodded in understanding. "'Tis fine."

"Forgive me, I–I do not drink wine any longer." She regarded her lady's maid, who had taken a seat beside Durham. "I believe Freya might enjoy it, however."

Freya's gaze slid to the goblet. "My lady, 'tis too fine."

Before Cat could press her insistently, Geordie put the goblet in front of the maid.

"If you don't drink it, I will." Durham grinned and moved his hand closer to the wine.

Freya caught the cup in her palm and drew it toward her. "Not unless ye want a sound beating."

Durham waggled his brows. "I do like a woman with a feisty side."

Eldon snorted. "So say you, until Peter finds out you've been flirting with his lass."

Cat laughed then, a ghost of what her joyous tinkling used to be, but it was a laugh all the same. And it was the first Geordie had heard from her in a sennight.

While they ate supper, he could not help but notice how her nails had been shorn down to the quick once more. The once smooth edges were ragged from being torn at by her teeth. To make matters worse, she did not eat much of anything. The past several nights, he'd noticed the same. She nibbled at bread and pushed the pottage around in her bowl, but seldom ever took a bite.

That night, a small trio of musicians were staying at the inn. As often happened with traveling troupes, they performed for their room and board. The hall filled with the gentle notes of the lute, pipe and harp. Eldon, Durham and Freya had all sat closer to better hear them play, while Geordie stayed back with Cat. It was a perfect opportunity to apologize. Again.

"Cat," he began. "Please forgive me."

"Geordie, you've done nothing wrong."

After his insistence in their conversation at the monastery, it had seemed wrong to press her into a conversation she clearly did not want to have. However, his apologies had done little good and whatever was causing her a considerable amount of distress continued to do so.

"I should not have said what I did," he said gently.

"You were ill." She put her hand on his forearm. "And I...I know it is confusing. I know I am..." She offered a shadow of a smile. "I know I am different than before."

"What is it that troubles you so?" He ran his finger lightly over her finger where raw, red skin showed beneath the torn nail.

She curled her hand inward to hide her fingers and gave a stiff shrug.

"You know you can tell me anything." Geordie sat up straighter to regard her.

Her head lowered. "It is nothing you have done," she said softly. "And everything that I have."

"Tell me, Cat."

She shook her head slowly.

"You used to tell me everything when we were children." He brushed a stray lock of hair from her face and tucked it behind her ear. "If you tell me, I will try to make it right."

He'd always liked that he'd been able to do that when they were young, making her sorrow lighter with some silly game.

"We aren't children anymore, Geordie." She slid him a sorrowful look. "Life is not so easily solved."

Something was indeed bothering her. "I could try." The not knowing was driving him mad. To be aware that Cat was hurting, and yet he could do nothing to help her heal, was more than he could bear.

"I don't want you to." She slid from her seat and rose to standing. "Please."

He stood as well.

"I find I am quite tired and would like to retire early." She raised her gaze to him, and he saw for the first time how deep the hollows under her eyes were. "Do excuse me."

"Of course." He bowed low to her and watched her departing back as she made her way through the crowd. There was indeed something amiss with Cat, and he suspected it had something to do with Lord Loughton.

12

Geordie didn't have the opportunity to speak with Cat alone again over the next several days. Mayhap it had been through her orders that Freya be at her side every time he might have otherwise spoken to her. Mayhap she did not wish him to learn what troubled her.

But what could possibly be so terrible?

He ought to let the matter go as she had asked, but, how could he? The unknowing rattled about in his brain like a loose stone, the clatter of it kept him from sleeping properly. Between worrying over her and cursing his own humiliation at admitting his love for her, there was room in his mind for little else.

Geordie shifted in his saddle and glanced over to Cat, who stared blankly ahead, not noticing his attention on her. Eldon said something and pulled Geordie's attention to the warrior.

The man nodded to the road in front of them. "The grass."

Geordie's attention lowered to the ground where lush, thick grass grew over the trail. Too lush for a path often traveled. Energy spiked through him. "Turn back."

He spoke so sharply, even Cat snapped from her haze to glance at him. But it was too late.

Men were already rushing onto the road with weapons drawn, demanding valuables and coin. The waymarks on the road had been switched to lead Geordie and his party down this deserted road. It was an old trick—one Geordie knew to avoid.

He'd been distracted and had led them all into danger. His foolish oversight might cost them their lives. He looked to Cat to warn her, but she'd already nocked an arrow and positioned Star in front of Freya.

"I am Sir Geordie of the king's army." He slid his blade free of its scabbard. "Leave and we will allow you to go unharmed. Stay and you will suffer the consequences."

The men didn't bother to reply. Instead they rushed from the close sides of the forest toward Geordie's retinue. Men kept coming from the brush until at least twenty surrounded them. Many wore the stained gambesons of poor soldiers, most likely land tenants forced into battle by their lord, and then cast aside when the king couldn't afford to feed them anymore. It was a sorry state Geordie had seen many times.

Geordie cut free the bag of food from his saddle and threw it to the men. "There's food enough there for several men for a sennight." One man darted forward and grabbed it to his chest. Three others followed his departure into the woods, as Geordie anticipated some might.

Soldiers who turned to theft were either hungry or pillagers by nature. The lingering sixteen men were evidently the latter. God have mercy on their souls, for Geordie would show none to their earthly bodies.

The first man charged, slicing toward Geordie's horse.

Geordie shifted Bentley, and placed his blade between man and beast, blocking the brigand first before punching the weapon through the man's paltry armor and into his chest.

Something darted through the air, and a man charging toward their party fell with a white fletched arrow jutting from his eye.

Geordie grinned, admiring Cat's skill, even as he expertly wielded his own weapon.

He easily cut down the three men trying to take him down as he edged Bentley back toward Cat. She didn't need his protection, of course, but he'd be there to ensure she remained unharmed, to give himself the peace of mind to better focus. As it was, he found his attentions divided between the need to fight and the constant desire to reassure himself of her safety.

One by one, she pinched an arrow to her bowstring, and one by one, the men fell.

That is, until a tall man with shaggy blonde hair leapt at her, grappling at her leg to pull her from Star. Geordie turned from the brigand he fought for only a fraction of a moment. A blade caught him on the left arm. The dull thud on his body told him there would be a wound bleeding there after battle.

He blocked a second blow with his sword, his attention still shared with the man trying to pull Cat from her horse. In an instant, she snatched up the sword from where it hung on the saddle near her thigh and plunged it into the man's neck. Only when the man sank to the ground with blood spurting from his mouth did Geordie turn his full focus on his opponent once more.

The attacker jerked back and looked around wildly. His brethren lay around him, motionless in growing pools of blood. He was the only among them still standing. Slowly, he backed away toward the forest.

"If you still fancy a fight, I can accommodate you." Eldon gave him a leering grin.

The man shook his head vigorously and continued to walk backward until he disappeared into the brush.

Immediately, Geordie gave his full attention to Cat. "Are you ladies well?"

Cat tossed him a saucy look, wiped the blood from her blade and slid it into the scabbard. Of course, she was well. She was a woman who knew battle. Freya, however, appeared ready to fall from her horse. Still, the lady's maid lifted her pale face with determination. "I'm safe, with thanks to my lady for her protection."

Cat's mouth fell open. "Geordie, you're bleeding."

In that short time, he'd forgotten he'd been struck in battle. He glanced down at his left arm. There, on the bulk of his shoulder, was a great gash. Blood had seeped out, staining the sleeve of his yellow tunic. The sting of a new wound made its way to his awareness, a sensation he'd grown familiar with in these last four years.

He lifted his good shoulder in an uncaring shrug. "'Tis only a scratch."

"It needs to be tended to." Cat walked Star closer to Bentley and peered at Geordie's shoulder. "If nothing else, we need to ensure it's clean."

He shook his head stubbornly. "'Tis fine." He clicked his tongue to lead his horse, and their party, away from the field of dead men.

"As it was fine when you were with fever?" Cat persisted, appearing beside him.

Geordie bit back a scoff. "It will take more than a fever, or a nick to the skin for that matter, to fell me."

Durham watched the entire exchange back and forth without ever moving his head, his eyes gliding between them. Geordie raised his brows to him in question, but the soldier simply smirked as if to silently lament the concern of ladies.

"If it was me who had received an injury, what would you do?" Cat inclined her head toward Geordie.

"I'd have you seen by a healer immediately." He looked behind them to ensure no brigands followed. "But as I told you, I am fine, and don't need a healer."

"Then let me look at it," she said softly. "It was I who found the meadowsweet to treat your fever when you were ill."

He nearly declined yet again, except he caught the furrow of concern at her brows and it nipped at his heart. She had not wanted him to say he loved her, but she obviously still cared for him. He could not turn down such affection when he wanted it so ferociously.

Finally, he nodded. "Aye, you may see to it."

Cat's face split into a smile and it was like the sun finally emerged from behind a stormy sky. He wanted to turn his face to its warmth, to revel in its beauty. But she was already urging Star in another direction. "I saw a cottage earlier on the trail, not far from here. Come, Freya. You look about ready to faint."

The lady's maid did indeed look ready to slide to the ground. She gave a weak groan. "Forgive me. The sight of blood always makes me rather weak."

"You may rest at the cottage," Cat pressed.

Freya gripped her reins and swayed. "Please, my lady. If his wound needs to be sewn…" Her mouth pursed as though she was ready to be relieved of her last meal.

"We'll go on ahead with the cart," Eldon suggested. "And you can join us when you're done. It'll be faster with you on your horses to reach us than if we all wait and resume together."

It was a good plan. Geordie nodded. "Aye, that is a fine idea. See to Freya to ensure she doesn't fall from her horse."

"It will be done," Durham said in a firm tone. "Peter will never care for my steed again if I let anything happen to her."

Color touched Freya's pale cheeks at Durham's claim as he passed a wineskin to Cat. He gave it a regretful stare. "Ye can use this for washing the wound."

This time when Cat led the way back to the main path, Geordie did not protest. If she wished to see to the wound, so be it. And mayhap he could speak with her while she did so–to learn what it was that troubled her.

CAT FORCED A SLOW PACE AS SHE LED THE WAY TO THE SMALL cottage she had seen. The others of their group returned to the main road, going the opposite direction of she and Geordie. She knew he wished to be left alone rather than tended to, but she couldn't leave the wound gaping and bleeding so.

Smaller injuries had taken down larger warriors than Geordie. It was nearly impossible to fight off infection, even for the strongest of men.

Cat found the house again quickly and dismounted from Star. Perhaps the occupants had basic herbs inside, garlic to clean out Geordie's wounds properly, or even chamomile to aid with the pain. Not that he appeared to be in pain. But at least something to safeguard against infection.

He came to her side to wait patiently for someone to answer her frantic knock on the roughhewn door.

No one came.

"There's no smoke rising from the chimney." Geordie indicated the sky.

Cat took a step back and gazed up beyond the roof. He was right. No smoke billowed out against the clear blue sky. In her eagerness to see to his wound, she'd failed to notice the obvious absence of people within the hut.

The sooner the injury was treated, the less likelihood there was of infection, or so Isla said. Considering all the lives the older woman had saved, Cat was not inclined to take her word lightly.

"This isn't necessary, Cat." Geordie backed away from the cottage. "'Tis a simple wound that can be addressed at the next inn."

"And you suspect a gaping wound will stop bleeding on its own?" She nodded toward his shoulder where blood continued to trickle freely. "You forget I've been involved in battles as well and have aided Isla and Leila in their ministrations of the injured." She tried the door latch. It clicked open. "That wound needs to be cleaned and stitched closed, or you'll likely suffer another fever."

She didn't wait to see if he followed as she pushed into the abandoned home. Though she called out a pleasant greeting, she kept her hand on the hilt of her dagger. One never knew what to expect in a lone building, even one that held no furnishings and smelled musty with disuse and fires burned out long ago. Sunshine shone in like patches of gold from the damaged thatch roof.

"It appears there was a fire here." Geordie's voice sounded from across the open space, making Cat nearly leap from her skin. He had entered the hut with the silence of a stable cat, his footsteps muted on the earthen floor.

He gestured to one scorched wall and the greatest piece of missing roof. Now that Cat was looking directly at the ceiling, she noted the bits of singed thatch where the fire had eaten through.

"Then this is perfect." Cat set her bag on the floor and began to sort through it, gathering everything she would need.

She tried to keep her thoughts fixed on what needed to be done to have his wound cleaned and stitched, rather than their being alone together.

Warmth swirled low in her stomach. It was all too easy to recall the gentleness of his kiss, and the way it made everything in her melt.

She pushed aside those memories and drew out the flagon of wine Durham had given her. It wasn't garlic or chamomile or any other herb that might help, not that Cat could remember most of them anyway, but it was better than nothing for cleaning a wound.

She strode over to Geordie with purpose. "Let me have a look."

Obediently, he turned his bad arm toward her. She lifted the torn cloth of his tunic and carefully prodded the edge of the slice. Blood trickled from the gash. There was no indication of white bone beneath, so the cut had not gone that deep. It was nothing that would kill him immediately, but still wide enough that it would not close on its own. If left untended, that might make him lose consciousness before the sun set.

"This will need to be stitched, or it will continue to bleed. You'll need to remove your tunic so I can access the wound." She rummaged through her bag again, seeking her needle case and some thread. The silk embroidery thread was not as sturdy as Isla's catgut, but it would have to do in a pinch. "Do you still hold an affinity for blue?"

She glanced up from her bag to find Geordie's torso completely naked, as she'd requested. But she hadn't expected...

Her mouth went dry and she nearly dropped the materials she'd gathered.

Nay, she certainly hadn't expected him to be so very strong. She'd felt the raw power beneath his tunic when they'd kissed before; she'd even been able to make out the line of his shoulders with her eyes. But she hadn't expected a narrow stomach banded with tight muscle, his broad chest and powerful arms all sculpted from countless hours of training.

It wasn't only his strength which caught her breath. Jagged scars lined and puckered his otherwise smooth skin—from his collarbones down to a nick of a line just over the muscular ridge of his hip.

He was a man chiseled by war.

"Are you going to sew me up like a tapestry?" Geordie chuckled, oblivious to her stupefied gawping.

Cat blinked and carefully pulled the needle from her case to ensure she didn't drop it to the ground. It was the only one she had.

"I have red if you prefer," Cat said in a weak voice.

Mayhap it was how she said it, but he met her eyes and spoke suddenly. "Cat."

Heat blazed in her cheeks. She ducked her head, breaking the intensity of his gaze, and unspooled the blue thread from the bit of leather it was wound around. "You may wish to sit as this will hurt."

"I'll be fine." His voice was rich, lush, the same as it'd been when they'd kissed at the feast.

Excited currents tickled through her stomach as she recalled how soft his lips had been. This man who had the body of a warrior, battle-scarred and powerful, was so tender with his touch.

"I may not be as fine as you with this," she confessed. "Will you sit, please?"

At that, he immediately lowered himself to the ground. The action caused the muscles across his abdomen and chest to flex. Cat forced herself to avert her eyes from the magnificence of his body and focus instead on his injury.

Nervousness swirled in her stomach. She could do this. She *had* to do this. And yet every part of her cringed at the idea of sewing Geordie's shoulder, of causing him any more pain. She drew a deep breath and unstopped the wine.

She *would* do this.

13

"First, the wine." Cat gave Geordie a moment to prepare before splashing wine over the wound.

His jaw flexed, but that was his only indication of discomfort for something no doubt very painful. The ruby liquid ran down his arm, mixing with his blood. The sharp scent of wine filled the air and stuck in the back of her throat, cloying. She shoved back at memories that tried to claw forefront.

She would not think of Sir Gawain now. Her focus would not go to a man so undeserving of her thoughts when one far worthier needed her.

Her hands shook so badly, she could barely get the thread through the eye of the needle. By some miracle, she finally succeeded, sliding the thread through and putting the iron needle to the edge of the wound. She flicked a glance up at him. "Are you ready?"

He gave a resolute nod, his gaze locked across the room. Judging from the number of scars on his body, he'd likely been sewn a time or two. Most likely by a burly man who pulled the thread from his own dirty tunic. Cat shuddered to think.

She pushed the needle to Geordie's skin as she had seen Isla do, but it did not give easily. She had to shove at the needle with the pad of her thumb before the point pushed through his skin.

Geordie did not so much as flinch. Cat, however, cried out as though it were she who had a needle jutting from a wound.

He reached up and brushed her face with his fingertips. "'Tis fine, Cat. I scarcely feel it."

She sucked in a breath and nodded. Bolstered by his reassurance, she sewed the wound closed the way she'd seen Isla and Leila do countless times before. She kept her stitching loose enough on either side to account for future swelling and went far enough away from where the injury split to ensure the skin wouldn't give way and tear.

When at long last she was done, she tied off the thread and sat back to admire her work. She'd never made a more perfect line of sewing, if she did say so herself.

"Finished?" He asked.

Cat nodded weakly. Nausea rolled through her stomach at what she'd just done, at the agony he must have felt and that he hid so well.

"I'm sorry to have hurt you, Geordie," she whispered.

He gave her an easy smile. "I've had much worse, I assure you."

She indicated his torso. "So I see." Her heart flinched at how many injuries he'd endured on the battlefield. How many battles had he fought? How many times had his life nearly been cut short?

Her throat went tight.

How many times had she nearly lost him?

Before she could even think at what she did, she reached out and gently brushed a small scar on his chest, silvery white beneath a sprinkling of dark hair. His skin was soft and warm. But the gentle caress wasn't enough. She had to touch each one, as though to offer her comfort for every injury he had sustained that she had not been there to care for him.

She brushed her fingers over a star-shaped wound on his ribs, still pink with having healed within the last year or so. He pulled in a sharp breath as though the wound still caused him pain. She looked up at him and found his gaze fixed on her, his eyes glittering with something she couldn't discern.

"Did I hurt you?" she asked.

His chest rose and fell with his steady breathing. "What are you doing, Cat?"

"I'm..." She regarded his scarred body once more and swallowed. "I'm trying to heal the hurt of four long years." She reached for him again, but this time he stopped her, catching her hand midair.

"Tell me you care about me, Cat."

She dragged her attention to his earnest expression.

"Be honest," Geordie said. "But tell me how you feel about me. Do you care?"

She knew what he was asking. She knew where the conversation would go. To her potential marriage with Lord Loughton's son, to the reasons why she wanted to go to court, and inevitably the crushing weight of her shame at having ruined everything.

Even still, she could not tell him she did not care.

"I do care." She pulled her fingers free and lightly grazed a crescent-shaped scar on his uninjured shoulder. "I did not realize you had seen so many battles as this." Her voice trembled with emotion when she spoke. "You could have been killed."

"I wasn't," he said resolutely.

Cat drew in a shaky breath. "But you could have been. How many battles did you fight?"

Geordie exhaled heavily. "Several. Aye, I got struck occasionally. Every man does. But I was never reckless." His heartbeat thudded hard beneath her fingertips where she touched a newer scar on his chest. "I knew I had to come home to you."

Cat pressed her lips together.

He gently pulled her closer, so they were eye level. "It's always been you. I thought of you so often on the battlefield. I read your letters until the creases went soft with use and started to split."

The knot in her throat hardened. He *had* always cared for her. *Pennyroyal.*

The small vial was still in her bag. The very one she had in the cottage with her. It would be so easy to drink it down, the extract no doubt bitter. Not nearly as bitter as the decision. And yet, she would be free from her burden. To begin her life anew, to have everything she wanted with Geordie.

But she could not bring herself to take her babe's life. Not when it was the most innocent victim of all.

"I'm glad you came home," she whispered. Her fingers swept over a scar along his abdomen. "I hate that you've endured so much hurt and that you were at risk every time you went into battle."

"I survived." He watched her as he spoke, his gaze dark with something that gave a decadent ripple of chills over her skin.

A warning at the back of her mind told her to withdraw her hand, to stand and walk away. The greater pull within her, however, nudged her onward and she touched the small wound near his navel. His stomach flinched in a lovely show of taut muscle. She let her hand linger for a moment longer than was necessary and met his gaze.

His stare dipped to her mouth and she knew immediately that he intended to kiss her.

※

GEORDIE'S SKIN HUMMED WITH THE DELICATE TOUCHES CAT delivered to the scars over his body, the perfect balm after her excruciating task of sewing his shoulder closed. Her tentative stitches had dragged the process out for far too long, despite the care she used. In truth, he preferred the brute force of the barbers on the field. They were merciless, aye, but they were swift and the mess of it was done in only seconds.

The interminable process, however, had been worth every slow puncture of her needle for this moment with her hands whispering over his body, her gaze locked on his.

She cared for him; he knew that much. Or she wouldn't have stayed by his side when he had fever or insisted on closing his wound. She tucked her lower lip into her mouth and shifted her touch to the side of his hip where there was obviously a scar or mark that he didn't bother to acknowledge right now.

He wanted that fragile touch on every inch of him, running over his chest, his back, down his stomach. Feather light strokes over his cock. Heat effused his body and his loins responded in kind.

He reached up for her face with his good arm and her eyes closed in expectation, as though she'd been anticipating his kiss. He closed his mouth over hers, sweet and tender as he had before, savoring the softness of her lips. She lifted her chin and kissed him back, this time with a little sweep of her tongue.

Her boldness, the sensual touch, having her in his arms again —all of it sent tingles of pleasure raking over his skin.

Her fingers on his torso drifted upward, teasing with her touch. He held the back of her head with his hand and tentatively let his tongue graze hers. She gave a low moan and opened her mouth to him. Geordie's pulse went wild with the sound, encouraged by her enjoyment and wanting to give her more.

The next brush of their tongues was not as tender; it was stroking and tasting. This time, it was Geordie who made a sound of desire with his low groan. Cat's fingers trailed over his chest, apparently no longer seeking scars, but wanting to mold her palms to the shape of his body.

Oh, and how he wanted to caress her as well, to sweep over her flawless skin, cup the weight of her silken breasts in his palm, to trace the line of her legs with his fingertips. Their kissing intensified, losing all sweetness and giving way to passion. The sounds of their lips parting and touching, the panting of their breath, all of it swirled around them and poured into the well of his need.

He moved his hands over her, mindful of his new stitches. First, he caressed the dip of her waist, then up higher to where her breasts swelled against her bodice. Her fingers continued to wander over him as well, no longer at his chest, but down his abdomen. His cock raged with hardness in his trews.

They continued to kiss, their tongues mating with one another in wild abandon. They should stop, he knew. His training and duty rushed forefront, to be chivalrous at all times, to respect women. He began to draw back when her hand brushed the tip of his cock. Pleasure rocketed through him and overwhelmed his senses.

Cat gasped. No doubt in horror at seeing such a thing on a man.

"Forgive me," Geordie said raggedly. "I...you..."

She kissed him then, with her lips and the hot stroke of her tongue. This time, the grazing of her hands over his hardness was no doubt intentional. The warning in Geordie's mind went dim, shoved to the back of his lust-hazed mind.

Geordie's kisses became hungrier, desperate. His fingers skimmed the top of her bodice to the delicate line of her collarbone and the silky-smooth skin of her bosom where the swell of her breast began.

Her hand bumped over the head of his cock again and he nearly burst with need. Unthinking, he put his hands to her backside and drew her against him. She spread her legs to fit over his lap. The pressure of her weight settled over his arousal and they both gasped in unison at the awareness of how very close to such intimacies they truly were.

It was wrong what they were doing. He knew better. He was stronger than this.

Or perhaps, he was not. Mayhap Cat was as much his weakness as she was his strength. His hips lifted and thrust his swollen shaft between her legs, and though the cloth of his trews and her skirt separated their sexes from one another, pleasure gripped them both. It raked over Geordie's skin and made him pull her more tightly to him. Cat's eyes fluttered closed, dark lashes sweeping down over her flushed cheeks as she gave a breathy cry.

He needed to stop.

His hips flexed upward again, grinding their pelvises together with the most wonderful heat and friction.

He *had* to stop. He broke off their kiss and gritted his teeth against the searing power of lust.

"Cat." He said her name on a ragged growl.

Her fingers trailed over his naked chest and sent a shiver teasing down his spine. She nuzzled her chin against his, letting their lips brush against one another in delicious little grazes.

"Cat," he said again and rested his forehead against hers. "Say you love me."

It wasn't what he'd meant to say. It wasn't what he should have said.

"Say it only if it's true," he added quickly. He hadn't felt this awkward and foolish in years. His gaze lifted to find her watching him with her large blue eyes. "Do you love me?"

Her brows flinched. "Geordie, it's..."

He shook his head. "It wasn't right to ask. I shouldn't have even..."

Lust clouded his mind and made his thoughts scattered. He was making things worse. Like last time at the monastery.

When would he learn?

"It's so much more complicated than simply love." She bit her lip.

"Complicated." He threaded his hand through hers and ran his thumb over her ragged nails. "Is that what makes you do this? Is that why you push your food around on your plate? Because of a complication you won't share with me?"

"Geordie..."

He shook his head. "When you kiss me like this, make my body burn for you, it feels like you love me." He shouldn't say it, but the words slipped from his mouth once more. "The way I love you."

14

Cat stared into Geordie's familiar gaze, knowing she ought to offer him some sort of reply.

She should say she did not love him, to dissuade him for good. If she didn't love him, she knew he would leave her be. But if she spoke such words, they would be the greatest lie of all time. For she did love him.

As a girl, she'd loved him as a companion. As a woman, she loved him as a woman loves a man, in the truest way. She admired his strength and his confidence, his drive to get the redemption he'd wanted so long by proving himself a better man than his father.

Cat had not divulged the real reason for her desire to go to court, and doubtless had told small mistruths along the way to cover her condition and shield him from hurt. But in this one thing, Cat knew she could not lie, not when it would wound him deeper than any weapon. And not when she loved him so fiercely.

"I do love you." Cat closed her eyes against the admission.

"Cat." His hands were on her face, gentle and stroking. "My Cat."

He kissed her again, as hungry and eager as before. His tongue met hers and made everything in her go soft. Desire still hummed through her from their shared passion before he'd spoken, burning in her veins and demanding satiation of a need beyond anything she'd ever felt before.

She knew he wanted to know about what she'd summed up as "complications." Such a simple word to encompass so much. Giving in to her lust was easier than explaining, than thinking.

He pulled her against him and the hardness rising from his trews pressed at her skirts, directly between her legs. She gasped in pleasure and ground her hips against him to feel more. Her fingers moved restlessly across his powerful body, dipping and rising over muscle and scar alike.

He lowered his hands from her face to trace a sweet line over her collarbone, then trail lower to the tops of her breasts just beneath her bodice. She pressed more firmly into his touch, wanting him to continue down into her dress to brush his fingertips over her aching nipples. Their bodies moved and flexed over one another in desperate need, grinding their sexes with layers of cloth separating them.

This was how her first time should have been. Not like what she'd experienced with Sir Gawain. Not while she was drunk and pressured.

The spice of wine floated in the air still from when she'd washed Geordie's wound. It stuck in the back of her throat now. A night of too much wine, of allowing herself to be taken without a fight.

She gripped Geordie's back and sat more firmly atop him, kissing him with desperation, longing to live in the moment. To forget the past. Geordie growled against her lips and met her passion with his own.

His fingers went to the hem of her skirt, resting just at the ankle of her stocking. She squeezed her eyes shut and kissed him harder, knowing it to be his hand and not that of Sir Gawain. Higher and higher the hand went, up her skirt until he went over her stocking just above her knee, onto her naked skin.

The odor of wine swirled noxiously around her. It pounded in her head like it had that fateful night. Geordie's hand going higher, higher, higher, like Sir Gawain's had.

Cat's breathing came fast, but not with lust—with fear.

"Stop." She'd meant it as a command, but it came out only in a thready whisper, one barely audible even to her own ears.

But it had been enough. The hand immediately pulled from her skirts.

"Forgive me, Cat." It was Geordie's voice, not Sir Gawain's.

She opened her eyes and found Geordie's long-lashed brown eyes stretched wide.

"Forgive me." He gently eased her from his lap and got to his feet before pulling her up beside him with his good arm. "I never should have kissed you like that, touched you like that, put you against me." His hands clenched into fists. "I did not act like a knight." He shook his head angrily. "I acted like an animal, driven only by lust."

"You were not alone." She lifted his tunic from where he had folded it carefully on a dry patch of dirt and handed it to him. "I wanted to kiss you, to feel your body against mine." Her cheeks went hot. "I enjoyed it."

"I won't do this again," he vowed. He took his tunic from her and tugged it over his head, mindful of his bad arm.

Cat helped him work his injured arm through the sleeve and said nothing. If he did not kiss her again, her strength would not be tested against the heat of his kisses, and yet a greater part of her was disappointed to think she might not taste him again.

Yet it was for the best, she knew, for she was finding it difficult to control her desire for him.

It had been a mistake to tell him she loved him and then to

kiss him so. Sir Gawain had been right about her playing the wanton. She'd done it with him, and the cost had been high. She did it now, and Geordie would be the one to suffer for it.

Nay, she could not allow his kisses anymore, nor any of his affection.

She pressed her lips together, knowing she should tell him about the babe, about how she had been one of those empty-headed women who fell for a man's smooth words at court. Mayhap she could tell him and refuse to divulge who it had been. Energy pumped through her veins and nausea swam in her nearly empty stomach.

Nay, not now. She couldn't now, and she knew her hesitation for what it was: cowardice.

For she did love Geordie, enough to wish every day and night that her life had turned out differently, that her admissions of love could be given without pause or thought.

Anger flared through her suddenly, white hot with intensity. Sir Gawain had taken everything from her, and though she had the ability to fight him off, she had not. She had let him ruin her life. And she could not now ruin Geordie's as well.

※

Geordie had apparently exacerbated Cat's "complications" further. In the following days of their journey, she went out of her way to avoid being in a position to speak privately with him. And he had tried.

Not only had he wanted to apologize for his behavior, he wanted her to know what his ultimate plan was for them. If only he'd been granted a position within a baron or an earl's household like some of the knights.

Geordie was left with no knowledge of his future; made to wait and hope. Everything hinged on the king's generosity with land and employment. It had been in Geordie's mind to wait until they arrived at court to talk to Cat, once he ascertained what reward he might receive for his efforts on the battlefield. However, now with London on the horizon and Cat avoiding him, he had no choice but to tell her now.

If he did not, he might well lose her to Lord Loughton's son.

He waited until she had finished her pottage and was straightening in an attempt to get to her feet.

"A moment," Geordie said in a soft voice he'd meant only for her.

She paused and slid him a wary glance.

"I need to speak with you," Geordie said. "Please."

She dropped her gaze to the table as though she could not bring herself to meet his gaze and nodded.

Geordie glanced around their surroundings, where people gathered in groups, drinking and laughing. Durham spoke in low tones with Freya, who listened intently and nodded to whatever it was he said, while Eldon had made his way across the room to converse with a comely redhead. "Somewhere with more privacy."

The trepidation in her gaze was a barb to his heart. He leaned toward her to ensure his words remained private. "I told you I would not kiss you again. I am keeping to my word."

Her cheeked reddened. "The hour is drawing late, and we will be at Westminster on the morrow."

"Which is why I must speak with you."

She lifted her eyes to his and nodded once more. He got to his feet, then offered his hand to aid her to hers. Her fingers touched his palm and his heartbeat came a little more quickly. It was time to tell her, before any land had been granted to him, before he even had employment secured. This was not how he had wanted to tell her, with nothing but hopes to recommend him, but if he did not do this now, he might lose her forever.

He said nothing as he led her to a corner where they could speak with a modicum of privacy.

After a quick glance about to confirm they were indeed alone in the corner, he gave a quiet sigh. "I didn't want to say anything until I was fully ready."

"About what?" She crossed her arms over her chest, clearly discomfited by his sudden need to speak with her.

He couldn't botch this, not like before. Nay, he was clear-headed this time, not addled with illness or lust.

"I want to marry you." Geordie wanted to reach out to hold her hand, or stroke her face, but suppressed the desire. "I had wanted to wait until I had land and income. I believe I may be given both at this meeting with the king."

Cat blinked up at him and the muscles of her neck stood out. She swallowed. "You want to marry me?"

Anxiety coursed through Geordie and knotted his stomach at his admission. "I haven't told you because I've been working to build a future for us first. I had to be worthy enough for you."

"Geordie." Her face softened and she reached out to him. "There's nothing you've ever had to prove or attain first. Especially not when it comes to me."

"Always when it comes to you." He folded his hand around hers and drew her closer. "You are the sun in the sky, spreading light and joy. You are the strength that kept me alive in battle. You are the reason I fought so hard to come home. You are beautiful and pure and everything any woman could ever aspire to become."

She drew in a shaky breath and shook her head. "You think too highly of me."

"I think everything of you, but it is never too highly." He gave into temptation and stroked the back of his index finger down her cheek. "You deserve every compliment I have given you and more."

She shook her head again, tears welling in her eyes. "You put me on a pedestal where I do not belong."

Her humility was admirable, as with everything she did. He

wiped at a tear that trailed down her cheek. "I love you, and I know you love me. Marry me, Cat. Be my wife."

"But…Lord Loughton." The excuse stammered from her lips.

A sharp pain twinged in Geordie's chest. "You don't love him."

She shook her head. "I do not even know him. I…I imagine I will love him in time."

"Have you already become betrothed?" Geordie was breathing faster. Had he missed something? A legally binding agreement between Cat and another man?

"Nay."

"And you do love me," Geordie confirmed.

Her eyes squeezed shut and another tear slid down her cheek. "I never should have said that."

He gritted his teeth. "Because it isn't true?"

She shook her head. "Because I'm not the person you think I am."

The fear raising his shoulders abated and his muscles relaxed. "The complications," he murmured. "If you tell me, mayhap we can resolve it together. Nothing is so bad that it could prevent two people who love one another from being together."

"It isn't that easy." She cast an anxious scan about the room and returned her gaze to him, as though trying to determine if she could trust him. "Not everything can be fixed."

"But it can be." Geordie felt the shift of her trust back toward him. "Together, we can do anything. Cat, marry me."

She sucked in a deep breath and stared at him, her face crumpling. "I…"

"Please." Geordie was nearly begging now. It was pathetic, he knew, and yet he could not stop. Never in all of his life had he wanted something more than he wanted to take Catriona Barrington as his wife. "I will always treat you well and be forever faithful. I will love and cherish you every moment of our lives together. Be my wife."

A sob choked from her throat. "I can't, Geordie."

He shook his head, nearly wild with frustration. "Why not?"

She gazed miserably up at him. "Because I am with child."

15

An ache pulsed in the depths of Cat's heart and spiraled out through her entire chest. *I am with child.* She had finally said those four damning words.

Geordie's brows raised in surprise and then furrowed. "I beg your pardon? I believe I did not hear you properly."

Cat squared her shoulders. "You did."

He regarded her a long moment, his mouth opening as if to prepare for speech, then closing again. His stare dipped to her stomach, which appeared flat beneath her kirtle. But she knew well the intimacies of her own body. The bump was now swollen enough for her to cover with the expanse of her hand, the budding life able to be cupped in her palm.

She self-consciously smoothed her dress and had the urge to cross her arms over her stomach to protect the babe within from Geordie's judgment. "I am not far along."

"How?" he demanded.

"At court." The threat of tears pulled at her once more and she swallowed hard to hold them back. "I am apparently one of those empty-headed women you spoke so highly of."

His expression flinched. "Who did this to you?"

She did cross her arms over her lower stomach this time. "I will not tell you."

Geordie's chest rose and fell with heavy breath. "Why not?"

She knew how this game played out. If she told him and confessed that she feared he would kill the man, he would vow he would not. Then, he would pick at her until she finally divulged the truth. In which case, he would doubtless kill Sir Gawain, and make all her lying and hiding an utter waste.

She simply remained silent.

"Lord Loughton's son?" he said, more to himself than to her. "But you swear you have not met him."

Cat said nothing.

He narrowed his eyes in thought as he worked through it all to figure out what she would not say. "If the father of your babe was a worthy enough man to wed, you would have asked your father. You would not be meeting Lord Loughton's son. Unless he was baseborn, or..." He sucked in a breath. "Or already married."

Cat slid her gaze away, unable to meet the accusation in Geordie's stare.

"Was it Lord Loughton?" he asked. "Now ready to pass you off to his son?"

"Nay," she exclaimed.

A group of men nearby began singing a bawdy tune. Geordie edged back against the wall, leaving Cat with no choice but to join him.

Geordie was staring down at her, incredulous.

She wanted this conversation done, for Geordie to say his piece. To bear the weight of the wretched conversation and be done with it for good. "Say something," she said.

Geordie shook his head. "It is too horrible to say aloud."

Cat steeled herself. "Say it and be done."

Even with her permission, Geordie hesitated before speaking, his words slow and careful. "Lord Loughton's son. You have not yet met him, yet you plan to wed him. Was that why you were so determined to travel so soon? So that he would not know you were with child, so he might think the child was his own?"

Her stomach churned. She wanted to protest that she'd never intended to meet Lord Loughton's son, that she'd wanted only to speak with Sir Gawain. All of this had only ever been to find a safe home for her child.

But she could not tell Geordie as much. Better that he believe her capable of such perfidy, better that he see her knocked from a pedestal she had no right to be on, than to put him at risk.

Her silence was answer enough. Geordie dragged a hand through his thick dark hair. It fell becomingly around his handsome face, highlighting his high cheekbones, straight nose and square jaw. He was truly a beautiful man. One who would have to belong to someone else. Someone worthy of loving a man as good and just as him.

"You have gotten with child by a married man at court," Geordie said. "You seek to pass his bastard off to another man before you are too far along for him to suspect as much. And as we have traveled to court, you have kissed me." Pain sparkled deep in his eyes. "You have told me you love me."

It was too much. Too much. All of it too awful to agree to. And yet, she must. To protect Geordie, for he was an innocent in all of this as much as the babe in her belly.

She lifted her face to him, accepting the entirety of his accusation, to leave no question in his mind. It was better for him think poorly of her and move on with a life with a woman deserving of him, than to try to save her.

"Aye," she said firmly. "That is the whole of it."

He stared at her for a long time, his face a mask of horror. "Cat, you are..." He blinked, and she realized that he was near tears.

The ache in her chest squeezed into something far more acute and wrought an agony unlike anything she had ever known.

"Cat, you are not the woman I thought you were," he said at last.

Cat absorbed the barb of his words and somehow managed not to flinch. "No woman can be what you thought me to be, Geordie."

"You were." He drew in a shaky breath and lifted his hand as if he intended to touch her before it fell away. "I loved that woman, Cat."

Loved.

The word was so devastating, it nearly cracked her carefully held composure. "And now?"

"And now I realize I have wasted four years of my life." He clenched his jaw hard enough for the muscles to stand out. "Thinking myself unworthy of a woman who was herself unworthy."

Cat swallowed down a sob. No woman could ever be worthy of a man like Geordie, who did no wrong in his life. "It is better for you to know before we go to court."

He looked away and sniffled. "If there is nothing else, my lady, I believe I shall retire for the evening." He narrowed his eyes at her. "There is nothing else, is there?"

"Nay."

With that, he inclined his head, coldly bid her good night and departed up the stairs. She went to her own chamber moments later, not bothering to summon Freya to join her. She wanted the solitude, the darkness of the empty room wrapped around her, cradling the hollowness of her chest. Once inside, she threw herself on the bed and allowed her composure to shatter into a million tears.

༺༻

GEORDIE LAY IN BED WITH HIS THOUGHTS ON FIRE. CAT, HIS Cat, bedded by a married man and now trying to coerce another man into wedding her so she could pass off the bastard as his. It was too much.

He flopped over in his bed, restless with the miserable agitation of rage. How could four years have changed her so much? How could he have been so wrong about her?

He was glad he had found out at the end of their journey. It would have been impossible to face her all those days on the road knowing what he did now.

What was more, she did not even appear remorseful, accepting the guilt with a defiant set to her chin. Mayhap he never should have left to become a knight. He could have stayed at Werrick Castle. He would have gone to court with her no doubt and could have prevented her from what had happened. He could have protected her.

What had happened. His heart twisted with ugly pain.

What had happened was sex. Fornication. Intimacy.

All the things he had put off for those long four years to remain pure of heart and body for Cat when he returned home and was worthy of marriage. Never had he allowed a woman's flirtations to turn his head; never had he defiled his body with that of another. It had always been Cat. Thoughts of her in his mind and a fist ready to slake out his body's lust.

Yet for her, it had not been him, but a married man.

Four years wasted.

These were the thoughts that plagued him through the stretch of one of the longest nights of his life. His mind and body alternated between rage and hurt and soul-crushing sorrow. When at last the morning came, it brought no relief, for it also brought Cat.

She did not appear as composed that morning, her eyes swollen as though she had been crying. Foolish though he was, he could not help but hope her tears might have been for him. She acknowledged him coolly, and they went about their usual routine with him aiding her onto her horse with a foreign stiffness.

The journey to London was heavy with oppressive silence. Durham attempted several jests that Freya had laughed too hard at, and all else had fallen quiet. At long last, they made their way down the long winding entrance to the castle where a bustle of servants greeted them, notified by Durham, who had gladly volunteered to ride ahead.

Cat scarcely looked at Geordie as she was helped from Star and led away to her chamber. She was gone in an instant, not just to her room, but to lead a life different than his while they were at court. Would she seek out the married man to carry on the affair?

A stab of jealousy dug into Geordie. He shouldn't care. She was not his to worry about any longer.

A page stopped in front of Geordie and bowed. "Sir Geordie, if you'll follow me, please. The king would like a word with you in his chamber."

Geordie straightened a little taller and tried to push Cat from his mind. The king wished to see him upon his arrival. Surely, good tidings would follow such a welcome.

Geordie was led into a long, narrow room with exquisite paintings along the walls. His lips quirked upward as he recognized the various virtues and vices. King Edward strode toward him, his brown wavy hair neatly trimmed to his shoulders and the full beard he wore likewise carefully cut and shaped.

"Beautiful, aren't they?" The king indicated the paintings. "Fire tried to take them once, and even an angry mob during the reign of Henry III wrought havoc upon them. All repaired with a careful hand and a considerable amount of time."

"They're exquisite," Geordie replied. And they truly were, depicted with vivid color.

"We're pleased to see you, Sir Geordie." The king put his hands behind his back and casually strolled along the wall, his gaze skimming the art. "Now that you are here, the planning for your feast may begin in earnest."

At the far end of the room was the stately bed with velvet

bedding. Several other courtiers milled about, waiting their own turn with the king.

"You honor me more than I deserve, Your Majesty." Geordie said reverently. He had not been an ideal soldier, for he had not followed all orders, only the ones his conscious could bear.

"You saved the life of your king and helped change the tide of battle." King Edward nodded to himself in confirmation. "If ever there was a man to deserve a feast in his honor, it is you, though we admire your humble reception. All our knights should be as humble and just as you, Sir Geordie."

Great pride effused Geordie, warming his chest to the point he feared his heart might burst. He could not wait to tell Cat of this moment. In that instant, the pride nearly deflated.

For he would not be telling Cat, not of this or of anything else, ever.

"We should like to have you on as one of our personal knights." King Edward led Geordie to the other side of the room to regard the other paintings.

"I would be honored." And truly, it was an honor greater than any other Geordie had ever dreamed of hoping for. The king only surrounded himself by men who were the strongest fighters, the most just of spirit and strong of body.

With the income from being a king's knight, Geordie could easily afford land, a home. A family. His stomach dropped.

He did not need land or a home any longer. There would be no family, not like he had been anticipating.

"We are of a mind to betroth you to a woman as well." The king had lowered his voice, clearly intending to speak only to Geordie. "Sir John Howard's daughter, Elizabeth Howard, has recently returned from the convent where she had been raised and will be in attendance at court on the morrow." The king raised his brows. "We hear she is quite a beauty and seeking a husband."

Geordie knew Sir John would have had to have given his

permission. That he felt Geordie would make a suitable husband for his daughter was an honor indeed. Except that he could not get Cat from him mind, or his heart, and doubted he ever could.

Still, he lowered his head at the honor. "Thank you, Your Majesty."

The king laughed. "You needn't look as though We're marching you to your death. Allow the introduction and make up your mind. If you want her, she is yours." He clapped Geordie on the shoulder as though they were old friends, and with that the king was gone, off to discuss something with a courtier who milled closely by.

Geordie followed the page moments later to his own rooms, ones far more finely appointed than his prior ones had been that he'd shared with several other men. Through it all, he could not stop thinking of the king's offer to meet Mistress Howard.

In Sir John's years of success, he had acquired a great amount of land and wealth. A marriage to Elizabeth would be advantageous, no doubt coming with land, coin and prestige.

But beautiful or no, Geordie dreaded his introduction to the fair lady, for none would ever be as fair as Catriona. No one's laugh tingled as beautifully, no one's smile shone as brightly, no one's presence warmed his heart as much as hers.

Dread squeezed in on him as he shut the door to his chamber. No matter how Cat had lied and deceived him, he knew in the depths of his heart that he still loved her.

16

Cat remained in the room longer than was necessary. It was a comfortable chamber assigned to Ella and her husband, Lord Calville, given to Cat to use during her stay at court.

Cat was grateful to be alone now. Even Freya had gone to fetch refreshment for her, giving Cat a precious few moments to succumb to the crush of emotion. Her heart raced impossibly fast and roared in her ears, sweat prickling at her palms and brow. The journey to court, the stretch of days it had taken—through all of it, she had planned exactly what she would say to Sir Gawain when she saw him again.

In her thoughts, she had been composed, deliberate in her speech and action. Now though... anger coursed through her like poison. Not only at Sir Gawain who had taken what she'd never meant to give, who had ruined her chance for happiness and love, but also at herself. She had been so eager to please a man who was older and seemingly in possession of greater sophistication. She had flirted and drank and drank and drank, she had followed him into the garden and then had tried to retract her affection when it was far too late.

Her hands balled into fists. She *had* to do this. For her baby.

She had to see if he would take the child from her, if he would at least aid her in finding a proper home for it if not in his own household. Once it was done, she could go to Ella's in privacy where the babe could be delivered, and Cat could then return to Werrick Castle. Without Geordie. Without her baby. As only a shell of herself, coming home with nothing left to give.

Tears burned her eyes, but she blinked them away as the door rattled and Freya entered the room. It was time.

"I should like to go to the gardens for a moment," Cat said, as though the idea had suddenly struck her. As if she hadn't been thinking of it for their entire journey to London.

She hadn't divulged her plan to Freya. The maid had kept Cat's discretion and had not asked any questions, but still Cat had been too frightened to share her plans with the young woman who had become a friend. Not because she worried Freya would talk her out of it, but because saying it out loud might make Cat realize how hopeless and ridiculous a plan it was.

And it *was* a ridiculous plan.

Freya did not question Cat's sudden desire to go to the garden. She simply set the flagon of watered-down ale she'd fetched and nodded. Cat steeled her resolve with a pleasant smile, and together they made their way out into the hall, threading their way down the path to the gardens. It was where Cat had first seen Sir Gawain, sitting in the sunshine while playing a lute and smiling charmingly. A rush of fresh anger roared through Cat's veins. How had she been so foolish?

So...empty-headed.

That last thought she had to shove aside, lest her heart crumple. She had lost Geordie. Forever.

Out in the gardens, she found many familiar faces, and several new. Lady Jane Steward, one of the many Janes at court and the snidest of all of them, approached first. She ran to her in short little steps that set her ample bosom bouncing, no doubt a display for the men nearby. And they all noticed.

"Lady Catriona," she cried as though they were the dearest of friends. "It is so good to see you."

"I am here for Sir Geordie's feast." It was not a lie. At least not entirely. For Cat did intend to stay at least for Geordie's feast. To see him honored.

Lady Jane's eyes went wide and she looked behind Cat. "Is he here with you now? Oh, I'd love to meet him. I hear he's terribly handsome, and of how intense he is on the battlefield. If a man has such physical prowess in battle, one can only imagine what other skills he might possess." Lady Jane's gaze dart around to see if anyone happened to overhear her loudly stated comment. "He isn't betrothed to you now, is he?" She gave a little pout.

Cat's cheeks went hot with the memory of Geordie proposing to her. "Nay."

"Wonderful." Lady Jane gave a feral smile. "I'd hate to have to steal him from you." She laughed playfully, but there had been bite to her words. "Has he told you stories? Like the time he took on twenty men at once? Or when he personally saved the king's life and then fought so valiantly that he turned the entire path of the battle? We ended up winning simply because of him. Oh, I'd love to hear them all."

Cat had not heard those stories. She had never even known they existed. Pride effused her once more. Geordie had not just become the knight he'd always wanted to; he was a hero.

How she hated that she'd wounded him so deeply and made him think such terrible things of her. She wanted nothing more than to throw her arms about him and congratulate him on his incredible success.

Truly, she wanted more than that. She wanted to kiss him, to start their life over again back at Werrick Castle, before she'd ever met Sir Gawain.

"Mayhap another time." Cat tried to give a coy smile to hide the fact that she did not know Geordie's tales. "For now, I'm seeking out someone else." She glanced behind Lady Jane to suggest urgency in the matter.

"Well, if you're seeking Sir Gawain, he is not at court." Lady Jane looked down at her immaculate nails and straightened a ruby ring on her left hand. "He's aiding his wife in preparing for her lying in." She glanced up, her mouth an "o" of surprise. "You did know he was married, did you not?" Her smug grin indicated she anticipated Cat did not.

"Of course, I did." Cat forced a smile and pleasant tone through the slamming of her heart. "I was actually seeking Lady Anne." For certes there were enough Annes about for the request to appear benign.

Lady Jane leaned a little closer. "If you *were* seeking Sir Gawain, I suspect he will be back by Sir Geordie's feast. You know that man never misses a celebration at court."

Cat didn't know that, but simply nodded with a nonchalance she didn't feel, as if she didn't care a bit for the treasure of information she'd been handed for free.

"I should very much like to receive an introduction to Sir Geordie," Lady Jane said with intent.

Mayhap the information did not come free, after all. Freya gave a little choking sound behind Cat, which Cat pointedly ignored. Jane slid her narrowed gaze to the maid before settling her attention back on Cat.

"I am sure I can arrange something," Cat lied. She'd cut out her own tongue before she used it to introduce Geordie to this viper.

But it was enough to remove Lady Jane from her presence, which had been Cat's ultimate goal. It wasn't until the vile woman departed that the disappointment of her news crushed in on Cat.

Sir Gawain was not at court. Her whole purpose of coming to court had been to see him, to have this conversation she had so prepared for. And now...what?

She had no choice but to wait until he returned. Hopefully,

Lady Jane was correct in her estimation that he would be back for Sir Geordie's feast, and Cat could confront him then. She couldn't even think on what she might do if he did not return. In the meantime, she would have to act as though everything was normal, as though her heart didn't ache with every beat.

And then there was Geordie. Would she see him? Would he seek her out? Or would he vow never to lay eyes upon her again?

Her chest was weighted with a heaviness she could scarcely hold upright. All her careful plans had gone so poorly, nothing could possibly make it worse.

"Should you like to return to yer room, Lady Catriona?" Freya asked.

Cat was about to nod when a masculine voice pulled her attention. "Lady Catriona, what a lovely surprise."

She turned and found an older man with silvery blonde hair and deep brown eyes. Lord Loughton. Her stomach sank straight down to her toes.

Perhaps it could possibly be worse.

"Lady Catriona." He indicated the man beside him, nearly a perfect replica of what the older man in front of her must have looked like when he'd been young. Shining blonde hair, an elegant nose and a mouth almost too wide for his narrow face. "Allow me to introduce my son, Tristan."

***

THE FOLLOWING DAY CAME FAR TOO QUICKLY FOR GEORDIE'S preference. And with it came the dreaded meeting of Mistress Howard. He walked slowly down to the great hall that evening for supper, fully aware the king would be introducing them.

The massive room never failed to impress. It was said to be the largest in all of Christendom.

The last of the day's light poured in through leaded windows along either side of the painted walls and one very large one at the end of the hall. Tables lined the length of the hall with the higher nobles and guests of honor nearest the dais, where the king sat at a great marble table. The servant led Geordie to one of the higher seats of honor.

Geordie tried to keep his gaze from wandering over the faces at the head table. He hadn't seen Cat since his arrival. Granted, there were many courtiers about, and finding one person in a sea of so many was nearly impossible. If he were a wiser man, he would not seek her out; he would meet Mistress Howard, wed her and forget he'd ever known Lady Cat.

It was a futile idea, though. He could no sooner forget her than he could imagine the world without the bright life-giving sun hanging in the sky. She was too engrained in his life, a thread woven into the tapestry of his heart. If one were to pull her out, the rest of him might unravel.

The king was settled on his dais when Geordie arrived. King Edward caught Geordie's eye and immediately waved him up to the dais as well as someone else from the crowd. The king gave him a wink and a trickle of dread ran down Geordie's spine.

Sir John emerged from the crowd, at least a head taller than most of those around him. At his side was a slender woman with long red hair.

"Sir John." Geordie inclined his head to the older man in greeting.

"Allow me to introduce my daughter, Elizabeth." Sir John nudged her forward.

She stepped closer and glanced around like a rabbit caught in a trap before settling her pale green eyes on him. "Well met, Sir Geordie."

Geordie bowed low in greeting.

"You will find you are seated beside one another." The king lifted his cup in silent toast and drank. "We expect you will enjoy each other's company."

"Thank you, Your Majesty." Elizabeth spoke in a rehearsed tone and gave a dramatic curtsy.

A flash of blonde hair in the crowd caught Geordie's attention as he and Elizabeth were led to their seats. *Cat?*

Geordie scanned those around him but did not find her again. A pang of disappointment echoed within the empty cavity of his chest.

Elizabeth sat in her seat before he took his own. She immediately lowered her head, casting her gaze downward.

Geordie chastised himself for seeking out one woman while sitting with another. He did not have to show interest in wishing to wed her, but he could at least be polite.

"What is your impression of court thus far?" he asked.

"It is loud." Elizabeth did not look up as she replied, and it left her words muffled. There was an indelicate odor of unwashed body about her. No doubt from her time in the convent when full body bathing was no doubt frowned upon as a show of vain luxury.

"I imagine after so long in a convent that court would be loud." He gestured to a servant to fill their goblets with wine. "I confess this is only the second time I have been to court myself."

He had said it to set her at ease, but she tensed at his words. Her reaction unsettled him. He eased to the far-right side of his chair to give her more space and took a sip of wine. Movement from the table across from theirs caught his eye. A man settled beside a woman and did as Geordie had just done, summoning wine for them both.

The woman was the most beautiful in all the world. Long blonde hair, wide blue eyes that he knew sparkled when she smiled, and a rosy, healthy hue to her cheeks. Her figure was slender, her breasts ample enough to tempt a man's imagination, and a flat stomach that would not remain that way for long.

Cat.

Elizabeth said something beside him.

He turned his head toward her to put Cat out of his line of sight. He would not watch her the entire evening when he had another woman at his side. He had morals, after all. "I beg your pardon?"

Elizabeth tilted her face up and met his gaze. "I have said prayers for all those you have slain."

"I say prayers for them myself," he said carefully. Truthfully. He had never enjoyed taking life, even if he was good at it. Those faces haunted his dreams sometimes. Night terrors he'd always chased away with thoughts of Cat.

At least he had not committed the sins many of his brethren had. The very thought left his stomach churning. He clasped his wine goblet and took another sip.

"Do you find pleasure in death?" Though she had resumed her stare into her lap, she asked the question with a pitch to her voice. Fear.

"I fight for our king." Geordie tried to keep his tone light. "It is an act ordained by God when our king wills it as such."

His explanation appeared to appease her morbid curiosities, for she did not speak again. An awkward silence descended the gap of space between them, widening it. "What past times do you enjoy?" he asked.

"Enjoy?"

"Aye." Geordie took another sip of wine. "Dancing, reading, sewing, anything of the like?"

"I enjoy prayer." She clasped her hands in her lap as though she would rather be praying at that very moment. "When I sew, it is strictly for aiding the poor with new clothing."

"That is kind of you," Geordie acknowledged. His gaze slid of its own volition to where Cat sat beside a man with golden hair. No doubt Lord Loughton's son.

Oh, aye, Geordie had asked around about him. Tristan was only slightly older than Cat at five and twenty, the only son of Lord Loughton who doted on him. Despite the full attention of his father and a wealthy upbringing, Tristan appeared to be a man of just morals and integrity.

It was irritating not having anything to latch onto Tristan to despise, aside from his interest in Cat. If nothing else, the baron's son would treat her well, and might even graciously accept the news that the babe Cat would bear was not truly his. Except that she kept her gaze as downcast as Elizabeth.

The latter realization brought his attention to the woman beside him, where he tried to force it to remain for the better part of the evening. They spoke of her life at the convent and how many times a day she prayed and the many small items of clothing she made for orphanages. Any mention of his time on the battlefield or on campaign with the king caused her to immediately change the topic, typically to something of a less secular nature. And while everything about Elizabeth was wholesome and pure and good, he found he could not wait to remove himself from her company.

A glance across the room found Cat with an expression on her face similar to his own, absent all sparkle and joy.

"I believe the music is about to begin." Elizabeth stood abruptly. "I should return to my room. I fear I am ill-prepared for the amount of revelry at court."

Geordie rushed to stand with her and nearly tipped his chair in the process. "Shall I summon a servant to see you to your room?"

"Nay, my nurse shall accompany me." She indicated the nurse behind her, who had remained as guardian to her mistress through the duration of their painfully disengaging conversation.

"It was a pleasure to meet you," Geordie lied politely and offered a bow.

"And you as well." Elizabeth gave one of her overly dramatic curtseys and hastened from the room.

His attention drifted to Cat in time to see her rising to her feet. She smiled gaily at Tristan and shook her head before turning to depart with a servant. Apparently, she meant to retire early as well.

Before Geordie could resolve in his mind what he was doing, he was making his way across the room in her direction. He didn't know what he would say when he caught her, only that he had to hear her voice, see her face tilt up toward him, to breathe in her beautiful, happy scent.

More than that, he wanted to kiss her again, to feel the vibration of her hum of pleasure through his bones and dancing over his skin. Cat. Whom he had judged harshly.

None of it mattered but her, and how desperately he wanted her.

"Geordie." A woman's awed voice came from somewhere behind him.

He'd heard awed voices saying his name since his arrival, though usually it was said with the preceding "Sir" as was befitting of his station.

The praise was generally unwelcome, for the attention left a discomfiting sensation twisting through him. After all, he'd merely done what he had been trained to do. Now though, the attention was especially unwelcome as he chased after the woman that he could not help but love.

"Geordie, please." A hand grasped his tunic.

The impertinence. He turned abruptly and found himself face-to-face with an older woman. Her mouth hung slack and her eyes swam with tears. The peculiarity of her expression threw off his ire and drew instead at his curiosity.

She released his tunic and brought her hand to her mouth. "Geordie Strafford?"

He winced at the surname, having always hated the memories it elicited. It was why he never used it.

"Just Sir Geordie," he said gruffly.

"I knew you as Geordie Strafford." Her lower lip trembled. "Do you not recognize me?"

Geordie shifted his weight uneasily and regarded the older woman. Her dark hair was threaded through with bits of silver, her face weathered by age and her brown eyes sad with the effects of a life not easily lived. And yet there was nothing about her features to recall her in his mind.

He slowly shook his head.

The woman gave a choked sob and put her fist to her heart as though he had greatly wounded her. "Geordie...my sweet Geordie."

People were watching now. Heat crept into his cheeks at this mad woman's lamenting. He stepped back, but she cried out and lunged at him.

"Please do not go." She clutched his tunic with her gnarled fingers. "I cannot lose you again. Look at me, please." She tilted her face toward him. Her eyes were bloodshot and her nose pink from her tears. "Do you truly not recognize your own mother?"

17

Geordie's breath rasped through his teeth as he swiftly made his way toward one of the tower rooms. He'd paid handsomely for the privilege of a few hours, and even more so for the discretion.

His eyes were gritty from lack of sleep after having spent the night speaking with his mother. The conversation had broken down the wall of emotions he'd spent sixteen years erecting. She had told him everything, from how she had protested how Lord Strafford had given him away to Lord Werrick in goodwill. How Strafford had known of his intent to lie from the start and that Geordie would pay the price.

Strafford had waited until she was asleep and stole away with Geordie. By the time she had woken, Geordie was already in the hands of Werrick. She had begged her husband to keep his word to Werrick, but Strafford had merely locked her in her room and left her to mourn the son her husband had left for dead.

Her other son had died five years later, and she declared her womb to be too sorrow-laden to take seed again. When Lord and Lady Strafford heard of Sir Geordie, they originally thought nothing of it. Until they learned he'd come from the wild north, and realized his description sounded like the very son they had lost.

The baron had been too much of a coward to come himself, and so he'd sent his wife to see if Sir Geordie was indeed their long-lost son, the one presumed dead. Lady Strafford had cried then, grateful to have found him after a lifetime of mourning.

Tears had stung Geordie's own eyes, but he had held in the emotion, though it all lashed at him: the hurt, the hatred, the desperation for love and acceptance and the barely controlled rage.

Lord Strafford wanted Geordie to return to Easton Castle in Strafford to take his place among the family. Not as a knight, but as heir to a baron, as was his right by birth.

Such knowledge had overwhelmed him. It sliced open his chest and drew everything held tightly inside outward, bared and vulnerable. He had left the woman who had been his mother as she sobbed her apology and let the door close behind him.

He had needed solace. He had needed air to fill the burning void in his chest. He needed Cat.

This was different from the times he'd been at battle, or at camp afterward, when thoughts of her had been enough to allay his terrible memories of war. She was too close now to merely summon her image in his mind. He needed *her*.

Was she waiting for him upstairs? He had paid his servant well to approach Freya, whom he knew to be discreet. Was it enough? Had Cat come?

He took the stairs two at a time and pushed through the door. Silence met him. Stark and ugly.

She had not come.

He couldn't blame her. When last they spoke, he had looked down upon her for the choices she had made with scorn and judgment. Why should he expect her to risk herself to respond to his request?

He braced his hands on whitewashed walls and let the cool

plaster dig into his palms until his wrists ached. His head hung down between his shoulders as he tried to catch the racing thoughts darting in too many directions.

"Geordie?" A soft voice spoke. A familiar soft voice, the loveliest in all of Christendom.

He spun around and there she was. Though he did not deserve for her to be there, she was. She closed the door quietly and turned the key to lock them within.

Her intake of breath was audible in the otherwise quiet room. "What is it?"

"My mother." Geordie shook his head, not even certain where to begin. "She recognized me last night."

Cat said not a single word, but instead ran to him with open arms. He fell against her, letting her wrap him in her warmth and comfort and sweet, wonderful scent of fresh summer roses. His heart fell open and the entire story came out, every piece of the conversation he'd had with his mother.

He remained locked in Cat's embrace as he spoke, unwilling to remove himself from the consolation he had been craving so desperately. She held him the entire time, never once interrupting. Never once reminding him of how terribly and thoroughly he'd cast her aside.

When he was done, she released him and gently stroked his face. He closed his eyes against the caress, wanting to feel it for a lifetime.

"I know you never felt wanted by your parents," Cat said in a gentle voice.

He opened his eyes. "You always made me feel wanted."

"But I am not your parents, and they want you now."

He scoffed, letting the bitterness of sixteen years show. "Because they have no more sons, and my wretch of a cousin, Robert, will destroy the land and wealth if he gets his greedy hands upon it."

Cat tilted her head in consideration. "Do you not want the barony?"

"Nay."

"Why not?" She went to a small table and poured a goblet of wine from a flagon set by the fire. "I know the obvious reasons." She pushed the goblet into his hand and nodded for him to drink. "Deferring the title to another would cause many problems."

Once his parents petitioned the king with him being their still living son, and the king accepted, Geordie wouldn't be able to decline the title. He could abdicate, but it would not please the king. Cat was indeed correct in her assessment. It *would* cause many problems.

Geordie took the goblet and drained the wine in two great gulps. It seared down his throat, burning at the hurt of emotion knotted in his chest. "To accept feels as though I'm forgiving them for their abandonment of me all those years ago."

She took the goblet and set it aside. "If you were a baron, you would not have to fight like a knight." She gently touched the scar along his collarbone that peeked just beyond the neckline of his tunic. "You would be safer."

"I worked hard to become a knight, to restore honor in my life," he said through gritted teeth.

"And now you can restore honor to the Strafford name, to make a new legacy." She gazed into his eyes. "If anyone can do it, you can." She put her hand to his chest. The heat of her palm bled through and warmed his heart. "Do not let an inability to forgive keep you from what you deserve."

"Will you join me? As my wife?" he asked.

The hope on her face wilted. "I cannot."

"I will take the babe in as my own, give him my name," he said. "We can all live a happy life together."

She shook her head.

Desperation scrabbled in his chest, clawing at his heart. "I would no longer be a lowly knight, but a baron. I would be worthy of you, Cat."

"Geordie," she whispered. "It was never because you are a knight, or because Lord Loughton was a baron. You have never, ever had to prove yourself to me. I have always believed in you."

"You have," he agreed.

He brought her closer to him and breathed in the lovely scent of roses that always brought back a rush of joyful memories. His forehead rested against hers. "And yet you will not marry me." His emotions were raw and unrestrained frustration welled within him. "Why?"

"If we wed, you will want to know who my child's father is." She set her warm hands on either side of his face and kept her brow on his. "Do not say you would not, for you know it is true."

Geordie did not deny it, only because she knew him too bloody well for him to try.

"I cannot ever tell you who the father of my child is." Her fingers stroked his face.

Geordie closed his gritty eyes. "Why not?"

"Because you would kill him." Cat took a shaky breath. "You would destroy everything you have built, and everything you are now working to achieve."

Geordie nearly protested that he would not kill the man, but he knew it to be a lie. A married courtier had taken advantage of Cat's naivety. She'd come from a life filled with innocence, raised far from the debauched courtiers with their calculated flirtations and false declarations of love. Aye, if Geordie knew which man had plucked her flower intentionally, knowing she would be left ruined, he would run the man through with his sword.

Still, he tried to offer a protest. "If it would mean having you, I could—"

She shook her head against his and tilted her mouth to capture his lips. It was a tender kiss, one borne of a love that could not be given or taken, a kiss of finality for what could never be. He reached for her, intending to draw her closer, when she pulled away from him and headed for the door.

He couldn't let her go, not like this. Not now. "Cat."

She turned and looked back at him, her eyes glistening with tears.

There was so much he wanted to tell her, to declare his love for her, to apologize for how he'd treated her, to say he didn't deserve the care and advice she'd offered him without question or reproach. "Thank you for coming." It was inadequate for all the emotions tearing through him, but he knew he could not bring himself to say more.

"It is better this way." She let her gaze linger on him a moment longer, and then she was gone.

He stared at the closed wooden door and his heart cracked open. "I love you, Cat."

Cat leaned her head back against the wall, composing herself outside the door of the tower room before descending the stairs. If she had left promptly, she might not have heard his beautiful, final words to her. But she'd lingered in her pain and had been rewarded with the most bittersweet words.

I love you, Cat.

She covered her mouth to suppress the sound of her jagged inhale. Tristan would be expecting her soon in the great hall to keep her company as she broke her fast. He seldom did so himself. Not for the arrogant logic of most nobles, being that only laborers ate a meal in the morning to sustain their energy through the day, but that he simply wasn't hungry.

Already, Cat had stayed too long.

She pressed her hands to her face as though doing so could reduce the redness her tears had no doubt caused. Several deep breaths later, she was prepared as well as could be expected to face another day at court. She made her way down to the great hall amid many others seeking to break their fast in search of Tristan.

"Good morrow, Lady Catriona." He approached her with a wide enough smile to bring out the dimple on his right cheek.

"Good morrow, Tristan." She inclined her head respectfully to him. "I trust the day finds you well."

"All the better now." He pulled the seat for her to take before a servant could do it.

She gave him a skeptical look before accepting the proffered chair. "None of that talk now. You know I am uninterested in marriage."

If nothing else, she had expressed her lack of desire to wed from the first. Despite her protests, he had continued to hover at her side. As she'd needed an excuse to remain at court while waiting for Sir Gawain to show himself, she had no choice but to allow his company.

Tristan settled into his own chair and leaned closer. "If we may speak candidly, I also am uninterested in marriage."

She reached for a loaf of bread. "And spending your time with me gives your father hope enough that he leaves you alone?"

"That, and I enjoy your cleverness." He winked at her. "Even if you are in love with the honorable Sir Geordie."

She lifted her brows at him. He saw much more than she had given him credit for. "Are you jealous?" she teased, knowing he would not be.

He laughed. "With all due respect, my lady, he would be the one to capture my interest more so than you. However, given the way he stares at you, I will answer your question with an emphatic 'aye.'"

Cat's mouth fell open in surprise, but she snapped it shut, recovering quickly. She understood now why Lord Loughton had been so eager for his son to meet her, and why he had been so driven to push them together.

"You will have to wed eventually," Cat said softly.

"More's the pity." Tristan reached for a slice of bread and spread a bit of salted butter over it. "But while we are prodding at open wounds, why do you not marry Sir Geordie? It is obvious to all at court that you both desire one another."

Cat took a breath to reply, but Tristan leaned closer still. "May I guess?"

She pressed her lips together, suddenly frightened at what he might suggest. Slowly, she nodded.

"You're with child. And it isn't his." Tristan leaned back in his chair. "Am I correct? I assume from your stricken face I am."

Cat immediately smoothed her expression.

"Do you know when you are nervous, your hands cup your lower stomach?" He glanced into her lap where her hands were protectively folded over that delicate little bump. "I've only ever seen women with child do such a thing."

She immediately unclasped her hands and settled them awkwardly on either side of the chair. "I will not be at court long," she warned him. "I am to confront my babe's father and then I will be gone."

"And he is already wed, isn't he?"

Cat made a face at Tristan. Was her situation so terribly predictable?

Tristan laughed good-naturedly. "It was honorable of you to inform me you were uninterested in marriage. Most women would have tried to pass their bastard off to a new husband." He glanced about the large room. "Is the sod at court now?"

Cat shook her head. "Nay, but I anticipate he will arrive in time for Sir Geordie's feast."

"And where will you go after you speak with him?" Tristan bit into his bread and chewed slowly as he waited for her response.

"To Berkley Place, where my sister and her family live." She brought her hands together and realized she nearly settled them over her stomach once more. Instead, she twisted her fingers together. "I hope once the babe is born without the prying eyes of court, or the rest of my family, that I can have it delivered to its father or to a good family."

"And after the child is delivered?" he pressed.

She shrugged. "Then I return to Werrick Castle."

"Such a barbaric land." Tristan shuddered. "It is no wonder your Sir Geordie came out as tough as he did. I'd wager you've got a bit of an edge yourself."

"No one can shoot an arrow like me," Cat said proudly.

"I'd like to see that." Tristan grinned. "Truly. You must show me later this afternoon in the gardens."

"Where everyone will see?" Cat glanced around the great hall filled with arrogant nobles, resplendent in their kirtles, tunics and doublets of costly fabric.

He smirked. "Let them. Sir Geordie will be looking on as well."

She hesitated.

"You are keeping yourself from love, but why not allow him to see you from a distance and be proud of you, just as you are proud of him?"

She tilted her head toward Tristan. "You really are curious enough to use that to goad me?"

He grinned. "Aye."

"Very well. This afternoon, then."

"Now that we've settled that, I have one more question to ask you." Tristan met her gaze with his long lashed brown eyes. "If the father will not have the babe and you cannot find another home for it, would you consider marrying me?"

Cat frowned. "I don't understand."

"You know who I am." He reached out and took her hand the way a lover might. "You know I will never be able to love you in the way a man loves a woman, and we would already have a child." He narrowed his eyes meaningfully. "You would be free to love

Geordie with the same discretion that I would use with my lovers."

Tempting though his words were, Cat knew she could never allow Geordie to take her as a mistress. She could never tarnish his shining reputation thus. However, Tristan's solution would offer her child legitimacy. A secret hope flared within Cat, a fledgling one that had begun to take shape with each tender stroke of her hand over her belly: the wish to keep the babe, to be its mother and love it as she had been loved in her own childhood.

She regarded Tristan's hand on hers, his fine, tapered fingers, the rhythmic tap-tap of his pulse ticking at the underside of his wrist. It was the second proposal she had received that morning, and it was one she would be foolish to not consider.

18

Several days later on the night of Geordie's feast, Cat dressed with extreme care. Not only for Geordie, who she was eager to see so rightfully honored, but also for her confrontation with Sir Gawain.

Many people had poured into the castle throughout the day and all now entered the great hall. Minstrels played a merry tune to welcome them into the feast and the tables sparkled with wealth. Golden goblets, jeweled salt cellars, costly plates gleaming and ready to be piled high with sumptuous food. The crowd made their way to their chairs in their best clothing and were greeted with hearty pours of wine. A feast was never an event to be missed, especially when the drink flowed freely and the food finely prepared.

For Cat, it was the culmination of everything she'd been anticipating since she left Werrick Castle.

Tristan guided her smoothly through the crowd to their places. The tension between them had melted away since he'd shared his own secret with her. Now they were like everyone else at court, tethered by promises to keep truths buried deep, while they put on a show of being who they were not.

How swiftly the court corrupted.

At least for all those who were not like Geordie. She saw him on the dais by the king in a seat of honor. He was slightly taller than the king, younger and far more muscular. Compared to those who sat around him, he looked like a god, perfect and powerful with strength.

"I hear he is heir to the Strafford Barony," Tristan whispered into her ear.

Cat smiled and cast a coy look up at him.

"You know." Tristan put on a show of mock offense as he took his seat. "The entire story is the stuff of a troubadour's tale, how his father used Sir Geordie in good faith and then lied, even though he knew his son would pay the price with his life. Is it true?"

Cat's smile faltered as she remembered that boy in his prison cell. His chin had been lifted high; his stance wide. There had been fear in his large brown eyes, and pain after such betrayal by his own family, but he had stood tall and brave in the face of death.

He'd been extraordinary, even then.

"My father never would have killed him," she said in the age-old argument she'd often had with Geordie. "I think it was more fortuitous for my father than for Geordie that I happened to be in the dungeon that day. It gave him an excuse to let the boy go free."

"I think the boy would disagree with you on that account." Tristan nodded toward the dais where Geordie openly regarded Cat.

Heat flooded her cheeks. She stared back in his direction, effusing her look with all the pride in her heart. And all the love as well. For how could she not allow him how truly happy she was at the level of honor he had earned?

The feast opened with several speeches made in Geordie's honor, and continued on until the end of the meal. Then, the entertainment began. One by one, the story of Geordie's accomplishments came to light. How he had truly fended off twenty men on his own, how he had saved the king, how he had single-handedly shifted the fate of battle, and so many more stories.

Hearing such harrowing tales made it easy to see how he had sustained so many wounds on the battlefield. He had continually inserted himself into danger and had been strong enough to survive every time.

Cat listened to all his accomplishments with her heart in her throat. She was not the only female to do so, as every lady in attendance kept her gaze locked onto Geordie's handsome face as he flushed with each story and met the rounds of cheers with shy smiles.

Cat knew the attention left him discomfited, but she reveled in the praise for him. This was his opportunity to shine and he had earned every moment of it. Let all the world see him for the man he truly was.

Everyone appeared enthralled, with the exception of a gentleman off to the side with his dark hair pulled back and held in a thong. He sat back in his chair with his forearms crossed over his chest as he glowered in Geordie's direction.

"Who is that man?" Cat asked Tristan and indicated the man.

Tristan scoffed. "You'd think he'd have more decorum than to show his irritation so baldly before the court." He smirked. "That is the former heir to the Strafford Barony, Robert."

A shiver wound down Cat's spine. "Is he dangerous?"

"From the stories I've heard of Sir Geordie, I wager he'll be fine." Tristan narrowed his eyes at the former Strafford heir. "But if Sir Geordie were any other mortal man, it would be prudent to employ a modicum of caution."

Cat hummed in agreement. "If all goes well tonight and I do not return, will you ensure Geordie is properly warned?"

"I will do it myself," Tristan vowed with a twinkle in his eye.

"Then I'm glad to have given you a reason to speak with him." Cat chuckled.

"As am I, my dear." Tristan winked at her. "Even if he'll only ever love you," he whispered into her ear.

Warmth washed over Cat at his words. She shouldn't wish them to be true. She wanted Geordie to have a happy life with a woman he truly did care for. Mayhap the demure red-haired daughter of Sir John who appeared to be pushed toward him in conversation while they all supped. From what Cat had heard of her, she'd recently emerged from a convent. She had the doe-eyed look of a lady released into a world she was ill-prepared to face.

Doubtless she did not carry another man's child in her womb and would not even be at risk to experience such a fate. Though it destroyed Cat to admit it, Sir John's pristine daughter was the kind of woman Geordie deserved: a woman as pure as him.

A man in the distance caught Cat's attention, dragging her focus from Geordie and recalling her second motive for her attendance that evening. It had been far too easy to forget as she'd watched Geordie being honored.

But there Sir Gawain was, standing and speaking with a comely brunette who flushed at whatever he whispered in her ear. Cat could only guess, though her assumptions would most likely be accurate, since the same words had been graced upon her once before as well.

Lady Jane was a liar in many ways, but in this one thing, she had been correct: Sir Gawain attended the feast.

***

WHILE IT WAS AN HONOR TO BE THE FOCUS OF A FEAST HOSTED by the king, Geordie had been ready for it to end as soon as it began. He did not like hearing his deeds in battle so publicly put on display. Especially when details got grislier as the hour drew later and the knights had more to drink.

With each passing story, Mistress Howard appeared to grow more and more disgusted. Not that Geordie minded. It was for the best. He'd already told the king of his lack of interest and confessed he was not yet ready to marry. The king had been gracious in understanding and had not forced the union.

Geordie's mother, however, listened to the heroic tales with affection glowing in her eyes. She stared at him the exact way he'd spent a lifetime wishing a parent would watch him: with love and with pride. His father had not come, citing illness.

It had been so easy for Geordie to forgive his mother, who had been yet another victim of his father's perfidy, but he would never offer clemency toward Lord Strafford.

The king leaned closer to Geordie. "We think we know the lady who has stolen your heart." His gaze fell on Cat. "Is that the one we hear hit the center of the target with every arrow she fired in the garden a few days prior?"

Geordie couldn't help but smile. The court had been in a flurry of gossip over it. "She's always been good with a bow."

"Mayhap we ought to allow women in our army." The king chuckled good-naturedly. "Her father is the Earl of Werrick. She is one of the few of his daughters left unwed. It'd be good to see another of his children with an Englishman, before they all marry those infernal Scots."

Geordie observed Cat for a long moment. It appeared the coldness between herself and Tristan had melted away into something far friendlier. Far more flirtatious. Energy flared hot through Geordie and left his muscles raging with the need to fight. Even as his body prepared for war, a slice of pain lanced his heart.

Jealousy. He knew it for what it was.

Cat would not have him. She wouldn't accept him when she knew he would demand to know who the babe's father was. Why couldn't he set that notion aside?

For her honor.

And he couldn't so easily set aside something as important as Cat's honor.

If he could, they could be together. Except the not knowing would be a rock in his soul, rattling about and painfully obvious. Nay, he could not so easily set such an idea aside.

"She is the reason you turned down the opportunity to wed Mistress Howard, eh?" the king pressed.

Tristan leaned toward Cat and whispered in her ear. She laughed at whatever it was he said, the sweet notes of her joy trickling over the din of conversations and made its way to Geordie.

He turned his attention from her. "I am not ready to be wed."

The king nodded and then tilted his head, not fully accepting Geordie's declaration. "We hear your father is unwell."

Your father. The words turned Geordie's stomach. "Baron Strafford has been suffering from poor health, as I understand it from my mother."

"When his soul departs this world, it will be good to see a just man in the barony." The king raised his goblet toward Geordie. "It is difficult to endure one's parents using them as a pawn in political games." The flinch to his lips told Geordie he understood. And how could he not, with what his own mother had put him through for years in her grasp for power?

The king recovered quickly. "Strafford has never done anything so grievous that we could strip him of his lands and title, but never have we given him our full trust." He paused to drink. "You, however—we are alive because of trusting you. We release you from your promise to be our personal guard so that you may pursue your birthright as baron."

"Any of your men would have done the same for you, Your Majesty," Geordie protested.

"But not nearly as well." The king grinned. "Off with you. Go let the ladies of court have at you. We can see them eyeing you like a flock of birds at a fish market. Good luck to you."

Geordie rose from his seat and almost immediately ran into a woman whose brunette hair was coiled beneath a layer of fine gold netting.

"Sir Geordie." She curtseyed and flashed him a saucy smile. "Lady Catriona was supposed to introduce me, but it appears she's otherwise occupied this evening."

He flicked a glance toward Cat to find Tristan helping her from the table. One only knew where they would go from there. The dance floor mayhap, where he would be forced to observe Tristan touching her subtly as Geordie once had? To the garden, to steal a kiss? Geordie's cheeks went warm.

"I should like to know more of your stories," the woman said.

"I don't even know you," Geordie murmured.

"Lady Jane Steward." She purposefully let her stare drift down his body. "It is a pleasure to finally meet you."

Her forwardness unnerved him, especially when it was unwanted. "Well met," he replied. "I bid you good evening."

Her mouth fell open in protest, but already someone was approaching him. Sir John. Geordie nearly groaned. Hopefully, the king had told the knight of Geordie's decision not to wed the man's daughter.

From the corner of Geordie's eye, he caught Cat moving through the crowd.

"I hear you're to become the next Baron Strafford." Sir John held out a hand to Geordie and they clasped forearms. "Fortune falls in your favor."

"Forgive me." Geordie cast a glance toward Elizabeth. Better to air out the truth than let lies and distrust cause unrest among them on the battlefield. The knighthood was a brotherhood with a trust to transcend all else.

Sir John shook his head. "Nothing to forgive. My daughter is highly sought after. I only hope the man she finally marries has as good a soul as you."

Geordie regarded his brothers-in-arms surrounding them. "There are many good souls here."

Cat was moving quickly now, nearly directly behind Sir John, easy to watch. Tristan was not with her, but she had her attention fixed on someone.

"Enjoy your feast." Sir John clapped him on the shoulder. "You deserve it."

Geordie nodded his appreciation and moved toward Cat, trying to see where she went. A dark-haired man turned toward her and the smile spreading easily over his face told Geordie what he had been seeking. The expression was too quick, too eager, too intimate.

He knew the man. Sir Gawain. One of the knights who seemed to always find his way out of battle rather than into it, a man known to enjoy loving over fighting.

Cat tilted her head and said something to him that caused him to look about and nod with a sly grin. With that, the two of them began moving toward one of the doors exiting the great hall.

Geordie's stomach twisted. Surely, she was not going for a tryst with the man after she'd been flirting with Tristan. Geordie clenched his hands into a fist, refusing to believe it of her. Especially with a man like Sir Gawain.

He tried to walk through the crowd toward her, but a man stepped in front of him, a baron something, to introduce his eligible daughter. Cat and Sir Gawain exited through one of the side doors to where the hall was no doubt quiet and filled with darkened alcoves.

Geordie politely accepted the introduction and moved five paces toward the door, when yet another person appeared in front of him. Frustration burned along the back of his neck.

At this rate, he would never get to Cat, but he knew he had to at least try.

19

Catriona followed Sir Gawain through the masses toward the door. It had been so easy to convince him to be alone with her, requiring only a flirtatious wink and the suggestion of intimacy.

He turned to face her briefly before they were fully free of the feast's attendees. "Wait a moment before following me." His blue gaze wandered down her body. "The second alcove on the left."

The second alcove on the left.

His usual cave of debauchery, no doubt. And he'd said it with such ease.

Cat swallowed her disgust and simply smiled in reply. He raised his brows in a way he obviously thought charming. In a way *she* had once found charming.

He strode from the room with his arrogant gait. How had she ever even been attracted to him? He oozed cockiness and overinflated confidence she'd been so naïve as to interpret as worldliness and authority. Her sisters were right—she truly was a bad judge of character.

She paused by the door and adjusted her belt to ensure her dagger was within reach. She'd swapped out her eating dagger for one with a sharper, longer blade. He would not take advantage of her again.

After a careful sweep of the room, and a supportive nod from Tristan, Cat slipped through the door. While the feast had been lit with candles and alive with the chorus of conversation and music, the hall was cast in shadows and empty.

Her heart raced with what she was about to do, but she willed it to calm. There was no turning back, not when she had put far too much into this endeavor. She was nearly to the alcove when Sir Gawain stretched out a hand and grabbed her to him. Immediately, his touch was on her, pawing at her bosom, grabbing her bottom to press her to his arousal. His tongue thrust into her mouth, nearly choking her with the lingering taste of sour wine.

He overwhelmed her with the onslaught of his lust. Like last time. The odor of his costly musk and ambergris perfume slammed at her memory with fresh reminders of that night.

For a brief moment, her head swirled with panic.

"Cease this," she growled against his lips.

He did not.

"I'm with child."

That stopped him. He pulled his head away from hers, breathing heavily from his gaping mouth. He glanced down at her stomach.

She resisted the urge to cover the small bump. He did not need to witness any weakness on her part. She had to be strong.

His brow lifted. "Who shall I congratulate?"

The knave. It was tempting to pull the dagger from her belt and turn the sneer on his face into a mask of terror.

"You." Cat forced her word to remain steady. "You are the father."

He laughed, a hard, brittle sound that echoed down the empty hall. "You came to me with such eagerness, I'm sure you've slept with half the court."

Cat clenched her hand into a fist. "I was a maiden when you took me."

"A virgin?" He scoffed. "You fell open with the ease of a whore."

Cat's chest blazed at the offense, even if she knew it for what it was: a ruse to discourage her from his own accountability.

"I've been with no man but you." She lifted her chin with a pride she did not feel. This was it. Even if she no longer held faith in the outcome, she had to say it. "Will you take the child as your own?"

He stared at her as if she'd asked him to carry the child in his own belly. "Are you actually trying to pass off another man's bastard to me?" His lip curled in disgust. "I have a child on the way. I've no need for your lovers' leavings."

She did cradle her womb at that. "This child is yours, though I wish to God it was not."

Footsteps sounded in the hallway.

Sir Gawain stiffened. "Stop saying that."

"How would your wife feel knowing that you've taken so many women at court?" Cat demanded.

His eyes narrowed and she was struck with how very much he looked like a rat with half his face buried in shadow. "She's a proper lady who knows well how to turn the other way and hold her tongue."

"Would she still be so obliging if she knew I carried your child?"

"Cease your accusations at once," Sir Gawain said through clenched teeth.

"May I remind you that I am an earl's daughter and you are a mere knight?" She lifted a single brow, haughty in her delivery. "If my father were to make a complaint against you to the king, he would believe my father over you."

"Then your father would know you're ruined, and your life

would be destroyed." Sir Gawain smirked. "I refuse to listen to another word."

He made to step forward, but she shifted to stand in front of him. He shifted to go around her, but she put herself before him once more, their feet scuffling off the hard floor and echoing around them.

"My life is already destroyed." Anger heated through her veins at the truth in her words, at what Sir Gawain had cost her. "I never asked for what you did to me. How dare you refuse to listen? How dare you deny culpability?"

"Culpability?" He straightened his doublet and suddenly did not look as arrogant as he had only moments before. "You were the one who flirted shamelessly with me, fluttering your lashes and catching my eye at every turn." His words pressed a sore spot within her, and he knew it.

"You took advantage of me," she said without the strength she would have liked.

He tried to move around her once more. "I didn't make you seek me out while you were at court."

She blocked him again. "The wine."

"You mean the wine you drank as freely as any alehouse slattern? I asked you to join me in the garden and you said aye." He tilted his head so that he gazed scornfully down his long nose at her. She hoped her child would not inherit that terrible nose.

"I told you to stop." The breath panted from her, a heady blend of rage and fear and shame.

He gave a harsh bark of laughter. "What did you think we were going to do in the garden? Kiss sweetly while I whispered of your beauty in the moonlight?"

Heat prickled at her eyes. That was exactly what she'd assumed.

Sir Gawain scoffed. "You're even more foolish than I initially thought." He shoved her. The action was unexpected and done with such force, she was sent stumbling backward.

She staggered in her surprise but managed to remain upright.

"Leave me be, little slut." He strode past her. "Seek out one of your other lovers to pin this offense on."

"This is your child." Cat grabbed his arm. "You will not leave me to deal with this on my own. You will accept responsibility."

He spun about and his hand struck out at her like a snake, too fast and unexpected to block. It smacked her cheek with an audible pop that reverberated off the walls.

"You will learn your place among men," he snarled.

Stars danced in her vision, but she shook them off. She'd been hit worse before in training.

"As you will learn yours among women." She lunged at him, throwing the force of her elbow to his jaw. His head snapped to the side and blood spurted from his mouth. He cursed and stared at her, dumbfounded. His shock did not last long.

He roared in rage and ran at her with blind fury, his moves erratic and his foe sincerely underestimated. She ducked to avoid his clumsy punch.

She straightened and delivered a blow to his nose with the heel of her hand. Blood exploded from beneath her palm followed by a grunt of pain.

The hit had been done to diffuse him, but it had the opposite effect. Rather than fall beneath the pain, something in his eyes flashed and he went wild.

He shoved her back again. This time before she could steady herself, he pushed her against the wall with his forearm pressing into her neck.

A burning ache filled her throat as her head slammed against the stone wall. Her lungs screamed for air, but her inhale only resulted in a ragged choke.

"You broke my nose, you slattern." He pressed harder on her throat.

A door opened in the distance and light flooded the darkened hall.

She could no longer draw breath. Her hand skimmed the smooth edge of her belt to where the hilt of her dagger jutted from its sheath. In a single motion, she slipped it free and pressed it to his groin. Just enough for the sharp edge to remind him of the damage a knife could do to such delicate skin.

The pressure on her throat eased.

"Hit me once more and I'll ensure you never touch another woman again," she rasped.

A bellowed cry of rage in the distance was followed by the force of a massive shadow, sweeping in and dragging Sir Gawain from her. Cat's heart caught in her throat.

Geordie slammed Sir Gawain against the wall. "How dare you treat a woman thus?" He pushed his elbow into Sir Gawain's throat as Sir Gawain had done to her. "You defile what it is to be a knight."

Sir Gawain made a terrible choking sound. That was when Cat realized Geordie was not only holding him against the wall but lifting him completely off his feet.

Sir Gawain's heels scrabbled silently against the tapestry behind him in a vain effort to find purchase. Geordie's eyes were cold and intense, fixed on his task.

Alarm prickled at the back of Cat's neck as her worst fear just became a real possibility. Geordie intended to kill Sir Gawain.

※

GEORDIE GRITTED HIS TEETH AS HE SHOVED HIS FULL BODY weight against the wall, digging his forearm into Gawain's skinny neck. For that was how he would think of this blackguard, not as Sir Gawain. He was undeserving of such a noble title.

Blood spurted from the man's nose and ran hot down Geordie's sleeve. Geordie had no intention of stopping, not until Gawain had ceased breathing and didn't plan to remove his arm from the man's throat even then. He'd killed enough men to know choking had to continue beyond loss of consciousness.

And he wouldn't stop until Gawain was dead.

Cat pulled at his arm. "Stop, Geordie," she cried. "You'll kill him."

Gawain's eyes fluttered and started to roll up into his head.

"That is what I intend," Geordie growled.

"And that's why I didn't tell you." Cat pulled at him. "Stop."

A door banged open in the distance and light spilled into the hallway, illuminating Gawain's slackening face.

"You will be executed for murder." Cat's hands tugged at him now, making Gawain's head limply roll back and forth against the tapestry.

Death would be worth facing if it meant the bastard who defiled Cat was dead. The man didn't deserve to be a knight.

"I can't lose you." There was a breathless desperation to her voice that plunged through Geordie's blind fury. He relaxed his hold.

"Sir Geordie!" An authoritative male voice echoed down the hall, which was now brightly lit, but Geordie was already releasing Gawain.

The man slid limply to the floor.

"This man assaulted Lady Catriona," Geordie said in a level voice.

"He is for the castle guard to attend to." Sir John put a hand on Geordie's shoulder and squeezed.

Geordie resisted the urge to shrug the man off. The gesture was well-meaning, even if it was unwelcome.

"Looks like you beat him soundly enough." Sir John nudged Gawain with his toe.

Cat stepped forward. "That was me." She lifted her right hand where the palm was smeared with Gawain's blood. "It is as Sir Geordie said. Sir Gawain assaulted me."

Gawain coughed, then sucked in a choking gasp as his eyes flew open.

Sir John looked away from the pathetic form of Gawain and fixed his gaze on Cat. "You're the one who hit all those targets dead center with the bow and arrow, aye?"

Cat nodded.

Sir John nodded appreciatively. "I'd say this fool accosted the wrong lady."

Cat lifted her head with pride.

Sir John glanced behind him to where a crowd of people had amassed and were staring at the scene. "I cannot say this was the ideal place to be meeting a man." Sir John lifted his brows with the weight of his suggestion.

Geordie tensed at the implication behind Sir John's words, but Cat simply straightened and met the older man's eyes.

"I would like Sir Gawain arrested." She delivered the demand with all the haughtiness one would expect from an earl's daughter. "For assaulting me." She touched a hand to her cheek and neck where the light coming in from the door illuminated her reddened skin.

Geordie had not noticed her injuries until that moment. Horror swept through him. He wanted to wrap her in his arms, to soothe away all the hurt she'd endured. He wanted it as desperately as he wanted Gawain to get what he deserved.

Sir John grabbed Gawain and hauled him to his feet. Gawain wavered, touching his throat as he gave a painful swallow.

"Leave me be," he croaked.

"You've assaulted an earl's daughter, Sir Gawain." Sir John tightened his grip on the man's doublet. "As the father of a daughter myself, I will ensure you face punishment for your actions." Sir John glanced at the floor, and his eyes narrowed.

Geordie followed his stare and found a dagger laying on the ground. Cat stepped toward it and covered the weapon with the sweep of her skirt. "Thank you, Sir John."

The large knight gave a hesitant nod. "I would recommend going the opposite direction." With that, he dragged Sir Gawain toward the assembly of the feast where curious courtiers stared with fascination. The door to the great hall banged shut behind Sir John, plunging Geordie and Cat into near darkness. A metallic scrape of steel on stone told Geordie Cat had picked up her dagger.

Geordie's eyes adjusted to the dim light. "Let us get you to your room." He reached for her shoulders to lead her in the opposite direction, as Sir John had suggested.

"Your feast," Cat said miserably.

Geordie led her down the corridor. "It is over."

Admittedly, this was not how he had anticipated the night of his feast ending. But he had saved Cat from a man who meant her harm. He squeezed Cat's shoulders a little more firmly, confirming to himself she was safe.

"Where is Freya?" he asked. "Why was she not with you?"

"I told her not to come."

Geordie led her up the back stairs, usually reserved for servants. If nothing else, it would keep them from the prying eyes of the courtiers. And there would be prying eyes, digging in to find fodder for gossip.

So many questions fired through his mind. Why had she told Freya not to come? What had she hoped to gain from speaking to Sir Gawain on her own? But he held all these questions back lest someone overhear them. He wanted the conversation with Cat to be private, to get the full truth from her.

Of one thing he was entirely certain—she had not gone to the empty corridor for a tryst.

Geordie walked Cat to her rooms. Blessedly, they saw no other souls on their way. As suspected, most were still at the feast and not roaming the halls.

He stopped in front of the door to Lord Calville's apartments, where Cat was staying. She did not make a move to enter to room. Instead, she looked up at Geordie, her eyes large in her slender face. The mark at her neck had begun to fade, but the injury on her cheek was still red.

"You have questions," Cat said softly.

Geordie swallowed them down. "You've had a trying night…"

"Come in with me." She reached out a hand and took his. "Please."

"You needn't tell me anything you do not wish to."

Cat put her free hand on the door latch. "I believe it must be said."

She opened the door and pulled him inside.

20

Cat knew she shouldn't be alone in the royally appointed apartments with Geordie. But after having the court see her with Sir Gawain in the hall, and after everything that had transpired, what did it even matter anymore?

A fire had been lit in the hearth by one of the castle's many servants. The cheery glow and the snapping of the flames were a stark contrast to the cold hollowness within her chest. While walking up to the room, she had been determined to tell Geordie everything that had happened that terrible night.

Now that he was here, now that they were alone, it was all too much. Too shameful.

She watched tongues of fire lick over logs and tried to ignore the weight of his presence.

Geordie, who had always been so adept at reading her moods, gently rubbed his thumb where their hands were joined. "Cat, you don't have to do this."

But she did. This was Geordie. The only person who knew everything about her. Everything, except this one thing that had kept the love between them from being able to blossom.

"Sir Gawain will be punished for what he's done," Cat said.

Geordie nodded.

"And you will doubtless be watched around him to ensure you do not do anything foolish," she surmised. Like kill Sir Gawain and ruin his entire life.

Geordie's gaze slid away with displeasure. It was as much of an agreement as she'd likely receive.

"I can only tell you all of this now, if I know it will be impossible for you to kill Sir Gawain." She clenched her teeth at the word "impossible," for nothing was so when it came to Geordie.

"It would be exceptionally difficult," he conceded.

Cat nodded, unable to speak for a moment, as her heart was lodged firmly in her throat.

"He's the father of your babe, isn't he?" Geordie asked.

"Aye." Cat swallowed. "I tried to get him to accept it as his, to help me figure out what to do. In truth, confronting him was my sole reason for coming to court."

Geordie furrowed his brows. "Tristan?"

Cat shook her head. "I had hoped not to meet him. I anticipated Sir Gawain would be here, that I could speak with him, get his assistance in finding a solution for the babe, stay in my room until the night of your feast and then leave. But Sir Gawain was gone until just this evening and I had no choice when I was introduced to Tristan."

"Then you don't love him?"

"Tristan?" Cat smiled affectionately at the thought of her new dear friend. "Nay, there would never be love between us. He is simply a friend. Our affections both lie elsewhere."

Geordie gave her a shy smile that told her he liked her answer.

"I got Sir Gawain alone as quickly as I could." She gave a mirthless laugh. "He refused to help, of course. He accused me of having been with half the court. Which I have not." She emphasized the last words. "It didn't go well, to say the least."

"I presume you do not love Sir Gawain."

Cat turned her stare back to the fire. This would be the

hardest piece to confess: her own responsibility in the mess of it all. The flames blurred before her, and a choked sob rose up in her throat. "Oh, Geordie. I was one of those empty-headed women who foolishly fell prey to a man at court."

Geordie put his strong arms around her and squeezed. "Jesu, Cat. I never should have said that. I...I was so angry about you wanting to go to court to meet someone who would take you out of my life that I said cruel things. I had no idea...I didn't mean..." He turned her face toward him and gazed down at her. "You are not an empty-headed woman. You are strong and beautiful and clever and it's for all those reasons and so many more that I love you."

Cat smiled sadly at the kindness of his words. "But I *was* one of those empty-headed women, Geordie." She looked down at where he still rubbed his thumb over their joined hands. "I've been the little sister for so long, always overlooked. Coming to court was so exciting. I wasn't overlooked but regarded as an eligible lady. Men flirted with me, and I was giddy with the attention." She closed her eyes. "I didn't know you loved me, not like this. If I'd known that, if I'd known you would return, that you had plans to wed me..."

"You didn't know," Geordie said. "I should have told you, but I wanted to be with you when I said the words. I wanted to have everything ready for you to become my wife."

A hot tear tickled down Cat's cheek and she had to pause a moment to collect herself before continuing. "I drank too much wine that night. Sir Gawain continued to fill my cup. My head spun and I knew it was too much, that I should have stopped." She released her hold on Geordie and put palms to her burning cheeks. "So many times that night I should have stopped or turned away. Like when I knew I drank too much, or when he led me into the alcove, or when he kissed me."

Geordie gently took hold of her hands and lowered them from

her face. "He knew perfectly well what he was doing, Cat. You've always been so trusting."

"Too trusting." She sniffed.

"Aye, and he took advantage of that." Geordie ran his finger over her cheek with such tenderness, it nearly broke her heart.

"It all felt so wrong." She drew in a shuddering breath. "When he...touched me." She closed her eyes again, unable to look at Geordie. "I knew it was wrong, but I was so surprised, I-I didn't say stop until it was too late."

Geordie stiffened. "You told him to stop."

"Before he..." She grimaced.

"You told him to stop and he continued?" There was a hard edge to Geordie's voice.

"I was not blameless." Cat shook her head. "I went willingly with him. He was right when he'd said I'd flirted with him, teased him. I didn't stop him when he put his hands under my skirt."

"But you told him to stop after, and he didn't," Geordie ground out. "Cat, he raped you."

Tears flooded her eyes then, and all of her hurt with them in soul-shattering sobs: the shame, the sorrow, the unfairness.

Geordie caught her in his arms and let her cry against his chest, never once uttering a word. He didn't have to. She could feel his rage in the hammering of his heart against her cheek, in the way he gathered her to him as though he could form a protective shell around her and never let her experience pain again.

"This isn't your fault, Cat." He whispered those words in her ear again and again and again, while smoothing her hair.

It only made her cry harder at first. But after the truth of those words sank in, the anger towards Sir Gawain took over, white hot and deep. She recalled asking Geordie to stop when they kissed at the abandoned cottage, after she'd stitched his wound closed, and he had.

Immediately.

Without question or argument.

Sir Gawain had not only countered her protests with persuasions, he had ignored them. Stolen what he wanted, then had the temerity to put the blame on her shoulders. And she'd accepted it, bearing the burden of the heavy cloak of shame.

Cat pushed her head into Geordie's chest and growled through clenched teeth. "He took everything from me."

"Cat—"

She pulled from his arms, anger induced energy lashing through her, unspent and wild. "He took my innocence, he took my joy, he took away my future." Her heart crumpled as she regarded Geordie. "He took you."

Geordie shook his head. "Never." He caught her face in his hands so their eyes locked. "No one will ever take you from me."

"I'm carrying a married man's babe in my belly. A married man who wants nothing to do with it." Cat pulled from Geordie's touch. "I have no idea what to do with this child, and I cannot bring myself to drink the tea Leila gave me."

"Nay, do not drink the tea." Geordie knelt on the ground in front of her. "Catriona Barrington, love of my life, will you do me the immense honor of not only allowing me to marry you..." Slowly, purposefully, he lifted his hands to gently touch her lower stomach. "But also giving me the pleasure and joy of raising this child with you, together, as our own?"

※

Geordie remained on his knees before Cat, his hands gently cradling her small stomach. She blinked down at him.

"Will you marry me?" Geordie asked again.

"This child may look like Sir Gawain." Despite her protest, she put her hands over his, securing his touch. Her stomach was firm and slightly rounded beneath his palms, filled with a growing new life.

"It is possible for a man to love a child who is not his own,"

Geordie said with the whole of his heart. "When he loves the mother enough to see past the violence of the child's creation and the man of his or her making."

He was referring, of course, to Lord Werrick and his love for Leila. Cat's youngest sister had not only been the result of a terrible assault on Lady Werrick when the castle was taken eighteen years prior, but Leila's birth had killed Lady Werrick. And still, Lord Werrick had loved Leila as his own.

It was not something Geordie had fully understood until Cat had first told him she was with child, until this moment when he knew she truly did love him, and not another. He realized then he would love the child she bore with as much of his heart as he loved Cat.

Recognition of his intent showed in her eyes. "Are you certain, Geordie?"

He bowed his head toward the woman he loved, gently resting his forehead against their joined hands cradling what would be their child. "I've never been more certain of anything in my life."

"Aye."

Geordie snapped his head up to regard Cat, certain that he had heard her incorrectly. Had she finally, truly accepted his offer of marriage? "Aye?" he repeated hesitantly.

She nodded, her face splitting into a wide smile. "Aye, Geordie. I will happily marry you."

He leapt to his feet and caught her in his arms.

The door opened suddenly, and Freya stepped into the room. Geordie froze with Cat in his arms. Freya gasped and slammed the door behind her lest someone in the hall see.

Geordie quickly released Cat and stepped away.

"My lady." She bobbed a quick curtsey and nodded respectfully in Geordie's direction. "I've been looking for you, Lady Catriona. I heard of the commotion and wanted to ensure you were well." Her face went red. "Now that I have confirmed as much, I shall assist with the clean-up from the feast."

"Freya." Cat beamed at her maid, who hesitated at the door. "Sir Geordie and I will be getting married."

A smile spread over Freya's face. "In that case, I shall leave you to celebrate." She paused once more. "And if you don't mind me saying my lady, 'tis about time." She threw a grin over her shoulder and was gone in a flash, with the door securely closed and locked behind her.

Geordie went to Cat once more and ran his hand down her cheek. "You've made me so happy."

"As you have me." She searched his gaze intensely. "You must promise me one thing."

"Anything," he vowed.

"Promise me you will not try to kill Gawain," Cat said fiercely.

Extreme love for Cat warred with extreme hate for the man who had hurt her, leaving Geordie cautious to answer. He would be watched around the other man going forward. Mayhap Gawain would lose his knighthood. It was possible Geordie might never see the man again in his life.

But then, he might. And he could be presented with the perfect opportunity to end the bastard's life. To exact revenge for Cat.

"I thought I had given you up forever when I had to turn you away," Cat said, interrupting his thoughts. "I couldn't tell you because I knew you'd kill him the first chance you got. I have trusted you with what I've confessed. And I cannot bear the idea of you being removed from my life forever in punishment for murdering him. I'm begging you to love your family more than you hate him."

His family. What he had always wanted and never truly had. Now he would have a wife and child, as well as a mother who cared greatly for him. In these few short days, he had been given everything. The power of love would have to outweigh the force of his hate.

Geordie nodded, realizing for the first time what revenge would truly cost him.

"I'll never do anything to lose you." He pulled her closer. "Not even kill a man who fully deserves it."

"Thank you." She tilted her face up, rising higher as she did so to brush her mouth against his. "Thank you, Geordie."

Her lips were as soft as rose petals and sweeter than any honey his tongue had ever tasted, for she was his. His woman. His wife. His family.

He eased his hand behind her head, wishing the stiffly plaited braids were loose and her hair was flowing around her like she wore it at Werrick Castle, so he could run his fingers through the silkiness of it. The tender kisses, however, were not enough, and he deepened them to something more possessive.

Their previous intimate moments had been brief, and done through a weakness of will, an overwhelming need against his resolve. This passion now was born of victory. She would be his *wife*.

She parted her lips and stroked his tongue with hers. Her hands slid up his back and fit him more snuggly against her.

He knew they ought to cease such intimacies until they were wed but could not bring himself to pull away. Not when she was finally his after a lifetime of loving her.

Her hands skimmed over his arms, avoiding his wounded shoulder, caressing him through his clothing, as he did with her. He ran his hands over the sides of her kirtle and wondered at the smoothness of her skin beneath.

A desperate, ravenous side of him wanted to pull open the ties at her back and peel away her gown. His cock ached for her, to experience the bliss of being sheathed inside her body, as close to her as it was possible to be. Two hearts, two bodies, becoming one.

It wasn't until she moaned into his mouth that he realized he had cupped her bottom to fit their pelvises together. The pressure of her body against the heat of his straining arousal was nearly more than he could bear, torture of the most enticing kind.

How he longed to give into the lust racing through his body. It had kept him up many nights as he thought of Cat; of this very moment. But his conscience now gave him pause.

Gawain had taken her by force that horrible night. Then, he'd attacked her only an hour prior. And though she'd agreed to be Geordie's wife, she was not yet in name. There was also a life growing within her womb.

Each of those three thoughts on their own could stay his longing. The three together nearly propelled him from her.

"Forgive me, Cat." He released her and ran a hand through his hair to tame the blaze of his lust. "I shouldn't have kissed you."

"*I* kissed you." The fire crackled behind him, the only sound in the room even as she stepped silently closer to him. The glow of the fire cast her in red gold light and shone off the braids coiled down either side of her face.

"I shouldn't have touched you," he said. "I shouldn't have pulled you so close to me like that."

She stepped in front of him. "I wanted you to."

He almost groaned at such words. "I'm not like Gawain." It was as much a reminder to himself as it was to her. "I can wait until we are wed."

"What if..." Cat pressed her lips together. "What if I do not wish to?"

Geordie swallowed. "You mean...?"

"Stay with me, Geordie." She ran trembling fingers over his chest. "Love me."

He gently brushed a finger across her cheek, beneath the reddened mark where Gawain had struck her. "I don't want to hurt you."

"I've been hurt." Pain sparkled in the depths of her sapphire eyes. "But each time you kiss me, every touch of your lips, every caress, you wipe away sorrow with something good and wonderful. It makes the ache heal in a way I never thought possible."

She put her hand to his chest, over the thundering of his heartbeat.

"I've been ashamed for so long," she whispered. "You made me feel wanted when most would have thrown me away. You lessened my burdens with your love."

Her words pierced his heart in the most tender of places. A stubborn tightening lodged itself in his throat, one borne of visceral understanding. For that was how he'd felt about her. So long unwanted by his own family, cast aside to die. When no one else had cared how his fate unfolded, Cat had been there. Not only to save his life, but also his spirit.

He wrapped his arms around her, cradling her and the whole of both their pain all at once. Separate, they were broken, unwanted. Together they would be mended, cherished.

"Love me, Geordie," Cat whispered. "Love me and take me away from all this."

He drew a long, slow breath to steel himself for his own admission. The perfumed scent of roses in her hair teased playfully at him. "You must know, Cat."

She shifted her head to gaze up at him.

His cheeks went hot with his admission. "I have never lain with a woman."

21

Cat's entire body flushed at Geordie's confession. He had not lain with a woman.

Cat had been in battle. She knew how women welcomed the return of soldiers who defended them, the pretty villagers making their interest known, and the men all too eager to accept their affections. And Geordie was no aging man with a soft stomach and thinning hair.

Nay, he was beautiful with his strong jaw and sensual mouth, his eyes filled with the emotion of his heart. Women would want a man like him. Women *did* want a man like him. She'd seen it firsthand at court as he moved through the room with so many sets of feminine eyes fixed on him, glittering with interest.

And yet never, in four years on campaign, had he lain with a woman. Cat shook her head in disbelief. "How?"

Geordie locked his gaze on her. "You've always been the woman for me, Cat. No other could ever compare with you."

She sucked in a pained breath, wanting any answer but the one he gave. "But I—"

He put his finger to her mouth to silence her protests. "I only tell you because I may be lacking in experience." His cheeks tinged with a slight blush in that endearing way she'd always loved.

"Then we will learn together," she said finally.

His face relaxed into a soft smile. "I'd like that."

Cat reached up to her bound hair and pulled free the pins holding the braids in place. They fell one by one like heavy ropes. She didn't want to come to him as a woman of court with her ornate hairstyle and stiff clothing. She wanted to be unbound, with her heart open, as though it could return her to the woman she'd been before she'd ever come to court, before she'd ever met Sir Gawain. Innocent, slightly naïve, ready to believe in the idea of love.

Her fingers worked through the plait, combing it out and leaving her hair crinkled with waves from where the strands had been twisted against one another. Geordie took the other braid and slid his fingers through it, mirroring Cat's movements. The subtle rose fragrance of her bathing oil surrounded her in a gentle, perfumed cloud.

Geordie's nostrils flared slightly as he drew in a slow inhale. "You always smell so good."

Cat went warm with the compliment.

He ran his fingers through her tresses. "I love your hair free like this."

"I know." She swept a length of her liberated tresses behind her shoulder.

His fingers eased to the nape of her neck. "If you wish me to stop, you need only say the word."

His featherlight touch swept over the sensitive skin of her throat like a whisper and left her skin tingling in its wake. She sucked in a breath of pleasure from the simple, thrilling touch.

"I know," she said again.

The affection in his eyes brightened and his gaze ran down her with interest. He made a quiet groan in his throat. "I've wanted you for so long." He brushed a strand of hair from her face. "I love you with the whole of my heart. And now I will love you with the whole of my body."

He kissed her then, not with the charged energy of their shared attraction, but with slow, purposeful strokes of his tongue against hers. As if he meant to take his time, savoring and cherishing every moment.

A true lover.

Nervous excitement raced in Cat's veins and left her hands shaking as she put her fingers to work at the first button of his doublet. She remembered all too clearly how his warm, taut skin felt under her hands, rippled with muscles and masculinity. She wanted to touch him again. All of him this time. Without having to stop.

Three buttons down, a light tug came from the back of her kirtle. Geordie regarded her carefully, as though wanting to confirm what he did was with her permission. She nodded.

They kissed one another as their fingers blindly worked to disrobe one another, as the laces pulled free behind her and his buttons popped open by her trembling hands. Cat finished first with Geordie's doublet and pushed it down over his shoulders, mindful of the one she knew had been injured. He wore only a quality linen shirt beneath. She grasped the hem and tugged it upward, over his head. He released her for the scant moment it took to divest himself of the garment.

A little hum of appreciation rose unbidden in Cat's throat. He was even stronger than she remembered, his body etched with harder lines, deeper valleys, smooth flesh turned golden by the firelight, with silver-white flecks of scars. White dots from her careful stitching showed over skin that was already healing, the blue thread cut away by now. She dragged her hand over his chest with a breathy moan, tracing such soft skin and powerful muscle. Desire thrummed in her veins and echoed the desperate beat between her legs.

She was so consumed by the sight of him that she scarcely

noticed when he pushed her kirtle from her shoulders. Its weight slipped free and whispered to the floor at her feet. She wore only her chemise now, a flimsy, insignificant bit of fabric separating Geordie from her nakedness.

A wave of self-consciousness rolled over her. In the last few weeks, the small bump of her unborn babe had started to round out her stomach, and her nipples had gone from a delicate pink to a rosier, darker hue.

He hadn't lain with any woman, but he had no doubt seen one naked at some point and would know her body was different.

She bit her lip. He was perfect and she...she was in skin that no longer felt like her own. His fingers grasped the tie at her neckline and gently pulled. Cat's hands moved of their own volition, crossing over her stomach.

"I'm different now." Embarrassment burned through her, hotter even than her lust. "I...I mean, I look different."

"I haven't anything to compare it to." Geordie gave a sheepish smile.

The tension relaxed from her shoulders. She took a deep breath and drew the chemise over her head. Her heart raced in her chest, fearful and nervous. However, once the linen was over her head and she could see Geordie's face, all traces of trepidation dissipated.

He regarded her with awe, uttering an oath, a word she had never heard him use before. Not her just and moral Geordie.

That she could bring him to such a state of mind empowered her. With that one small word, he made her feel beautiful without telling her she was. He lifted his hand and traced the line of her collarbone. Cat sucked in a breath and closed her eyes against the caress. A shiver of pleasure teased over her skin.

His exploration trailed lower, his careful touch so soft, it almost tickled. He grazed the outside of her breast before cupping it in his warm palm, pressing her sensitive nipple. Cat opened her eyes at the wonderful sensation.

Geordie groaned and pulled her into his arms once more, his naked torso pressing to hers as their mouths met and their hands explored. His fingers traced over every curve of her body, first circling her nipples before growing bolder and dipping lower to her inner thighs.

Her knees nearly gave out when at last his fingertips swept between her legs. The heat there went hotter, the pounding of desire grew more insistent. Her thighs parted, opening to him, wanting him in a way she had not known she could want a man.

And he did not disappoint.

※

Geordie's cock was impossibly hard, as though it was about to explode. He traced the line of Cat's sex with his middle finger, gliding through her wetness and groaning with anticipation.

Her eyes closed and she gave a long, slow exhale. Had anything been more desirable than Catriona Barrington as he loved her with his hand?

He probed lightly inside her, where she was wet and hot. He breathed faster. Cat grabbed his arm and clung to him, her thighs widening to give him better access to what they both wanted. He eased his finger from her and lightly ran it over the little nub he found at the front of her sex, exactly where he'd overheard his fellow knights mention it would be.

And her reaction was what they'd boasted, as well.

She cried out, a breathy, hoarse sound between a whimper and a moan that made his cock strain against his trews.

He hadn't told the men he'd never lain with a woman to get such information. He never needed to. They spoke of it every time they were on campaign, as soon as several tankards of ale had been consumed. And though uncomfortable, Geordie had noted every detail and was grateful for that knowledge now.

With his free hand, he cupped the weight of one of her breasts. Her nipples were dark against her alabaster skin, the buds hard with need. Beautiful. *She* was beautiful. All of her. Beyond what he had imagined.

Smooth skin, long, lean limbs, the sensual blonde hair between her thighs. He circled his finger over the responsive little bud of her sex and her hand dug into his shoulder where she gripped him. If he kept going thus, he would make her release.

He ran his thumb over her nipple while his other hand continued to stroke her sex. He bent over her and took the pert nipple between his lips. The tip was firm in his mouth and went harder still when he flicked his tongue over it.

She gasped his name and swayed slightly.

Was she close? He was unsure how to tell, and for the first time, begrudged his inexperience. She staggered and he quickly straightened, catching her with the hand he'd used on her breasts. He paused in his ministrations.

Her eyes were heavy-lidded, her expression sensual in the haze of her pleasure. "Kiss me."

He immediately complied, parting his mouth over hers. She moaned against him and played her tongue over his in a tease of lust. Her hips ground against his hand.

He kept one arm locked around her to keep her upright while he rubbed at the peak of her pleasure, that place the other knights had said would unlock a woman's greatest desires. Cat's breathing quickened and the muscles of her body tensed.

Before he could wonder if this was her climax, she cried out and her sheath clenched repeatedly. Victory rushed through his veins.

He had brought her to release. All the battles he had won, all the feats he had accomplished in his life, never had they felt more glorious than this moment in pleasing Cat. He grinned.

Cat slowly opened her eyes. "That was…" She didn't finish, but instead released her breath. Her gaze slid down his torso to where his arousal left an obvious bulge in his trews. "Only the beginning?" Her lips lifted at the corners.

He took her hand and gently guided it to his waist to allow her to remove what remained of his clothing. If she undressed him, she would have control over the situation, to see and touch as much as she was comfortable doing. To move at her own pace. He would never have anything forced on her or rushed beyond her wishes.

She ran her hands over his body in sweet torment, stroking over his chest, his stomach, lower. Heaven help him, lower still. She traced the outline of his arousal over his trews before cupping him with her small palm. He gritted his teeth.

It had been far too long since he'd brought himself to relief and now, he paid for it with aching stones. She gently tugged at one of the ties and the corner of the flap jutted out beneath the pressure of his erection. The second one of the four ties was all that was needed for his arousal to spring free.

Cat's eyes widened.

"'Tis not always so big," Geordie ground out. "Only when…"

She nodded and caught her lower lip in her teeth. Her fingers brushed over the length of his shaft. Light enough to nearly make him growl in frustration.

He swallowed his impatience. He had waited four long years for this moment. Another few moments of maddening touches were inconsequential.

Regardless of what he told himself, her curious ministrations were driving him mad. The delicate graze of her fingers up and down over him; how she circled the head.

"You can hold it." He panted for breath. "In your hand."

She immediately settled her hand under the base and curled her fingers around him. Pleasure raked over his skin. He nodded. "Squeeze."

The pressure around him intensified and his bollocks went tight. His body flinched with the overwhelming bliss of it.

Cat looked up at him. "Show me."

Geordie nodded and put his hand over hers. Slowly, he guided her over his shaft, her hand like hot silk against the power of his desire. She did as he showed her, taking over on her own, gliding up and down over the impossible hardness of it.

Sweat prickled at his brow. "Enough." He caught her wrist. "Please."

Cat regarded him with flushed cheeks and heavy-lidded eyes. "I want you, Geordie."

How long had Geordie dreamed of hearing those words? How many times had he fantasized about this while stretched out in a bedroll under a tent?

"I've wanted you for years." He undid the last two ties of his trews and pushed the leather from his legs to the ground.

Cat slowly backed up, toward the bed. Her lithe body was graceful and lovely. Delicate lines of her strength showed beneath flawless skin made gold by the firelight. Her hair fell over her shoulders, parting over her firm breasts.

He followed her, focused entirely on her.

"And now we'll both have each other." She stopped just before the bed.

With a groan, he wrapped his arms around her and drew her against him. Her nakedness pressed completely to his body, all soft skin and curves. The heat of his arousal pressed to her lower stomach. A reminder he was taking great care with her.

Cat kissed a searing path from Geordie's ear to his collarbone.

"Ella implied that intimacies while with child were quite enjoyable," Cat said between kisses. "You needn't worry about hurting the babe."

"I worry also about hurting you." Geordie ran his hands up her slender back, wrapping her fully in the protection of his arms.

Cat pulled back and regarded him with her wide blue eyes. "You would never hurt me."

Before further argument could be brokered or fears spoken,

her fingers skimmed down his abdomen and curled around his arousal. She pushed up on her toes and captured his mouth, her lips on his, her tongue sweeping against his, all of her needing all of him.

And finally, after years of sacrifice, of waiting, Geordie had exactly what he wanted. Cat, not only in his heart, but also in his bed, soon to be his wife.

22

Love and lust tangled into a heady rise of emotion within Cat. Geordie's powerful body beneath her hands reminded her how the boy with the remarkable character that she had cared for so deeply as a girl, was now the man she loved so completely as a woman.

Her fingers shook with nervousness, excitement and the force of her anticipation as they moved over his shaft as he'd shown her to do. He palmed her breast and teased at her sensitive nipples until she was crying out into his mouth. That was when his hand came to rest between her legs, his fingers against her and inside of her. He claimed to lack experience, but he had obviously learned what pleasured her quickly.

He circled the center of her pleasure with his thumb and gently leaned her over the bed. She lay back on the soft mattress with the smooth coverlets beneath her. He withdrew his hand and slowly, carefully eased over her; his weight braced on his forearms to keep from laying atop her fully.

"You're so beautiful, my Cat." He ran his fingers up the side of her waist reverently.

Cat drew in a sharp breath at the tingles radiating out from his caress. "I love you."

"And I you." He lowered his mouth to hers and kissed her thoroughly, wonderfully, until her head spun.

Their naked bodies moved against one another, grinding and flexing. She parted her legs and cradled his hips between her thighs. The heat of his shaft lay against her entrance, not penetrating, but rubbing. He made all of her hot with lust, her core impossibly wet and pounding with desire.

Their kisses turned hungry, more desperate as the rhythm between their rocking bodies increased. Geordie shifted his hand and the head of his arousal bumped against her entrance. A sliver of a memory came back to that night with Sir Gawain, but she shoved it aside. She squeezed her eyes shut and kissed him harder. She wouldn't think of that. Not now. Not when Geordie—

The pressure between her legs, at that intimate spot, increased. Cat's breathing sped as wild panic turned the heat in her veins to ice.

"Stop," she gasped.

Geordie immediately pulled away from her. His chest rose and fell with the labor of his breath. His cheeks were flushed and his eyes bright. "Did I hurt you?"

Cat shook her head in frustration. "I...it..." Shame burned in her cheeks. "It scared me."

"We don't have to—"

"Nay," she said vehemently. Sir Gawain would not ruin this for her, not this night and not the intimacy she experienced now with Geordie. Sir Gawain had already taken too much and she refused to give him more. An idea came to her. "Let me see you," she said. "I want to look at your face."

Geordie nodded. "Anything, Cat."

She took her hand and put it to his arousal. The tip was damp from where he'd entered her, and it pulsed wildly in her palm.

"You guide me in. I had meant for you to do that, but I..." He shook his head slightly. "Forgive, me, I lost myself with you."

She pressed a kiss to his mouth at his sweet words and positioned him at her entrance once more, angling her head to watch him. Geordie stared down at her, his lovely brown eyes tender with love. He always had shown his emotions in his gaze, and now she clung to that. She drew him toward her, and his mouth parted in a shuddering intake of breath.

She flexed her hips up to carefully nestle the pulsing head of him inside of her. His brows flinched. She released him and gave him a little nod. He pushed slowly, easing into her more deeply. This time the action did not fill her with panic, but an eagerness for more.

He exhaled as one does before battle, when they need their heart rate to slow. Cat nodded once more. He eased out and pressed back in, going further this time. The pulse of desire thrummed between Cat's legs again and her nipples prickled. Geordie's eyes closed in apparent pleasure and quickly opened once more, fixing on her with concern.

Cat gave a soft hum of delight. "All of it," she whispered.

Geordie swallowed. "You are certain?" he asked in a husky voice.

"Aye." Cat arched her hips to meet him.

He watched her as he carefully withdrew from her and thrust back in, filling her completely. She gasped at the satisfaction of it, to have all of him within her, fully joined together. Geordie groaned and dropped his head forward, his breathing ragged.

Every muscle in his body was tensed to the point of trembling. He uttered a quiet curse and slowly lifted his gaze to her.

Cat locked her stare on his and moved beneath him, rolling her hips back and forth as they'd done before he was inside her. He blinked and shifted himself from her, before pushing within her fully once more.

"God, Cat," he muttered. "You feel so, so damn good."

"So do you," she breathed.

He braced himself over her, thrusting in a careful rhythm as the tingles of pleasure dancing over Cat's body grew hotter and hotter and hotter still.

"Kiss me," she gasped.

He bent over her and took her mouth with his. She wrapped her legs and arms around him, pulling him deeper into her, as they panted and kissed one another. He shifted slightly and found the bud of her sex with his finger once more.

Cat cried out, everything in her tightening in preparation for another crises. His digit moved over her in deft strokes, bringing heat flooding through her, even as he thrust within her. Her center tensed, pausing on the brink for one more pass of his finger, two, three.

Cat gave a scream of pleasure that he drank in with his own mouth. Her core clenched around the thickness of his arousal pulling him deeper still. He pushed into her, burying himself. His forehead dropped to her shoulder and he loosed a low groan, gritted out through clenched teeth.

They lay there for a long moment, panting with their racing hearts and sweat-slick bodies. Geordie lifted his head first and gently touched her cheek. "I didn't hurt you? Or the babe?"

It was then she realized, he'd awkwardly leaned to one side of her to avoid pressing his weight on the small bump of her belly. Cat smiled softly and shook her head. "Nay. Quite the opposite." She lifted a brow. "I thought you said you had no experience."

He flushed. "That doesn't mean I didn't pay attention to the braggarts conversing around me."

Everything in Cat felt light and airy. She gave a soft laugh and pulled him down to her for a kiss. "You make me so happy."

"As you do me." He grinned and pulled himself from her.

A shudder of latent pleasure rippled over her at the subtle movement. "I look forward to a lifetime of this with you."

He gave a low growl. "Every night." He kissed her lips. "Sometimes during the day." He slipped lower and kissed her collarbone. "Mayhap even in the morn." He licked the line between her breasts.

She moaned with pleasure.

"There is so much more to this than what we did." Geordie gave her a wicked grin that set the hungry pulse of pleasure trilling between her legs. "I want to do it all."

Cat laughed again, caught up in the happiest joy she had never thought to actually experience. Their life would be perfect indeed. Perfect and happy and wonderful with not one thing ever going wrong.

༺❀༻

Geordie pulled himself regretfully away from Cat. He went to the ewer, for a splash of cold water. Not only to clean himself, but to quell the stiffening of his cock. Though he'd just had her, his body reacted to his carnal thoughts, craving more of her.

Except that she would no doubt be sore. He had been serious when he'd said he'd never hurt her, and that included being aware when she might be tender from having him inside her once already. He splashed water from the ewer onto a fresh linen and carried it to the bed. He rolled his shoulder slightly; the one Cat had stitched with such care. It ached from holding himself up for so long, a pain he would gladly take in exchange for the pleasure they'd shared. In fact, he hadn't even felt it twinge until that very moment.

Cat reached for the linen as he neared, but he pulled it back and shook his head. A languid smile curled at her lips.

God, but she was beautiful. Her hair crimped from her braids and tousled around a face that glowed with the effects of having been freshly loved. He would see her like this every night.

"So?" Cat said coyly. "Was is worth the wait?"

Geordie chuckled and swept his hand down her knee to part her legs. "Aye, well worth it. Enough that I would have waited another four years for certain." He paused thoughtfully. "Though I'm glad I didn't have to."

"I imagine so." Cat laughed and spread her shapely legs for him.

Geordie swept the linen over her sex to wipe her clean and the good-natured tinkle of her laugh faded into a soft moan.

"Thank you," she said. "For being so gentle, so understanding."

Geordie set aside the cloth, lay beside her on the bed and pulled her into his arms. "I'm glad it was pleasurable for you too. I always want it to be."

"It will," she said with a certainty he liked.

He drew up the blanket at the foot of the bed over both of them.

She nestled against him, laying her head on his chest. "I'm sorry you missed the rest of your feast."

The feast. It felt a world away.

He wrapped an arm around her to hold her close to him. "I'm not." He would give up a lifetime of feasts for having had this night with her, especially when it led to the promise of so many more.

Cat's breathing turned deep and even almost immediately and her body relaxed against him. Sleep tried to come for Geordie, but he pushed it away. He'd spent beyond four years wanting her.

From the moment he was old enough to have dreams of desire, from when he'd first started to notice the budding breasts at Cat's bodice—he'd wanted her since then. Only when he was older and truly understood the ways of the world did he understand he didn't want her merely for sexual satisfaction, but as his companion, as his wife.

He ran his hand up and down her slender arm. Her skin was like cool silk under his fingers. Cat gave a little sigh in her sleep and nuzzled closer.

Nay, he would not sleep, not for the entire night. He wanted to lay awake with his love held to him as he savored his good fortune. At long last, he had everything he could ever want and would not lose the moment to sleep.

His mind wandered over the life they'd promised one another, imagining her within Easton Castle in Strafford, bringing light to those dark halls of his memories. He could almost hear the happy squeals of their child and see her brilliant smile as she stood at his side.

And then he knew, there was one final thing he needed to make everything entirely perfect. Quiet and stealth, he slipped from the bed of his love with the skills he'd learned as a warrior and dressed. He would be gone briefly, before she even realized he had left.

With one final glance back at a sleeping Cat, he slipped from the room and let the door close behind him.

23

Cat woke to the glow of light from beneath the shutters, but she did not open her eyes. Not yet. Everything the night before had been too wonderful to be real.

She feared opening her eyes and being crushed by reality, if indeed it had all been nothing more than a dream. Except that she lay against something solid and warm, a strong body that was certainly not her imagination. She blinked her eyes open and found Geordie with one arm tucked behind his head, the other securely around her shoulders.

His stare was fixed on the underside of the bed's wooden canopy, as though he had been awake for some time. Cat shifted to better regard him and he turned his attention to her.

"Good morrow, my Cat." He smiled at her.

"Good morrow, my Geordie." She pressed a kiss to his naked chest. "Have you been awake long?"

He tucked a lock of hair behind her ear. "I didn't want to wake you. Did you sleep well?"

Cat rolled her shoulders inward, curling around Geordie. "I don't think I have ever slept so well." And it was true. She'd felt safe in his arms, cherished. "You?"

"It was the best night of my life." He winked at her.

Cat couldn't help but laugh at that. "I would have to agree with you."

Desire pulsed between her thighs as she remembered exactly how the night had been; how he'd felt inside her, filling her. Her nipples drew taut and her breath hitched. She bit her lower lip.

The happiness in Geordie's eyes went serious with what she now knew to be desire. Already, she had learned what it looked like on his face, and how her body reacted in kind.

But there was so, so much more to learn.

His gaze dipped lower to her breasts, then her mouth, before returning to her eyes once more. "Cat, if you're sore…"

She shook her head and let her touch wander over his torso, being careful to avoid his wounded shoulder.

His breath quickened and a suspicious lump appeared under the covers. She brushed her thigh over him and met the hot hardness of his ready arousal. Aye, suspicious indeed.

"I believe I was told mornings might be involved…" She arched her body against him.

He grabbed her to him with a growl, a low, primal sound that made the hairs on her neck stand up with a delicious thrill. He nuzzled her ear with his mouth and ripples of pleasure teased over her skin. She parted her thigh to better rub her body against him.

A knock sounded at the door. Geordie sat up, blocking her with his body.

She curled her hand over his tense shoulder. "'Tis only Freya."

"I'll be missed from my chambers." He looked down at her and frowned. "I do not want to sully your reputation."

Cat scoffed. "I believe I handled that well enough on my own at the feast."

"It isn't the same." He rose from her bed and quickly dressed. "I must take my leave."

He was right, though she didn't want to admit it. She pulled herself from bed and drew her chemise on.

The knock came again at the door, harder this time. "My lady," Freya hissed.

Geordie paused in his dressing and cast Cat a questioning look.

A trickle of cold apprehension ran down Cat's spine. Freya never insisted anything of Cat. Something was amiss. Quickly, she made her way to the door and unlocked it.

The servant entered the room swiftly and closed the door behind her. She pressed her back to it and huffed to catch her breath. Her cheeks were flushed. Evidently, she had come to the room in haste.

"Freya, what is it?" Cat asked.

Geordie came to Cat's side and put his arm around her shoulders, as though bracing her from any news she would hear.

"Everyone is looking for Sir Geordie," Freya panted. "I dinna say anything and slipped away at the first opportunity I could to come here."

Cat stiffened at her servant's words. Geordie did not flinch.

"Why am I being sought out?" Geordie asked with an immaculate calm.

"Because he's dead," Freya whispered. "Sir Gawain has been killed."

Cat staggered back. "Killed?"

"Aye." Freya gulped in a breath of air. "They found him in his cell with his guards knocked senseless and his throat slit."

"But Geordie has been here all night," Cat protested. "I will vouch for him."

Aye, it would destroy her ragged reputation to do so, but once she and Geordie were wed, it would be of little consequence.

"But he was no', my lady." Freya flicked a cautious glance up at Geordie. "Someone saw him leaving yer room in the middle of the night."

"I beg your pardon?" Cat turned to Geordie, her mind a

muddled wash of confusion and fear. He had promised her he would not kill Gawain. Surely, he had not gone against that.

She shook her head, unable to even ask the question.

"It wasn't me," he said resolutely.

"Where did you go?" she asked.

He shook his head and his cheeks colored. "It was foolish." He ran a hand through his hair. "I had no idea..."

"Where did you go?" Cat repeated. "What is going on?"

"I didn't kill Sir Gawain, but I did leave the room." Geordie reached into a pouch at his belt and pulled out something she could not see. "I've had this for two years. I thought..." He gave a helpless shrug. "I wanted to finally see you wear it."

He opened his hand and there in his palm was a gold ring with a sapphire winking at its center.

Cat sucked in a breath.

He had gone to his room to get the ring he had kept for her all those years, and now he might die for his romantic act.

※

GEORDIE CLOSED HIS FINGERS OVER THE RING, LOCKING THE cool metal in his hand. At the time, it hadn't seemed an issue at all to take only a few moments to retrieve it. Now, he realized how costly a mistake it might be.

"Oh, Geordie." Cat put her hand to her mouth.

Geordie clenched his jaw. "I couldn't possibly have known he would be murdered then."

"You could leave," Cat said hurriedly. "You could go now and ride hard to Werrick Castle. The king and his men never venture so far. You know that. And even if he did, the Scottish border is—"

"Nay." Geordie shook his head. "Only guilty men run. I will get a trial and there I will be proven innocent."

"But if you are not..." Cat pressed her lips together.

"Pray to God justice will be served and I will be."

"Nay." A sob erupted from her. "I cannot lose you, Geordie. Please."

"Cat." Geordie knelt on the ground before her and extended the ring to her. "Wear this, think of me daily and say prayers for my imminent release. Once the trial is done, I will be free, and we can wed."

She held out a shaking hand and he slid the ring on her fourth finger, the one with the closest path to her heart. He got to his feet and embraced her. "I must go to them now. I'll not have them thinking I am hiding."

"Give me a moment." Cat broke away and dashed to the trunk at the foot of her bed. "Give me a moment to properly dress and join you. Freya, your assistance, please."

The maid ran to Cat and set to work on the line of lacings at the back of the kirtle Cat had hastily pulled free. A fine gown with elaborate stitch work over vivid red silk, one meant more for an evening banquet rather than a day at court.

Geordie crossed the room and shook his head. "Forgive me, but I can't have you there."

Her lower lip trembled. "Why not?"

He ran a fingertip along her jaw. "Because I fear if you are there, I will not be able to be as strong as I need to be to do this. I love you far too much and the thought of losing you, even for the few days it will take for a trial to be held, is immensely painful."

A quiet sniffle sounded from behind Cat where Freya still worked at the ties on the gown.

"Stay here and know that I will return to you." Without waiting for her acquiescence, he cradled the back of her head in his palm and delivered one final, searing kiss: a promise of what he meant to finish when he was released as a rightfully free man.

With that, he strode across the room for the door.

"Tell them you were with me last night," Cat said. "I will tell all of court you were, so do not think to preserve my reputation or modesty."

Geordie regarded her over his shoulder. There was no time to argue, not when he knew how stubborn his Cat could be when she set her mind to something. "I love you."

"I love you too." Her face crumpled and so too did his heart.

He turned to the door, opened it and was gone. He did not have to go far before a guard caught sight of him, cried out in alarm and a horde of men rushed in his direction. Geordie put up his hands in surrender.

"I know what you think I have done," he said, choosing his words carefully. "And I am here to tell you, I am an innocent man."

The men roughly apprehended him and snapped a pair of heavy manacles to his wrists. "So you say," one of them muttered.

He was led through the castle, not to the dungeon, but to the king's painted chamber. Geordie's heart thudded in his chest as he entered the long, narrow room filled with light and vibrant paintings. The king meant to speak with him, and would no doubt be disappointed in him.

Geordie kept his back straight and his head held high as the soldiers led him through the ornate room, the way an innocent man would do in the face of false accusation.

The king met them halfway, his face devoid of all emotion. He flicked his wrist at the soldiers. "Leave us."

At the simple request, all the courtiers and guards cleared out the room, leaving only Geordie and the king.

"Many men would have given the entirety of their fortunes to have such a feast as the one we gave for you." The king arched a brow. "Yet, you did not stay."

Geordie bowed his head. "Forgive me, Your Majesty. I appreciate the grand gesture, truly. But with all due respect, I do not battle for glory."

"Indeed?" The king tilted his head. "Why then do you battle?"

"For England," Geordie replied. "And for honor."

The king nodded to himself. "As all our noble knights should." His mouth lifted at the corner in the ghost of a smile. "You were uncomfortable at the feast, were you not?"

Geordie shifted his weight from one foot to the other. "I believe I am not a man meant for such things."

"Which means you are the worthiest." King Edward ran his hand down his beard. "Tell us of Sir Gawain."

Geordie regaled the king with the events of the previous night, how he had found Cat being held against the wall, pinned at her neck by Sir Gawain and what transpired thereafter.

"You wanted to kill him," the king stated.

"I did, but Lady Catriona stopped me."

The king nodded to himself. "After you left the feast, where did you go?"

The king was acting the part of the magistrate, or the Captain of the King's Guard. That he had taken such an interest in Geordie's plight was in his favor.

"I escorted Lady Catriona to her chambers. She is staying in Lord Calville's royally appointed rooms."

"And after that?" the king pressed.

Geordie hated the heat scalding his cheeks and knew he was most likely blushing. "I did not leave from there, Your Grace."

"You entered Lady Catriona's chambers and remained there?" The king's brows rose, though obviously he already had heard Geordie had been in her rooms.

Geordie steeled himself against the shame that would come to Cat over the sordidness of it. "You once spoke of a woman I possibly loved. You were correct. I have loved Lady Catriona for most of my life. I stayed with her last night, with the exception of leaving the room to procure a ring from my own chambers that I'd purchased for her."

Her image flashed in his mind, the hurt on her face as she watched him go, how beautiful the ring had looked on her slender finger. "I mean to marry her."

The king's head lifted. "Did you seek our permission? She is a daughter of one of our wealthiest earls."

Geordie stepped forward and lowered himself to his knee in supplication. "Please, Your Grace, allow me to wed Lady Catriona. Despite what happens with the trial I know I will face, I want to ensure she will be well taken care of, her and my child."

A low sigh emanated from the king. "Your child?"

It was a lie, in a sense. The only one he'd ever told to the king, for he had not put the child within Cat's womb. But Geordie would not have a child brought up feeling unwanted or unloved by his or her father, as he had. This was a noble lie for all the right reasons, even if it tarnished his honor in the eyes of the king.

"I love her."

The king nodded solemnly. "Men do foolish things for love. You have our permission."

"Before the trial, please, Your Grace." Geordie was pressing his favor, he knew, but he would topple the king's favor if it meant Cat and the babe would have the protection of his name and not face the stigma of illegitimacy.

"Very well," the king conceded. "Before your trial. Until then, we will allow you to remain under arrest in your chambers. If you are truly innocent, you will not try to escape. But if you run, you will be caught and hanged."

Geordie got to his feet and bowed. "Thank you for your mercy, Your Grace."

The king summoned the guards, who arrived promptly and escorted Geordie from the room. Dread curled low in Geordie's gut. Trials had uncertain outcomes, especially if there was strong evidence against those accused. Like a death threat issued publicly, or an inconvenient time to be seen leaving the one person who could vouch for his innocence.

His only comfort was knowing Catriona and the babe would be safe and well cared for, regardless of how Geordie's fate fell.

24

Cat never had been one to easily give up, and Geordie's arrest was no exception. She had Freya dress her, not in the ridiculous gown she'd hastily selected before he left, but in a more fitting gown. It was a somber shade of gray, modestly cut and hid well the small bump of her growing babe.

No doubt the members of court would trip over themselves to get a glimpse of her as they whispered their gossip. She held her head high as she left her rooms with Freya at her side and did not lower her chin once.

People stared, as she knew they would. They bent toward those next to them, murmuring in low tones, as she knew they would. What she did not expect, however, were the glances toward her stomach. Some did not bother to hide their sneering disdain, while the others at least pretended not to see her or looked away.

They were all vipers, the lot of them.

Cat wanted nothing more than for the trial to be done with, for Geordie to be freed of the accused crimes and for them to get as far from court as was possible. That was why she had left the sanctuary of her rooms, to ensure Geordie would be ruled innocent. She did not put as much trust in the honesty of the trial as Geordie did. Men were poisoned with the need for power and prestige, and Geordie was well-liked by the king. There were many who would gladly see him fall.

Whoever had slain Gawain had willingly allowed Geordie to shoulder the blame.

Cat would find who that was. But she had only a short amount of time to do it.

"Good morrow, Lady Catriona."

She turned toward the friendly voice and smiled at Tristan. "Good morrow, Tristan."

He winked at Freya in quiet, friendly greeting as the maid moved respectfully behind them. "May I escort the most talked about lady at court to the great hall to break her fast?" He bowed to Cat with usual charm.

"So long as you do not mind being the second most talked about man at court." She offered a smile that nearly cracked her face for being so brittle. "I will not take offense if you decline."

"And miss the gossip firsthand?" Tristan grinned and presented his arm toward her in a courtly gesture.

Cat's smile warmed to something more genuine, and she accepted his offer to walk with her. "How bad is it?" she asked him discreetly.

The carefree lightness on Tristan's good-natured face darkened for a flash of an instant. "It is not good." He cast a glance around the many sets of eyes upon them. "I do not imagine we will be left alone to speak, so it is best to do so as we walk, before others can linger near us."

"What are they saying?" Cat asked.

"That he did it. To protect you." Tristan guided her around a group of women who refused to move from her path, offering spiteful stares in Cat's direction.

"Everyone heard his threats," Tristan went on. "No one spoke of anything else last night. And everyone knows he was in your rooms and slipped away for a bit of time."

Cat's face went hot despite her resolve not to care. "He didn't do it," she hissed.

"You're certain?" Tristan cast her a serious stare. "The guards keeping watch over Sir Gawain were quickly dispatched, only knocked unconscious but not slain. The mark of a good soldier and everyone knows Sir Geordie is the best."

"I would stake my life on it." Cat spoke with all the resolve in her soul.

"You don't have to," Tristan said with a chagrined expression. "He's already doing it for you."

They walked into the great hall together, and the usual hum of conversation and clatter of bowls and utensils fell silent as all eyes latched onto them.

Cat hesitated, her insides flinching at the intensity of all those glares. "It turns out I am not hungry after all."

"Don't you dare give them the satisfaction of leaving." Tristan flexed his arm, locking her hand in place. He was right, she knew.

She forced a laugh as though Tristan said the most humorous thing she'd ever heard, as though she truly didn't care a whit about their pummeling judgment. "Was that convincing?"

He chuckled. "Several people even looked away." He guided her to a seat and pulled the chair out for her. "There is more you must know," he murmured in her ear as she sat.

She took some bread and swept a bit of butter over it as Tristan sank into the chair beside her.

His gaze slid around the room. "Apparently the king is going to allow you to wed prior to the trial, as a special favor to Geordie. To ensure his unborn child will inherit Strafford, should things not go according to plan."

Cat's heart caught in a bittersweet knot of elation and dread. For she would finally marry Geordie, but under such terrible circumstances. And she did not even want to consider "things not going according to plan."

In Geordie's most perilous moment, in his own private audience with the king, he had thought not of himself, but of Cat. But it was more than that. Geordie wouldn't have asked for permission to wed her if he thought he would truly emerge from the trial unscathed. And further still, he had claimed her unborn child as his. In the eyes of the king and court and every man and woman of England.

She took a bite of bread in an effort to avoid the tears threatening her composure. It was dry as dust against her tongue and almost impossible to swallow, forced down only with a gulp of ale.

"While I'm mentioning it, I like your new ring." Tristan winked. "Though I confess to be downtrodden over losing you, my darling Cat. Not that I can blame you."

Cat glanced at the ring where it sat heavily on her finger. If she'd gotten it under better circumstances, it would not have felt like a manacle weighing her down. But to know that the small band of metal and elegant gem might be the one thing to cost her Geordie made it a hard weight to bear.

She touched her hand to her belly, an action she no longer had to hide. "I'm going to need your help, Tristan."

"Anything." He leaned forward to grab a slice of bread for himself.

"I need you to continue to listen to the gossip, to see if anyone seems particularly interested, or contrarily resistant to hearing any of it."

A smile blossomed over Tristan's mouth. "You're going to try to find the killer before the trial."

"Nay," Cat said. "I *will* find the killer before the trial ends."

"Then I think you'd best hurry, for it will come about in three days."

Cat settled back in her seat. Three days? That was nothing.

A woman on the other side of the table caught Cat's attention. Lady Strafford.

"Do excuse me," Cat said to Tristan.

He leaned back in silent invitation for her to go. "And on the hunt, she descends."

She smiled her appreciation and went to Geordie's mother with Freya trailing after her. "Lady Strafford," Cat said.

The seated woman glanced up. The veil over her head covered most of her hair, but Cat could make out several strands of white in the otherwise dark tresses. The woman had a generous mouth that stretched into a shy smile that Cat knew to be the very mirror of Geordie's.

"My lady," Cat inclined her head graciously.

The woman got to her feet and grasped Cat's hand. "You must be Lady Catriona. My dear, you are so lovely. It is no wonder my Geordie…" Lady Strafford's voice wavered.

"I wish to speak to you about Geordie." Cat glanced at the people around Lady Strafford. "Mayhap we can go somewhere to talk?"

"Of course." Lady Strafford allowed Cat to lead her from the great hall with their maids following at a slight distance behind them to allow for privacy. Cat led her to Ella's apartments. While Cat had been unable to bring Tristan to her room for private conversation, she could do so with Lady Strafford without issue.

They settled before the fire as their maids brought them each a cup of ale. As they made their way to the room, Cat had tried to plan out what she might say to Geordie's mother. Now, with the older woman sitting across from her, she found herself at a loss.

Her face flushed. "First I should like to apologize," she stammered. "I realize what transpired between Geordie and me was far from appropriate. We grew up together, you see, and have loved each other—"

"You needn't explain." Lady Strafford leaned forward in her seat. "I went from having no living children, to having a son, a daughter-in-law, and a grandchild on the way all in a matter of days." Tears shone in her eyes. "You have made me the happiest woman in all of Christendom."

Cat found herself immediately warming to the woman she had spent a lifetime hating. "I understand you had no part in Geordie's sacrifice."

Lady Strafford stiffened. "I can assure you I did not. Lord Strafford has been notified of Geordie's arrest and will no doubt be making arrangements to be here in time for the trial. You will meet him then."

Cat pressed her lips, suppressing the urge to share that she did not wish to meet him. She was not the only one holding back her words or ire. Lady Strafford's jaw clenched with her own apparent displeasure. And was it any wonder, after what he'd done?

"You don't think he did it, do you?" Geordie's mother asked.

"If you're referring to Geordie killing Sir Gawain, I know he did not." Cat took a sip of her watered-down ale, then went on to explain how Geordie had wanted to marry her for so many years and how he had gone to get the ring for her. "So, you see, I know for certain he did not do it."

"That sounds like my sweet son." Lady Strafford drew a square of linen from her sleeve and dabbed at her teary eyes. "He's always been like that, so focused on his love of others. When his father asked him to come to Werrick Castle, I was told he was so proud to do something for his father that he went happily to Lord Werrick." She began to cry in earnest.

Cat got to her feet and went to Lady Strafford, hugging her as Marin always did with her sisters. She waited until the baroness's sobs abated before releasing her and finally addressing what she'd wanted to say. "Someone killed Sir Gawain and it was not Geordie. We have three days to find who did it."

Lady Strafford squared her shoulders, appearing resolute, where moments before memories had so defeated her. "I will do anything to save him. If you are seeking out people with a wish to kill Sir Gawain, I believe he had many enemies."

Cat smirked. "I can see how that would be possible."

Lady Strafford lifted her brows in agreement and took a sip of her ale.

Cat thought hard and stared into the fire. "We might want to consider this another way. Who might have killed Sir Gawain, not out of spite for him, but to attack Geordie's character? Someone who was at the feast or heard the gossip about Geordie threatening to kill Sir Gawain."

"Ah," Lady Strafford exclaimed with such exuberance, Cat's attention was pulled from the dancing flames in the hearth.

"There are many who would see Geordie knocked from his place of honor," Geordie's mother said. "Out of sheer greed, for personal gain, for jealousy. However, one in particular may stand to be considered first: Robert, my husband's nephew. He is next in line for the barony and would do anything to inherit."

"Even murder?" Cat prompted.

Lady Strafford narrowed her eyes in a manner that suggested how she felt about the former heir to the barony. "Especially murder."

※

GEORDIE HAD ONCE THOUGHT HIS APARTMENTS WITHIN THE castle were quite large, especially in comparison to his previous cohabitational stay at court. Now though, as he paced the narrow floor so many times, he'd lost count and it seemed as though the room was becoming smaller with each step.

He'd been locked within them for a full day and night, and it felt like an eternity. The door opened and Geordie rushed to open it, hopeful for any news he could glean, whether the visitor be a servant bringing food, or a guard checking in on him.

It was Sir John's towering frame that entered and locked the door behind him.

Better still to have one of his brother knights see to him. "Sir John." Geordie came to attention as any good knight would in the face of so high a ranking knight. "Tell me, if you would please, how does Lady Catriona fare?"

"She does well enough." Sir John went to the small table and poured two cups of wine.

"I am aware of how the people of court treat those whose secrets have been bared." Geordie followed Sir John to the table. "Tell me the truth of it."

"She has loyal friends who see to her," Sir John said. "Tristan stays by her side despite her obvious lack of interest in wedding him, as do her father's soldiers, and your mother." He held a cup in offering to Geordie.

His mother. He accepted the wine. With all the worrying he had done over Cat, he had scarcely thought of his mother. Granted, their relationship was new, only just healing the bond broken between mother and son. But, aye, he would imagine his incarceration would leave her distressed.

"You might have more of a care for yourself, though." Sir John took a sip of wine. "Everyone says you did it. They all heard you at the feast or learned of what you'd said at the feast. When you slipped away from Lady Catriona's chambers, it was too coincidental. It happened exactly when the soldiers were attacked, and Sir Gawain was killed. Did you know that?"

Geordie took a sip of his own wine, grateful for the splash of it in his empty stomach. He had not realized the timing had been perfect.

"Lady Strafford is here to see you." Sir John took another sip of wine. "If you will accept the visit from her."

Geordie nodded, still too dumbfounded from the blow of news to properly reply.

Sir John put a hand to Geordie's shoulder. "You are the bravest knight in battle I've ever seen. I imagine that will garner loyalty in some. I pray it is enough." He set his empty cup next to the flagon on the table. "I'll let your mother in now."

"Thank you, Sir John."

The knight clapped him on the arm; thankfully not the one that was still healing after the attack on the trail to London.

Had that truly been only days ago? It felt as though a lifetime had passed since then: one filled with lofty highs and degrading lows. A child had been discovered and claimed in that time, a love declared, promises made for marriage, a mother reunited with her son and now the possibility of a death sentence. How could less than a fortnight carry such impact?

Lady Strafford entered the room and rushed to him with enough haste to send the veil over her dark hair billowing out behind her. When she got to Geordie, she reached out to him, then paused as her hands fluttered with apparent uncertainty as to whether she intended to touch him or not.

In the end, she clasped her fingers together and drew them over her heart. "Are you being well-treated?"

"Aye, Mother." He set aside his wine and put a hand over her clasped ones. She was icy cold beneath his warm palm. "Thank you for caring for Cat."

At the subtle touch between them, his mother collapsed against him with a sob. He settled his arms around her, embracing her for the first time he could remember.

Her slender body quaked in his hold, as though all of her was fraught with a chill. He led her toward the large wooden chairs near the fire, but she did not sit.

She drew in a shuddering breath and leaned close. "We are seeking the person who killed Sir Gawain," she whispered. "We suspect it may have been Robert, your cousin who was to inherit the barony before you were discovered alive and named heir. But it is so hard to find evidence against him. We are asking—"

"Do not." Geordie released her with a shock of alarm. "Do not place yourself in danger or put the lives of Cat or our child at risk."

"It was her idea." Lady Strafford's face softened. "Oh, my son, she loves you beyond measure. I could not have selected a more perfect woman for you if I had tried."

"It is not worth the risk."

"Not worth the risk?" She gaped at him in horror. "We cannot lose you. I think you do not understand how much is heaped against you."

Geordie ran his hand through his hair and scrubbed the back of his head. "I am well aware."

"Then you know we must do this." His mother braced herself on the back of one of the chairs and met his gaze. "For your unborn child and for the woman who will be your wife in only a matter of hours."

Geordie stilled. "Do you mean the king will indeed allow me to wed Lady Catriona?" The king had said he would, but Geordie had heard nothing more of it. With the trial approaching with such haste, he had begun to lose hope. But now...

"Aye, my son." His mother beamed up at him. "Within the next several hours." The joy on her face dimmed. "Your father will be arriving shortly, as well. I do not know that he will make it in time for the wedding, but he will be there for the trial for certes."

His father. The thought soured Geordie's stomach as much as it elated his mother. He shoved it aside, however. If he was to wed Cat, he would not let the thought of Lord Strafford sully the moment.

"You must promise me you will stop trying to seek out whoever killed Sir Gawain," Geordie said to his mother.

At his request, she braced her small feet wide and set her shoulders with the determination of a soldier. "Geordie Strafford," she said in a voice used by a mother to scold a naughty child. "I was not given a choice when you were taken from me all those years ago. I spent a lifetime under the burden of regret, wondering what I might have done to save you, what I could have done to stop your father. I wondered if I might have gone to Lord Werrick myself, rather than trust your father's flimsy word."

She folded her arms across her chest. "If there is any chance to sway the trial and prove your innocence, I will find it. I will not sit idly by and wait for the fates to decide your future. I will not lose you, not again."

Her tone brokered no room for argument, even though he had many.

"I do not want you getting hurt," he said. "What you are doing is dangerous."

"And living in a life of heartbreak is misery." She relaxed her stance and patted his cheek with her small, cold hand. "I love you, my son. I would do anything for you."

"Take care of Cat and our child."

"You will do it better yourself." She smiled at him with all the love he thought he'd never have. "Now, prepare yourself. You'll be a groom in only a few hours." After another embrace from her, she left him alone to prepare for the wedding.

A bath was brought up for him and the king, ever generous, gifted him with a fine blue tunic sewn with gilt thread. But that was not the king's only gift. Geordie was informed he would be allowed to spend the entire night with Cat, following the private ceremony.

With the trial set for the next afternoon and a stack of evidence against him, it could possibly be Geordie's last night alive.

25

The armed guard on either side of Geordie was unnecessary. But if being paraded through the castle under escort of two of his fellow knights was what was required for Geordie to wed Cat, so be it.

They made their way through the corridors, past countless courtiers who gawped open-mouthed, like fish sold on market day. Their gossip met his ears, but he did not allow himself to listen. He was to marry Cat, and that was the only thing that mattered to him.

Two additional guards stood on either side of the door to the chapel and opened it as he approached with his unwanted retinue. The priest rushed toward them, waving his hands. "Stop." The word rang out on the stone walls. "Do not enter this house of God with your weapons."

Sir John protested, but Geordie did not hear anything that was said after that moment. For there, standing at the altar in a kirtle of blue silk with her hair falling around her shoulders like a cape of gold, was Cat. His Cat.

She took an uncertain step toward him, but he shook his head.

He would not have her be surrounded by weapons and war. Not on this day. Instead, he strode forward to her.

A hand pushed against his chest to stop him. Geordie met the withered face of the priest, the same man who had attended him that afternoon to take his confession prior to the marriage.

"Swear by the blood of Christ that you will not try to escape," the priest demanded. "Or these marauders will fracture the sanctity of this holy place."

"I swear on everything in this world and in heaven above I will not escape." Geordie regarded Cat over the priest's shoulder. "I want only to marry the woman I love."

Lady Strafford stood beside Cat and covered her mouth with her hand as a little sob emerged from her throat.

Geordie's mother was not the only person in attendance. Tristan was there, as well as Eldon, Durham and Freya, each of them wearing their finest clothing.

Lord Strafford, for Geordie refused to think of him as "his father," had apparently not yet arrived. For that, Geordie was grateful. On his wedding of all days, he did not wish to see Lord Strafford.

The priest removed his hand from Geordie's chest and allowed him to walk to the altar where Cat waited for him. Once he arrived, she threw her arms around him. "I've missed you so," she whispered.

Geordie embraced her slender body. He put his nose to the top of her head and breathed in the sweet scent of roses, savoring her smell and the sheer wonderful feeling of having her in his arms. "I've missed you as well, my Cat."

Someone cleared their throat and they pulled apart. The priest stood at the altar once more, regarding them with a cocked brow. The armed knights were nowhere to be seen, though Geordie suspected they waited just outside the door.

"Thank you all for coming." Geordie nodded his gratitude to the small wedding party.

Cat put her hand on Geordie's. Delicate white flowers had been embroidered on the hem of her sleeves, ones that reminded him of those they picked as children at Werrick Castle. The sapphire ring sparkled on her finger. He ran his thumb over the stone, his heart heavy that the gift he'd meant to mean so much more had become this mess.

The priest began the ceremony. It was a swift affair, absent pomp or ceremony. Not that Geordie minded. All he truly cared about were the words forever binding their souls; words that made Cat his wife. There was no feast following the most joyous event of Geordie's life. Instead, they received the well wishes of their intimate wedding party and were sent out to the armed guards, and marched back to Geordie's rooms.

Through it all, Cat firmly clasped her hand in his, her head lifted with all the nobility of an earl's daughter. Together, they ignored the stares and whispers until they were delivered to the door of Geordie's apartments and finally left alone. They didn't speak until the key clicked in the lock, then Cat rushed into Geordie's arms.

"My husband," she breathed.

He smoothed her hair reverently from her face. "My wife."

"I have been trying to find proof against Robert, but I—"

He shook his head, cutting her off. "I do not want you endangering yourself or our child. Please, Cat."

She said nothing and instead simply looked away. Which was all the answer he knew he would get.

"Cat, it's dangerous."

She turned back to him, her gaze fierce. "I can handle myself, Geordie." Her features softened. "Let us not speak of it now. We have this one night…"

She did not say the rest of the words, but she didn't need to. They had this one night, which might be the only one they shared ever again.

Geordie rested his finger against her lips and shook his head.

He didn't want her to say aloud what they both knew in their hearts. What he did want was this night with her, beautiful and wonderful. The two of them together, sealing the love that had spent a lifetime growing between them.

Without saying anything else, he set about undoing the laces at the back of her kirtle, slowly pulling them free. She watched him as he did so, her gaze roaming over his face as though committing every detail to memory. He did the same, though it was unnecessary. He knew every curve and line of her, from the delicate slope of her nose to the sensual dip at the top of her upper lip.

She had a freckle just beside her collarbone, dotting her smooth shoulder. He had discovered it in the evening when they lay together. He bent and kissed it indulgently. He would do this to her entire body, memorize it as he had her face.

For though they had this night, he knew he had to make it last a lifetime.

However short that might prove to be.

※

CAT TRIED TO SWALLOW DOWN THE KNOT OF EMOTION LODGED in the back of her throat. Geordie's mouth moved in a slow, gentle caress over her skin as he pulled free the ties of her kirtle and pushed it to her feet. The fading sunlight of the day streamed into the room and melted into the glow of the small fire in the hearth.

Cat drew the hem of her sark up and over her head, standing before him now wearing only her stockings and shoes. This time she was not self-conscious for Geordie to see her naked. Not when he had shown her how beautiful he found her last time.

Geordie knelt before her and helped ease the slippers from her feet first, then untied her stockings and rolled them off her legs. As he did this, he used his body to brace her balance to ensure she did not fall. When he was done, and she stood before him without a stitch upon her body, he bowed his head toward her stomach and whispered something she could not hear. He pressed a kiss just above her navel with such tender affection, it made that stubborn knot of emotion clench even tighter.

His gaze slid up to hers as he got to his feet and let his hands travel up her body in a slow, teasing stroke.

"What did you say?" she asked. "To my stomach."

"That wasn't meant for you to hear." He rested his hand on the swollen bump of her belly. "That is between a father and his child."

"Then you can tell him or her when they're born." Cat hadn't meant to bring up the future at all, but how could she not? Especially when speaking of it made the reality of a future feel more likely.

"Cat." Geordie's voice cut off and his eyes filled with tears. "My God, I love you."

Cracks splintered through her heart. She shook her head "Don't."

Rather than offer a protest, he cupped her face in his hands and brushed his lips over hers. She opened her mouth and deepened the kiss with a sweep of his tongue. Pleasure tingled over her skin and made the ache in her heart hum.

She murmured his name as they kissed, and her fingers went to the hem of his fine tunic. Careful of his shoulder, she lifted it off him. He wore nothing beneath, and she let her hands roam over the heat of his powerful body. If she failed at uncovering evidence against Robert, Geordie would die.

His beauty, his spirit, his nearness, all of it would be gone. Forever.

She hadn't even realized she'd started crying until he brushed a thumb over her cheek. "Don't." He mirrored her wording for the same reason: don't focus beyond the night. Not on the trial, or the future. Think only of now, of being in one another's arms and the intensity of the love they shared.

He swept her into his arms and carried her easily across the room to the bed, where he set her gently upon the soft mattress.

"I am going to enjoy this night with you, my Cat." He worked on the ties of his hose and pushed them down his legs. His erection rose proud and hard, proof of his ardent desire for her.

"I'm going to explore every part of your body." He crawled onto the bed toward her, his movements lithe and purposeful, like a panther. "Every swell." He skimmed his fingertips over her breasts.

His touch grazed her nipples and left them standing hard with delight.

"Every valley." His hand swept lower, past her navel and to the apex of her thighs.

Cat's gave a shuddering gasp. She widened her legs, desperate for his sensual caresses.

"Every crevice." A finger dipped inside her.

The subtle pulse of desire leapt to a steady pounding of need. She whimpered and arched her hips against his hand.

"But not only with my hands." His finger ran over her inner thighs, tempting them further apart with the promise of bliss. "With my mouth and tongue."

Before she could ask what he meant, he lowered himself to the mattress with his face near her sex. He kept his attention fixed on her and slowly, sensually slid his tongue over her most intimate place.

Cat gripped the blanket beneath her with two tight fists, as though it might keep her grounded even as she seemed to float on a cloud of pleasure. Geordie moved over her with his mouth again, his tongue gliding over her, probing and flicking until she was crying out for release. He grinned up at her, wickedly pleased with himself.

His tongue circled the top of her sex, flexing mercilessly

against the most sensitive part of her until her lusty cries turned to a sharp scream and stars danced before her eyes. He continued to lave between her legs until the final waves of her crises calmed and she sank deep into the soft mattress.

"More overheard talk from your brethren?" she asked breathlessly.

He rose over her. "They had much to say."

Cat slid him a coy glance. "What else did they speak of?"

"Oh, many things." Geordie laid on his side next to her and lazily dragged his forefinger over her hip, up her stomach and to the side of her breast.

Cat closed her eyes as he drew the pad of his digit around the curve of her bosom up to the nipple.

"Such as talk of a woman riding a man," he murmured.

Cat blinked her eyes open. "Like a horse?"

Geordie shrugged, then bent and suckled her nipple. She caught the back of his head, holding him to her while he flicked his tongue over the tender little bud. Desire ached between her thighs, slick and hot with the need to be sated.

"Shall we try it?" Cat asked.

Geordie glanced at her from the side of his eye and his mouth curled into a smile. It was all the answer she needed.

26

If Geordie had felt pride the first time that he'd brought Cat to climax, that now paled in comparison to what he'd managed with his tongue. He could sense her enjoyment so much more acutely with being so close, his mouth on her sex, tasting her crises as much as feeling the clenching of her euphoria against him.

A fine sheen of sweat shimmered over her skin and turned her luminous in the firelight. Beyond beautiful.

This might be the last time he saw her. Kissed her. Loved her. The thought edged unbidden into his mind and left his heart knotting into a powerful ache.

He couldn't think on that now.

Cat grinned down at him, her expression coy and sensual. The suggestion in her gaze was a welcome reprieve from the crushing fear that kept threatening to consume him.

Her cheeks flushed. "If you wish me to ride you, you'll have to show me what to do."

Geordie's cock twitched in anticipation. He eased off her and lay on his back on the bed.

Cat sat up and tucked her knees under her. "I think I like this already." Her fingers trailed over his body in exploration, running over his chest and down his stomach to where his arousal pulsed in time with his rapid heartbeat.

"You'll need to straddle my hips." He grinned. "When you're done teasing me."

Her fingertips danced up his shaft and circled the swollen head of his erection. "I might tease you all night."

"Or we could try more things in that time." He looked over her body with slow, savoring intent.

A wicked gleam showed in her eyes. "Why didn't you say as much initially?" She got to her knees and parted them over his body, straddling his hips. Her teeth caught her lower lip. "I think I know how this might go." She sat back, lowering her pelvis so her sex rested atop his shaft, pressing the heat of his arousal against his belly.

He held his breath in anticipation. She put a hand on his chest to balance herself and slowly moved forward and backward so her slick center rubbed over him. The action elicited a groan from deep within his chest and her lips eased in a half-smile.

Without a word, she raised herself off him, and took his cock with her bold hand, angling it between her thighs. Slowly, she lowered onto him and gave a soft, happy sigh as he disappeared inside the grip of her heat. She rocked her body and her core squeezed around his shaft. She wriggled and the little move sent prickles racing over his entire body.

"I don't know what to do now." She gave him a sheepish smile.

She was doing pretty well by his account. He held her hips as he flexed his own, learning as he went as much as she was. He moved her backward first, then forward. The subtle shift made her sex clutch him tighter. He repeated the action again. This time, her lashes fluttered.

The next time, she shifted, rolling her hips in time with the action, and they both began breathing harder. As she rocked over him, he pushed up into her, their joining deep and powerful.

She was glorious above him. Her hair fell wild around her shoulders, her skin glossy in the firelight; her breasts gave a firm bounce with her actions while her body moved in the age-old rhythm of love and sex. She watched him as she pleasured herself with his cock, riding him in earnest, her hands firmly planted on his chest. He gripped the coverlet beneath him to keep from losing control too quickly.

Her breathing came faster; the grip of her sheath tightened. Her pace intensified with a driving need he understood all too well. She threw her head back and gave a little scream at her crises. Her sheath spasmed around him, coaxing his own climax. He held her hips in place and thrust up into her one final, magnificent time and let the waves of pleasure crash over him and drag him under.

Cat's body relaxed and she lay down upon his chest, their bodies still connected. "That was quite enjoyable," she panted.

Geordie hummed his agreement and folded his arms over her, securing her against him.

"I think I'd like to try other things you've overheard." She lifted her head and gave him a naughty look.

Geordie's lust was nowhere near completely spent, not with this beautiful woman straddling him. *His wife*.

His cock twitched at the idea of more. Cat's eyes widened in surprise, no doubt feeling the movement within her. A smile bloomed on her lips.

"I've heard a great number of things," Geordie warned.

Cat sat up and took his face in her hands. "We have all night, my love." With that, she rolled her hips and yet another bout of play began.

They went on and on throughout the night. They memorized each other's bodies and sampled the different ways to please until the gentle rays of dawn showed around the outline of the shutters in the dark room.

Then, they had lain together, much in the same way they had

the night Geordie first came to Cat's room. He was cradled between her thighs with his weight braced over her, their eyes locked as they made bittersweet love one final time. Most likely forever.

Their words were whispered endearments of love, promises they might never be able to keep, voices husky with emotion. When they were done, they held each other as though their lives depended on it.

Yet nothing could save Geordie if he was condemned to die.

Cat wept softly against his shoulder, and Geordie's own eyes grew hot with the threat of tears. He stroked her long, silky hair and caressed the slight swell of her belly.

He'd gone from having a family, to losing everything, in a matter of days. From having Cat after a lifetime of working to earn the honor to wed her, only to lose her so quickly.

A knock came from the door. Too soon, and heartily unwelcome. They held one another tighter and Cat began to cry.

"Come now, my Cat," Geordie said in a broken voice.

He had to be strong. For her. For the babe. For himself. If he gave in and allowed himself to crumble, he might never be strong enough to face what he must. He helped her from the bed and assisted in dressing her in the additional gown Freya had left for her.

Geordie dressed quickly, paying little attention to what he wore as he would have plenty of time before the trial to clean properly. A knock came again, along with a warning.

They had run out of time.

Cat turned to him, her eyes brimming with unshed tears. "Geordie."

He went to her, opening his arms to cradle her against him. "Be brave," he said into her ear.

"I cannot leave you," she said against his chest.

"You will." He held her tight, wishing his words were not true. "You must." He put his hand to her stomach, a silent reminder of why she must continue to go on. "I love you," he said fiercely. "Both of you."

"We love you," Cat said between sobs, securing her hand over his.

"Then you must go," Geordie said, his voice breaking. "Now before I lose the strength to let you leave."

She looked up at him one final time, searching his eyes with her own tear-stained ones. Then she turned and dashed from the room. Geordie staggered over to the chair before the fire and collapsed into it.

Would he ever see her again? At his trial, mayhap? At his hanging or beheading? Would she go?

His heart crumpled into his stomach.

A knock came at the door once more and he leapt to his feet. Had Cat come back?

Before he could walk toward the door where he anticipated a guard waiting to tell him of his visitor, a tall man with a scraggly gray beard entered the room. He was tall with a presence that seemed to consume much of the room. There was a sickly pallor to his skin, and his eyes glittered with a kind of malice Geordie had come to recognize in his four years on campaign with the king.

"Geordie." The man's voice scraped out of him, low and raw. "Stand up and show me the respect I deserve, boy. You recognize your own father, do you not?"

Geordie's blood turned cold. After all this time, he would finally be facing Lord Strafford.

※

CAT WALKED WITHOUT SEEING WHERE SHE WENT, HER FEET moving to follow Freya back to Ella's apartments. There, Cat did not protest as the maid stripped her down, bathed her and prepared her to face the day.

Cat didn't want to face the day. Not without Geordie. Exhaustion, paired with the aching reminder that she might never be held by him again, fractured her composure. Tears ran hot down her cheeks. Freya wiped them away with a cloth and spoke in gentle, encouraging words. No doubt saying whatever she thought might help get Cat through the upcoming trial. "I know ye dinna feel like breaking yer fast, my lady, but I think even a little will help ye." She took Cat's hand in hers. "For the bairn, aye?"

Cat nodded, unfeeling, as Freya dressed her and plaited her hair. She didn't want to go to the great hall, to be the spectacle all those at court watched for their amusement. If she bothered to eat anything at all, she would prefer it in her room, and yet the act of speaking her wishes out loud seemed too great a burden.

A soft knock came at the door.

Cat snapped her head up. It couldn't be Geordie. Of course, it couldn't. But mayhap it could be news of him.

Freya was clearly of the same mind, for she raced to the door and drew it open. "My lady," she said a moment later. "'Tis Lady Strafford. Will ye see her?"

Cat nodded again. Freya disappeared and Lady Strafford swept into the room, bringing with her a sweet lavender perfume. Cat breathed in the scent and was reminded of Marin, who always wore a similar fragrance. Her heart thudded hard in her chest, with loss and grief, leaving behind a devastating emptiness.

"Lady Catriona, my daughter-in-law," Geordie's mother said tenderly, which only served to make the ache within Cat's breast burn greater.

Cat looked up at the baroness, noting her fine brocade kirtle of dazzling blue and the bands of yellow at the sleeves and hem. Gold and gems glittered in the mesh caul holding her coiled braids in place and she wore a necklace studded with jewels. It was all too bright, too cheerful.

Cat turned away, but Lady Strafford gently caught her chin. "I wanted to wear black, but I refuse to mourn another child," she said. "If the court thinks I am optimistic about my son's outcome, mayhap it might sway one's vote. It is why I instructed Freya to dress you as she did. We must do this together. For Geordie."

Cat glanced down at her own kirtle then, noticing for the first time what she wore. It was a delicate pink kirtle with gilt thread sewn through it in a pattern of flowers and leaves. Also too bright and cheerful.

Lady Strafford leveled her gaze at Cat. "This is difficult, I know. The trial will be as well. But we must do this. We must give him our support and let everyone see it, even if we are not confident."

"Have you found anything to implicate Robert in Sir Gawain's death?" Cat asked.

Lady Strafford's shining eyes dulled somewhat, and Cat knew the answer before she spoke. "I know only that there is no one to vouch for his whereabouts that evening, save his servant who would lie to protect Robert. But there is nothing we can use to implicate him. Many people in court slept alone that night with servants to vouch for them. We cannot expect the king to question them all."

"And the guards who were attacked remember nothing?" Cat pressed.

"Nay."

It was a disappointing blow. Cat had been certain they would uncover something they could use to free Geordie by this point. Yet despite her efforts, as well as those of Lady Strafford and Tristan, and even Eldon, Freya and Durham, they had been unsuccessful.

"Shall we break our fast in the great hall?" Lady Strafford asked. "Let them see us, daughter-in-law. Let them know we are strong and that we believe in Geordie's innocence."

"Aye," Cat said with more resolve than she felt. For inside she was broken.

Once, when she'd been a small girl, she'd dropped a vase she meant to fill with flowers. It had smashed to the floor so completely that there were only a few recognizable pieces, with the rest little more than splinters and dust. That was what her heart felt like at that moment: splinters and dust. Irreparable.

But Lady Strafford was correct. Cat needed to appear strong, and so she allowed Lady Strafford to walk her down to the great hall, where they found Tristan waiting for them. He offered a smile upon seeing them, but it did not touch his eyes.

"You look at though you have not slept," he commented as he helped Cat into a chair.

Her cheeks burned.

"Now you're just making me jealous." He winked and settled in the chair beside her.

"Have you found anything we might use?" Cat tried to keep her hand from shaking as she reached for a bit of bread.

"Nay," Tristan replied in a lackluster tone. "And it isn't due to lack of trying. The guards mentioned only a shadow looming over them. I've seen the guards. They're tall, but so is Geordie, so that won't help."

Cat's shoulders sagged. It was as she had expected, but not as she had hoped. A servant arrived at her side, the brunette who now knew Cat's affinity for a watered-down ale in the morning, and deposited a cup in front of her. Cat nodded her appreciation and settled her hand on the cool metal goblet.

"There has to be something more," Cat murmured.

"And before the trial begins," Lady Strafford added.

Cat pulled in a long, deep breath to sigh and caught the scent of mint in the air. Absently, her gaze scanned the table to see what might cause such a strong smell. There was naught but a platter of bread, another of crisped slices of salted ham and bowls of butter and salt.

"How much longer do we have before the trial begins?" she asked.

Tristan frowned slightly. "Only an hour."

Helpless frustration threatened to crumble Cat's stoicism. She brought her ale to her lips to drink and paused. The minty scent was noticeably stronger. Recognition tapped at the back of her mind, through the fog of her sorrow and hurt.

Pennyroyal.

She gasped and set the cup to the table.

"What is it?" Lady Strafford asked. "Have you thought of something?"

"Someone has tried to poison me with pennyroyal." Cat scanned the crowd of faces, seeking out the young servant who brought out her ale every morning.

Tristan lifted the cup and smelled it before wrinkling his nose at the offense. "Is that not what ladies use to empty their wombs?"

"It is," Cat agreed.

"And I believe I know who best would want your womb emptied of a potential heir." Lady Strafford raised a brow. "In this attempt to harm your child, we may have the evidence we need."

From across the room, Cat caught sight of the serving woman. "Do excuse me." Without another word, Cat leapt to her feet and dashed across the room to the servant.

The woman moved swiftly through the crowd, but through determination and a lack of care for any of the court's consideration of her, Cat managed to reach her.

"My ale," Cat said sharply.

The woman spun about to face her with a pleasant smile that shifted to confusion. "My lady?"

"Who gave you my ale this morning?" Cat demanded.

"I got it from the kitchen, same as I always do." The woman offered a respectful bob of a curtsey.

"Did you see anyone unusual in the kitchen?" Cat asked. "Anyone who ought not to be there?" She put her hand protectively over her stomach. "Someone tried to poison me with pennyroyal. Someone meant to harm my babe."

The woman's brown eyes went wide with horror. She shook her head frantically. "Nay, my lady. I didn't know, I—"

"Ask the other servants." Cat hastily withdrew several coins from her pocket and slipped them into the woman's hand. "Please. A man's life depends on this."

The brunette's fingers closed around the coin and she gave a quick nod before departing back into the kitchen.

Cat's pulse did not cease racing after their exchange, nor did it in the following hour leading up to Geordie's trial. If anything, it raced faster still as the time approached when Geordie would be judged.

Her only hope was that the serving girl would be fast enough to do something to help.

27

Geordie could not have anticipated the prison of his room being any worse, but then he had not imagined being trapped in it with his father.

He did not bother to temper the hostility in his gaze as he regarded Lord Strafford. "Why did you come?"

"You're my son, the heir to my lands." Lord Strafford lifted his shoulders in a nonchalant shrug. "And you're high in the king's favor. I wanted to ensure you squeezed it for everything you could."

"I have everything I need," Geordie said through his clenched teeth.

Lord Strafford looked around the small room and gave a slow nod. "I see that."

Geordie's hands tightened into fists. "I suggest you take your leave."

The baron smirked. "But you are stuck in here, *Sir* Geordie, and a baron has more power than a knight. I'll depart when I'm good and ready to." He lowered himself to the large chair beside the fire and set his feet on a nearby tabletop. "I hear you married a woman who was already with child. I trust the babe is yours. I'll not have my legacy passed onto a bastard."

"That child is more mine than I ever was your son." Geordie squeezed his fisted hands tighter. "Do you know the reason I wished to become a knight?" He asked, his heart pounding in anticipation for everything he'd ever wanted to tell his father.

"Certainly not for royal favor, as you don't appear to bother with trying to get more." Lord Strafford scratched at the top of his head where his scalp was visible amongst the fine gray and white hair.

"Because I wanted to be a better man than you." Geordie stepped closer to his father. His feet were bare as he hadn't time to put on boots prior to the baron's arrival. "You sacrificed your own son to get what it was *you* wanted."

"And you're better than me?" The baron scoffed.

"I am," Geordie said without hesitation. "Every time I felt as though I might fail, I thought of you and how much I loathe you. Of how I never wanted to be anything like you."

Lord Strafford stood in a single, swift move he had not appeared capable of. "And yet it's you who will be losing his head for murder at the end of all this, even as mine is still attached to my body." He clapped Geordie on the shoulder.

Pain stabbed through Geordie's wound, but he ignored it. God knew he'd had worse.

"Why even claim me as your son?" Geordie demanded. "You didn't love me enough to keep me as a boy, you don't care for me now. Why bother?"

"Love." Lord Strafford gave a snort of laughter. "That'll make you weak. You're my blood. It's why you're such a damn good fighter. That cousin of yours, Robert, is as spineless as they come. At least you've got a set of stones on you."

Geordie glared at the man he'd spent a lifetime hating. "Leave."

"It'll be hard to look down on me if you don't have a head."

Lord Strafford shook his head with apparent disappointment and quit the room.

After the baron left, Geordie set about preparing for the trial. He harbored regret as he ran the cool, wet linen over his body, erasing Cat's sweet rose perfume from his skin. He wanted to leave her scent on him, as though the memory of her could wrap him in a blanket of comfort.

Once he was clean and presentable, he was led down to the great hall. It had been set for his trial with stands erected for spectators on either side and a platform raised at the rear for the king and members of the house of lords. The stands were packed full of the people, all of whom turned to watch his slow entrance into the court. Despite the large room, the air was thick with the heat of too many bodies packed together and the silence was filled with the occasional rustle of cloth as people shifted restlessly.

Twelve of the realm's peers sat aside, their faces solemn with the information they had spent the prior three days gathering to make their judgment. Geordie already knew what their efforts had uncovered and none of it would be in his favor.

He scanned the room, desperate to find the source of his strength. There, in the front, was Cat. She wore a lovely pink gown that made her cheeks and lips appear rosy. A veil sat over her golden hair. A pity. He'd wanted to see it one last time, to be reminded of how she'd looked above him, tresses tousled by their intimacies as they spent the night loving one another.

The trial was interminable. Stuffy with pomp and formality. Through it all, Geordie kept his gaze fixed on Cat. He didn't listen to the accusations made, nor did he bother listening to the twelve peers offering their findings on his guilt. He knew well how it would end.

Nay, he wanted to gaze at Cat who stared at him in return, their eyes locked over several dozen people, through several thousand lengthy words that would see him condemned. He was glad he had not bothered to listen. It wouldn't have mattered as he was utterly helpless in changing the outcome. For at the conclusion, the twelve peers of the realm stood together in their final verdict: guilty.

Within two days' time, Geordie would die by beheading.

※

CAT SAT IN STUNNED SILENCE AT THE COURT'S DECLARATION. Beheading!

She put her hand to her throat, unable to breathe, as though it were she who was preparing for the executioner's block. The men who had sentenced him to death did not flinch as they gave their verdict.

Frustration blazed in her veins and made her want to scream. Those men knew better. Not all of them, but several. She had managed to go to them after hearing back from the kitchen maid who had informed Cat that there had been a suspicious man in the kitchen. Not just any man—Robert's own personal servant. The one who had lied for him.

Cat had rushed to find as many of the twelve jurors as she could. She'd found seven, a majority of the twelve, even if only by a hair. She'd thought it would have been enough. It hadn't. Not one single man mentioned the evidence she presented to them.

Lady Strafford wept softy beside Cat. This earned a stiff rebuke from Lord Strafford, a beast of a man who it seemed impossible to have fathered someone as good and just as Geordie.

Guards led Geordie away in manacles, his gaze locked on hers until the last moment when he was led from the room. Only then did Cat breathe. She drew in a deep, stabbing breath as all the pain of realization rushed over her. Geordie was going to die.

After having finally found happiness together, it had slipped through their fingers, as intangible as sunlight. She put her hands over her stomach. Only three days prior, Geordie had spoken softly to the babe cradled in her womb, making promises it would be impossible to keep.

Anger seared through her at the unfairness of it all. How Sir Gawain continued to destroy her life, even in death.

The assembly of spectators had begun to disperse once the source of their entertainment had been escorted away. The twelve men who had judged him chatted amongst one another, their jovial banter bringing smiles where moments before they had been solemn. As though they had already forgotten the man they had fated for death.

Somewhere, in the inky darkness of Cat's despair, came a flicker of an idea, a spark of hope. Mayhap if she could get Robert to confess, she could circumnavigate the court. If the truly guilty party was brought to light, Geordie might still be saved.

She leapt to her feet.

Lady Strafford startled. "What is it, Catriona?"

"This can't end like this." Cat's voice quavered; proof she did not feel as strong as she would need to be.

"But it has," Lord Strafford said in a low tone. "It is good we have Robert to at least inherit the barony."

"Do you not even care?" Cat hissed. "Geordie is your son. First, you abandon him to be killed and now, after finding him alive, you welcomed him as your heir, then do nothing as he is condemned to die? You would lose him twice without so much as blinking an eye?"

Lady Strafford put a fisted hand to her gaping mouth and looked fearfully at her husband.

"You've got to have a head to blink an eye." Lord Strafford's narrow gaze scanned Cat up and down. "And I intend to keep mine. You know nothing of the affairs of men, you foolish chit. Mind you stay out of the business of them."

Cat caught sight of Sir John in the crowd and spun on her heel.

"Off to go have a good cry?" Lord Strafford called after her in a mocking tone.

She turned about to glare at him. "Off to handle a task you are too cowardly to attempt." Without waiting for a reply, she hurried off toward Sir John, lest the noble knight become swallowed up within the crowd.

"I don't know what you are about to do," Tristan said from beside her. "But I can't let you go about something foolish without anyone there to keep you safe."

Now nearly to Sir John, she could spare a side glance at Tristan and gave him a grateful smile. "Sir John," she called.

The large knight turned toward her, his face grim. "Lady Catriona, my heart aches for you."

"Do not let it ache yet, as this is not over." She stood still in a moving crowd. Tristan and Freya remained near her, trying to deflect as many of the bumps and jostles as was possible.

Sir John stood against the passing people like a great tree that lets a river part over its roots. "What pray tell do you mean by such a thing?"

"I believe Sir Geordie's cousin, Robert, set him up." Cat rushed on to explain about the servant saying his master slept the night Sir Gawain died, and how that very servant turned up in the kitchens when pennyroyal was added to her ale.

Sir John nodded as he listened. "It sounds suspect indeed, but the trial is over. It will not be heard again. The jurors have made the decision based on their own investigations, which were quite thorough."

"But they were not." The burn of desperate frustration tightened in stomach. "They knew more but omitted it."

Sir John shook his head. "My lady, there is naught I can do to reverse this verdict."

Anger welled inside her and exploded in a sharp curse.

Sir John blinked in surprise. "Lady Catriona, I..."

"This is ridiculous." She gestured to an open door leading to the hall where a majority of the people had departed. "In an entire court of men who speak of little more than bravery, you are all cowards when it comes to doing what it is right."

Sir John opened his mouth, but Cat rushed on. "If you will not help me, I will see to it myself."

"Lady Catriona, whatever you mean to do—"

"I will not be talked out of. Good day." With that, she rushed from the large hall.

Tristan trailed behind her. "Are we going to confront Robert?"

"Aye, that is exactly what we are doing," Cat said. "But first we must find him. Freya, you come with me. Tristan, seek Robert out and find Eldon and Durham as well, please. Once you find Robert, have a servant sent to me. All of us working together will make it easier to locate him. It will be better to confront him in public, of course, to get a confession all can hear."

Tristan nodded and rushed off in the opposite direction.

Cat immediately set off through the denser areas of the castle, the smaller halls where people milled about, the gardens, any other place she could think of to find him.

All the while, her stomach knotted with the desperation of a ticking clock. She had failed in finding sufficient evidence against Robert before the trial. Now, with Geordie's death looming closer with every minute, she would not fail again.

28

Cat had searched everywhere for Robert in her pressing fear for Geordie's life. It was near the door to her own apartments that she finally caught sight of the man. Mayhap she ought to have discreetly followed him to a more populated area. She was, however, worried that he would slip into his apartments and she might not get the chance until much, much later. If at all.

So concerned she might not get another opportunity, she rushed toward him without pausing to think. "I'd like a word with you, please."

The man stopped and regarded her with disdain. "Lady Catriona Strafford, I presume."

Cat nodded. "I must speak with you. Will you join me in the gardens?"

"Nay."

Cat hadn't truly anticipated he'd accept her offer. Very well, she would work with what she had. "You are aware of my husband's predicament?"

The dour look to his face lightened into a courtier's pleasant expression. Without his brow furrowed, he appeared far more attractive a man than his glower suggested. "I'm quite aware. You have my condolences on the impending loss of your new husband."

His words carried no regret.

Cat's pulse quickened with what she was about to do. "I imagine it must be difficult for you to wonder at the sex of the child within my womb." She set her hands to her stomach. "Knowing that your inheritance hinges on whether I birth a girl or a boy."

The glower was back on his face, dark and full of hatred.

"I know you tried to poison me to make me lose the babe." She stepped toward him, but he did not step back. The distance between them was too close, too uncomfortable, but she refused to retreat her advance. Regardless, she raised her voice in the hopes it carried down the hall and to anyone who might be in their chambers. "I know you killed Sir Gawain. I know you allowed Sir Geordie to take the blame so you could eliminate him from the path to your inheritance."

Robert's face darkened. "And where is your proof?"

"It was your servant they saw in the kitchen, before I was given my cup with pennyroyal in it." She hugged her arms over her babe. "You were willing to kill an innocent child, just as you are condemning an innocent man."

"I sent my servant to the kitchens to fetch me some garlic for a nasty bout of gout I've been suffering from." He smiled at her and a chill slid down her spine. "Though I will say, an unfortunate loss of your child would be most convenient on my behalf. Now if you'll excuse me..."

Cat shook her head. "I refuse to leave until you admit to what you've done."

"Move yourself from my path, Lady Catriona."

Cat widened her feet. "Not until you confess to what you've done." Her voice was becoming louder still, nearly a shout. "I know you killed Sir Gawain to cast blame on my husband and I know you tried to poison me."

Robert's gaze slid coolly around them, up and down the narrow corridor, as if confirming no one had heard her outburst. "I've warned you."

No sooner had he spoken the words than he drew his fist back and drove it toward her stomach. Cat's forearms were already crossed where she hugged her unborn child and that made it easy for her to block the force of Robert's blow. Pain shot up her forearms at the impact, but her child was safe. Which was the only thing that mattered.

Freya screamed somewhere in the distance, but Cat was too focused on Robert to pay her any mind.

He drew back to try to strike her again, but she spun away. She had to get the upper hand. He darted after her and put himself directly where she needed him to be. On the offensive, thinking he might get a hit.

She charged forward and slammed her forearm into his face.

Blood spattered out of his mouth and he staggered back, holding his jaw. "I forgot you know how to fight, you feral wench."

He pulled a dagger from his belt and ran at her. Cat slid free her own blade in preparation for his attack. She'd long since stopped bothering with an eating dagger at her side and carried a true weapon.

Robert crashed into her despite her anticipation. The weight of his body against her chest knocked her hard to the floor. The blow forced the air from Cat's lungs, but it was not anything she hadn't experienced before. She gritted her teeth and swept up with her blade. It caught against his shirt, splitting it and revealing a slice of red beneath from where the point slicked at him.

With a roar, he pinned her to the ground. His dark eyes were wild with intent. He turned his blade to her stomach. "You're right. I did kill Gawain. The man was a wastrel and after Geordie defended you against him, I saw the opportunity to place his death on Geordie's shoulders to restore my inheritance. Until he stepped forward and told the world what a whore you are. This child will ruin everything. *You* will ruin everything."

Cat kicked her leg up at him, but the skirts she had to wear for court impeded the blow and made the attempt seem little more than a helpless struggle.

A series of fluttering bumps flickered against Cat's stomach, from within. Her child. As though it was scrambling for its own life inside her womb. With a cry of defensive rage, she drew her knee up with all the force she could muster. It landed perfectly between Robert's legs. He loosed a howl of pain and dropped to the side, rolling off her.

Cat scrambled over to him with her hand protectively over her stomach. With her other hand, she put her dagger to Robert's neck. "Do not move."

He gave a high-pitched squeak and clutched his wounded manhood. His blade lay several feet away, dropped no doubt by the impact of her blow.

"Freya, I—" Cat glanced about, noticing for the first time Freya was not there.

Footsteps thundered on the floor in the distance. Robert obviously heard them as well, since he straightened and struggled as though trying to get to his feet. Cat pushed the dagger more firmly against his neck and a drop of blood trickled to his collarbone and soaked into his white shirt.

Sir John rounded the corner with Freya at his side and the king's guard behind them. Cat gasped out her relief.

"Don't kill him," Sir John said as he ran to her. "Back away from him, Lady Catriona."

Cat immediately lowered her dagger and backed away, leaving Robert for the king's guard. "He confessed to his crimes." She hugged her arms over her child as it bumped against the inside of her womb. "It was he who killed Sir Gawain, just as he tried to kill my unborn child."

"A trial will handle this." Sir John bent and hefted Robert to his feet. Or as much to his feet as he could be with his knees still bent in apparent agony.

"Thank you for assembling the guards with such haste," Cat said with gratitude.

"Oh, I assembled them the moment you left me." Sir John chuckled. "You've got a penchant for mischief, Lady Catriona."

Cat couldn't help but smile. Everything in her felt light and free. Geordie would be safe; they could finally have their life together.

"She's mad," Robert ground out. "I made no such confession. She attacked me. I'll admit to nothing I didn't do."

Cat turned an outraged look to Sir John, but before she could bother to protest, the door nearest them opened. An aged woman in an elegant blue silk kirtle with her white braids twisted into rolls on her head peeked her face out. "He lies," she said in a fragile voice. "I heard his confession myself." She gave Cat an apologetic smile. "Were I as brave as you, my dear, I would have come out to help you."

Cat lowered her head in thanks. "Thank you, Lady…"

"Lady Ellington," she said with purpose.

Cat's heartbeat quickened. Lady Ellington was wife to Lord Ellington, one of the twelve men of the jury who had judged Geordie.

"She lies too," Robert hissed. "All of them—"

Sir John drew back his fist and smashed it into Robert's face. "Enough out of you. Guards…"

The king's guards came forward and took Robert, who had ceased his protests long enough to transfer his hands from his groin to his nose.

"Geordie…?" Cat asked.

Sir John nodded. "I shall go and speak to the king on his behalf now."

Cat nearly collapsed with relief. Surely after hearing of

Robert's confession, especially coming from Sir John, Geordie would be freed. He *had* to be freed.

Didn't he?

※

GEORDIE WAS GOING TO DIE. HE SAT IN FRONT OF THE CHAIR by the fire, his focus consumed by the flames licking over logs in the hearth.

After finally having Cat and everything he had ever wanted, it would all be for naught. Tears welled in his eyes at the hopelessness of it all. The key clicked in the lock of his door and he swiftly blinked away his emotion.

He would die like a man and refused to be seen as weak. His door opened and Sir John entered.

"That wife of yours..." Sir John chuckled.

Geordie regarded his brother knight with confusion.

"She sought out Robert on her own when no one on the jury would listen to her." Sir John gently closed the door but did not lock it. "She came to me for help as well, but sadly, I did not listen to her either."

A prickle of fear scraped down Geordie's spine. "Is she well?"

"Aye, as is the babe," Sir John confirmed. "She got a confession out of Robert. He killed Sir Gawain to make it look like it'd been you, and he then tried to kill your wife's unborn babe. First with poison, then he tried to stab her in the stomach."

Geordie leapt from the chair. "You are certain she is well?"

Sir John lifted a brow. "You know your wife above all others. You already know the answer to that question."

Thanks be to God. He couldn't help but smile at his fellow knight's words. "Should I be asking then after the welfare of Robert?"

"He could scarcely walk to the dungeon." Sir John chortled.

"Not that he'll need to be walking anywhere but the gallows soon."

The gallows. He would most likely be hung then, not even beheaded as a peer. Geordie suppressed his shudder.

What he had gone through, the anticipation of a guilty verdict, the pain of it being said aloud, the excruciating time of living while waiting for death—he would not wish it on anyone. Not even on Robert. Though he was grateful Cat could no longer be hurt.

"What of my sentence?" Geordie asked.

Sir John grinned. "You have been exonerated; you are free."

Geordie almost sank back into the chair once more with relief. "Cat. Where is she? I must—"

"Do you really think I'd come see you without her waiting nearby?" Sir John opened the door and in walked Catriona, lovely as a new day and wholly perfect.

They ran to one another and met midway between.

"Geordie," she gasped. "You're free, my love. You're free."

He smoothed the hair back from her face where it had come loose from the careful braids bound around her head. "You could have been killed. The babe—"

"I wasn't." Cat touched his face, her fingers wandering down his cheeks, over his jaw and neck, to his collarbones, as though she could not get enough of him. "The babe is fine. I felt it move within me." She took Geordie's hand and put it over her stomach. "Our child is doing so again now," she said. "Can you feel it?"

The silk of her kirtle was smooth and cool against his palm, and he could feel only the firmness of her belly. He shook his head. "I believe women sense it before men can. God be praised that you are both safe. Cat, you should never have taken such a risk..."

"And if I did not, you might be dead." She buried herself in his embrace. "I could not lose you, Geordie. Not when so much has pulled us apart for so long. Not when we have finally found one another."

He wrapped his arms around her and gently stroked her hair. Never had he thought to hold her thus again, to feel the sweet warmth of her against him, to breathe in her lovely rose scent that held notes of sunshine and happiness. They were all alive and well and safe.

"How can I ever repay you for your courage, my Cat?" he asked into her ear.

"With a lifetime of joy and love." She drew away to smile up at him. "And mayhap, we might return to Werrick Castle to deliver the babe there."

"I'd rather be there than Easton Castle for certes." And truly he would. The idea of letting a child start their life in such a hard and hostile home. He had no plans to take the child there, not until Lord Strafford was dead and they could bring their own warmth to those cold halls.

Cat beamed up at Geordie. It had been far too long since she'd looked so cheerful. After all she had been through, he was glad to see her jubilant spirit return.

"Would you mind terribly if we invited Lady Strafford to stay at Werrick Castle as well?" Cat asked. "So that she might be there when our child is delivered."

Geordie could only smile at her request, knowing what it would mean to his mother. He pressed a kiss to Cat's smooth brow, loving her for her consideration and kindness. "I am certain she would be overjoyed to receive such a request."

"I shall write to my father immediately." Cat locked hands with Geordie and regarded him once more. "I am eager to leave court. I confess I lied when I said I enjoyed it. I needed you to believe it at the time to ensure I got to court, so I could confront..." She pressed her lips together, rather than put a name to the man who had brought them both so much pain.

"I understand." He pulled her more snugly against him. He

too was ready to leave court. In fact, he'd been ready to leave as soon as they arrived. The king would need to give his permission, of course, but with war having been temporarily set aside, he doubted the king would refuse him.

If all went according to plan, they would be able to leave within a sennight and could travel at a comfortable pace to ensure Cat's safety, as well as that of their child.

Soon, they would be back at Werrick Castle. Away from court intrigue and gossip and carefully spoken words. And when the babe came, it would be surrounded by family and friends and all the love a new child deserved.

Aye, it would be good to go home.

29

The horses were loaded with packs and the small carriage piled with several more trunks than they had arrived at court with. In the last sennight, Cat had noticed the distinct shift in the atmosphere at court. Her name still seasoned every tongue, but now with praise.

She was a hero, a woman who pushed beyond the duty of any wife and found a way to free her husband from certain death. Not that she cared for their exaltation any more than she had their slurs. All that mattered was that Geordie was safe. And that they were soon to depart for Werrick Castle.

Eldon and Durham were already on their horses while Freya fussed over Lady Strafford's horse to ensure as much comfort as possible for Geordie's mother. Cat knew part of it had to do with Freya's anxiety to return to Werrick Castle where she would see Peter once more.

Cat watched the archway to the castle with anticipation.

"Tristan will be down in a moment," Cat promised Geordie. "He said he'd see us off, and he will."

Geordie grinned. "I'd never dream of making you leave without bidding farewell to Tristan."

No sooner had his name been mentioned than the man stepped through the archway and out to where they stood on an expanse of cobblestones. "Did you think I wouldn't make it?"

He opened an arm, revealing blue silk undersleeves.

Cat went to him and embraced him. "You've been my only true friend while I've been at court. Thank you for everything you've done. For me, and for Geordie."

"This has been the most enjoyment I've ever had at court." Tristan released her and bowed. "Trust me when I say life without you will be terribly dull."

"I think dull might be a good change," Geordie offered. "Thank you for all you've done for us. Your kindness will not be forgotten."

"God's bones." Tristan leaned close to Cat and eyed the emerald necklace about her throat. "Was that the king's gift to you?"

Cat flushed and touched the massive stone. It was far too extravagant for her taste, and nothing she ought to be wearing for travel. But she did not want to offend the king when he had made such a generous gift for her efforts in saving the life and honor of one of his most trusted knights.

"It may pull me off my horse," Cat said in light jest.

"I'd be there to catch it." Tristan winked at her.

"Do not dare leave." An authoritative voice boomed out.

Cat's chest tightened with dread. They had hoped to avoid this moment.

Lord Strafford stepped around Tristan, purple-faced and sweating with the fatigue of walking from the castle to where they readied to depart beyond the stables. "Lady Strafford, I said you could not go." He shoved the servant at his side forward. "Pull her trunks from the cart. Now, you wastrel."

"Nay." Lady Strafford stood in front of the cart with her feet braced wide.

"I told you that you will be returning to Easton Castle with me." Dots of spittle caught the sunlight at the vehement words Lord Strafford ground out. "Get to my side now, woman."

Geordie took a step forward, but Cat pulled his arm and shook her head. Lady Strafford had spent a lifetime doing her husband's bidding and suffering the consequences of actions she had no hand in making. If this was the first time that she declined to be biddable, doubtless she would have more to say.

"Please leave them," Lady Strafford said gently to the servant. The man bowed his head in acquiescence, as though unsure what to do. Geordie's mother, however, did not suffer from such hesitation. Nay, she strode forward to her husband, her back straight and her head lifted high.

"I lost Geordie to you once before." She kept walking until she stood directly before him. "I almost lost him again." She jutted her chin upward. "I lost young Tom as well because of you. I will lose no more. I have sacrificed enough for you."

Lord Strafford drew back his arm to strike his wife. Lady Strafford did not move from her position, but Geordie did. In a flash he was in front of her, shielding his beloved mother.

"If you weren't frail as an old woman, I'd crush your nose into your skull," Geordie snarled.

"The son so pathetic, even Werrick couldn't bring himself to kill you." Strafford snorted. "It matters not." He waved a hand with disinterest. "Her womb has been dried up for years. She's of little use to me now."

Geordie drew back his fist, but his mother put her hands to his forearm to stay the action.

"He isn't worth it, Geordie." Then, without another look back at her husband, Lady Strafford turned away and allowed the Master of the Horse to aid her onto her steed.

"Go on with you," Tristan said. "I'll ensure he doesn't follow."

Cat gave her friend a grateful smile. Within minutes they were on their horses and departing, leaving behind happy memories as well as horrible ones, bitter enemies as well as lifelong friends.

Soon, they would be among family and friends with a wedding to celebrate, a babe to birth, and a new life to begin.

※

WHEN THEY RETURNED TO WERRICK CASTLE, THEY WERE welcomed back with genuine affection. Geordie's mother had been drawn into the fold, not as a guest, but as family, and the news of the marriage was met with much joy. Perhaps no one was happier to see them returned than Peter was at seeing Freya. Cat had told Geordie of their budding romance and they could not help but share a smile as the two met once more with shy excitement.

While Lord Werrick had appeared pleased with Geordie and Cat's marriage, Geordie could not help the twist of guilt at his gut. A knight knew better than to wed a woman without first seeking her father's blessing.

Though the journey back to Werrick took twice as long as it had to get to Westminster, nearing on two months, Cat and his mother were both exhausted upon their arrival. Geordie waited until they were settled and resting peacefully before doing what he ought to have done the moment he'd arrived at Werrick after the king's campaign ended: to seek the Earl of Werrick's permission to wed Cat.

The earl was in the solar, seated behind the large desk as he went through a ledger. He looked up as Geordie entered and a smile lit his face.

"I'd like to speak to you for a moment." Geordie entered the room and tried to hide the sudden sheepishness creeping over him.

"Of course, my boy." Lord Werrick closed the journal and gestured to the seat before the desk.

The room was brilliantly colored with tapestries on the walls and painted animals, flowers and whorls along the beams overhead, all lit with sunlight spilling in from the leaded glass windows. There had been so many wonderful memories in that room over the years. Its familiarity set Geordie at ease.

"Forgive me for not seeking your permission prior to wedding Lady Catriona." Geordie slid into the chair, taking the right as the left always gave a terrible squeak. "It had been my intention, but not until I was established with land and income. Not until I was worthy of her. I feared if I asked you prior to having a suitable life attained for Lady Catriona, you might have given me the funds to do so, and..." Geordie met the earl's steady blue gaze. "I wanted to do it myself."

Lord Werrick nodded appraisingly. "Aye, I would have paid for you to be established to wed Cat. Regardless, you've always been worthy of her, lad. Always. Before you were to inherit a barony, before you had wealth, before you were even a knight. No one has ever been more worthy of our Cat than you."

Geordie lowered his head in reverent acknowledgment of the finest praise he'd ever been given by a man he'd always admired.

"You seek my forgiveness, but it is not needed," the earl continued. "You did exactly as you were always meant to."

"Thank you," Geordie said solemnly.

"And thank you for accepting Cat."

Geordie looked up at that. "For accepting her, my lord?"

"Simple mathematics." Lord Werrick raised his brows. "I am certain you know the months do not add up."

The pregnancy. Heat effused Geordie's body.

"After you departed for Westminster, Isla approached me and told me her suspicions." The earl lifted from his seat and took the chair beside Geordie. The chair gave a low squeak. "When Cat announced her pregnancy upon your arrival, I knew her condition to be further along than only one month. I'm certain you do as well."

Geordie met the earl's level gaze. "I know well what I am lucky enough to have in my life with Cat."

Lord Werrick nodded. "I think you will find that a child born of the woman you love can bring as much joy and affection as a child of your own loins." He patted Geordie on the back.

"I fully expect it." Geordie grinned.

"Get you to your wife, lest I be laid to blame for your absence." Lord Werrick got to his feet and went to his own chair once more. "It is good to have you home, Geordie."

"It's good to be home," Geordie said earnestly.

He slipped from the solar and wound his way down the hall to the chambers he shared with Cat. He entered the room without waking her and eased onto the bed at her side.

She gave a contented hum and rolled toward him. He pulled her into his arms, reveling in the heat her sleeping body gave off. She smelled of roses and everything that had ever brought him joy. He watched her as she slept, noting the sweet pink of her cheeks and lips. Her hand was slung over her stomach, which had grown fuller and firmer in their travel to Werrick.

Geordie smiled down at Cat. "I love you," he whispered softly.

As if hearing him in her dreams, her lips twitched into a soft smile. He put his hand to the rounded belly. "And I love you," he said quietly.

A gently tapping sensation tickled against his palm. He froze, fearful of making the small movement cease. Emotion knotted in his throat as he felt another little bump at his hand. He had felt their baby move for the first time.

Surely his life could not be more glorious than it was at that moment, when he had everyone he loved with him and safe.

30

Three months later

Cat held Lady Strafford's hand on one side, and Marin's on the other, as she gave a final push. A scream rent from her throat and pain split through her core.

The pressure ceased, and a thin wail filled the room. Cat fell back, exhausted. Both Lady Strafford and Marin were no longer looking at her, but at Isla at the end of the narrow bed. At Cat's baby.

Cat lifted her head, despite the jelly-like feel of her stomach, straining to see just one glimpse of the babe.

Isla came around the bed with a small bundle swaddled in her arms, calming the child's cries with a gentle rocking. "'Tis a girl, Lady Catriona. The bonniest wee lass I've ever laid eyes upon."

A girl. Catriona laid her head back. They had decided long ago if it was to be a girl, they would name her Evelyn, after Catriona's mother.

"May I enter now?" Geordie asked from the other side of the door, his voice strained.

The women all looked at one another and shared a soft chuckle at his eagerness.

"You have the caul to deliver still." Isla shook her head. "I dinna let the men in before that part is done. Even barons."

Geordie's father had died in his sleep two months prior, an unfittingly kind end for a man who had hurt so many in his life. Geordie inherited the barony, making him the new Baron Strafford. Cat was simply grateful he could find closure in his father's death, and love in his mother's affection.

Isla passed Evelyn to Catriona.

The child's weight was almost nothing in her arms. Marin hovered protectively over the babe as Cat drew her new daughter to her chest. Wetness coated Evelyn's face and slicked down her dark hair, but she didn't seem to notice as she blinked her squinted blue eyes at Cat, as if even the candlelight was far too bright for her.

Her face was delicate, so small it was scarcely the size of Cat's palm. Evelyn moved her mouth and furrowed her brow, testing both out for the first time.

Cat laughed at the expressions on such a tiny face. It was clear Evelyn had inherited Geordie's dark hair. The thought sent an unpleasant jarring through her joy. Because the darkness of her hair was not Geordie's, but Gawain's. She and Geordie had spoken of their child together so often, it had made Cat feel as though Evelyn as truly their daughter.

But then, her own father loved Leila as his own when it was evident she was not. They all had.

Suddenly, Cat did not care who had given her baby such lovely dark hair, only that Geordie would raise Evelyn as her father had Leila, and that they would grow to be a family of love and happiness together.

"She's beautiful," Dowager Lady Strafford whispered, her voice choked with emotion.

There was a pressure at Cat's lower stomach, but she was so enthralled by the precious face gazing up at her, she scarcely noticed what more went on at the foot of the bed.

Marin smoothed Cat's hair. "You've done so well, sweet Cat. You will be a wonderful mother. I'm so happy for you."

"I was afraid to tell you initially." Cat's cheeks flooded with shame. "I didn't want to hurt you."

Marin smiled and brushed the back of her finger delicately over Evelyn's round cheek. "My heart is stronger than my barren womb. I love all of you far too much to ever begrudge your happiness."

"And all good things come to those who are patient." Leila set a steaming mug of tea on the table. Cat had been so consumed by Evelyn's small face that she hadn't heard Leila come in.

Marin kept her face impassive, but Cat's heart fluttered with hope. Leila was careful not to speak of her visions for fear of how they might be misinterpreted, or how it might impact the future. Cat hoped this truly was a vision she'd had and not a simple statement of encouragement.

She hugged Evelyn to her chest and prayed that Marin would experience the same beautiful joy of having a child. While Cat could not have her own mother at her side for Evelyn's birth, she had Marin, who had always served as their mother in the years following Lady Werrick's death.

And Cat had Geordie's mother, who loved Cat as completely as any mother ever loved a child. Lady Strafford bent over and cooed something at Evelyn, who screwed up her lips in reply, much to the entertainment of all in the room.

"Now may I come in?" Geordie asked from the other side of the door. "I assure you, I am trying desperately to be patient, but..."

Leila smiled. "I suppose we ought to let him in." She lifted her brows at Isla, who nodded her consent.

Lady Strafford and Marin departed the room as Geordie entered. He paused at the entrance, his gaze locked on Evelyn.

"We have a girl." Cat's heart glowed with pride at their perfect babe.

"Evelyn." He said their daughter's name with a catch to his voice and came closer. He knelt by the bed. "Oh, Cat, she's perfect."

Cat smiled to watch the joy play over his features as he gently extended one finger to caress Evelyn's cheek.

"Would you like to hold her?" Cat asked.

"Aye." He hesitated before rising to standing. "But she is so small, I worry that—"

"You won't hurt her." Cat shifted the delicate bundle into Geordie's strong arms.

Those massive arms and hands that had slain many men, that had saved the king, turned the tide of battle, kept all of England safe—they now carefully cradled their daughter with all the gentleness in the world. Geordie drew in a soft breath and his eyes shone with happiness as he stared down at Evelyn. "You've done well bringing such a lovely daughter into this world. Thank you for this gift." He slowly lowered into the chair beside Cat. "Thank you for this life."

Cat was exhausted and her body still ached from childbirth, but she wouldn't trade anything to be anywhere else at that moment. Not as she watched her husband gaze at their daughter. Their whole lives stretched ahead of them like chapters in a book yet to be written.

"It is a good life," Cat said with the entirety of her heart. For truly it was.

EPILOGUE

November 1348
Easton Castle

Cat smiled as she watched her children play. Evelyn, now seven, was a tall beauty with curling brown hair and large blue eyes. She shepherded over her younger brother, Eversham, with such care that Cat was reminded of Marin.

Eversham, however, was at the unruly age of three and wanted none of it unless he was hungry or injured and Cat was not about. But Cat was there now, and he turned his brown eyes on her with the full force of his charm. "Mama, may we play outside?"

Lady Strafford stiffened. Cat put her palm to her mother-in-law's hand to set her at ease.

"Mayhap later." Cat pulled him into her arms and kissed his sweaty blond hair. He struggled against her affections before wriggling down and hopping onto a wooden pony Ella had purchased after he was born.

"You've mussed your hair," Evelyn chided gently and

smoothed down Eversham's tresses as he rocked back and forth on his toy.

He waved her away with one dimpled hand. "Mama did it with her kisses."

Cat and Lady Strafford both chuckled at the complaint. Eversham was an affectionate child, always eager to snuggle into a waiting lap and endure a multitude of kisses. Unless he was at play. Then, he wanted nothing more than to be wild and unfettered.

Which drove Evelyn to distraction—her life was one of peace and order.

Cat wished she could let them outside. She knew it would be best for Eversham, especially. The boy needed to run about, to climb trees and throw rocks into streams. But it was far too dangerous.

They had been lucky thus far that the great pestilence had not reached Easton Castle. In truth, it had been more than luck. Leila had sent them a missive the year prior, warning them of great death on the horizon. First there would be great rains, which there had been. Then the cattle would die in great numbers, which they had. Lastly, illness would sweep through the land, killing men and women and children without mercy.

It had.

They were safe here thus far, but Cat would not take any chances. It took only one person with the contagion to wander onto their land, to get too close.

Her heart nearly seized in fear at the whisper of an idea of losing either one of her precious children. Or any of those in her household for that matter. These were trying times indeed.

The door to the nursery opened and Geordie stepped in. Cat leapt to her feet and threw her arms around her husband. "I'm so glad you're safe," Cat whispered into his ear.

Geordie said nothing. He released her and gently cupped her

jaw in his large, callused palm. Though he smiled at her, the joy did not touch his eyes.

A knot of ice tightened in Cat's lower stomach.

"How bad is it?" Lady Strafford asked as she embraced her son to bid him welcome on his return home.

He had been out of the keep for nearly a fortnight as he traveled to court at the king's command. Evelyn came forward, her expression uncertain in light of the dampened mood.

She glanced up at Geordie and beamed, unable to quell her happiness as she wrapped her arms around him. "Welcome home, Papa. I missed you."

Geordie's somber expression blossomed into a smile. "I've missed you and your brother terribly." He lifted her into the air and pulled her in for a great hug. "Have you been good while I've been gone?"

Evelyn's mouth fell open. "Of course!"

He chuckled and pressed a kiss to the top of her hair. "I figured as much. And your brother?"

Evelyn sighed like a strained mother and regarded Eversham over her shoulder. The boy rocked back and forth with fervor upon his pony.

"It is like that, then." Geordie laughed.

Evelyn gave a shrug just as Eversham let out a hoarse roar akin to a battle cry, eliciting a laugh from them all.

Geordie reached into his bag and withdrew a small red-bound leather book. "The king wanted you to have this, knowing how much you love to read."

Cat cast Geordie a nervous glance. Anything could carry contagion. Even a book gifted by the king.

Evelyn's eyes lit up. She immediately pulled it from Geordie's hands and went to the window bench to read.

"It came from the king's own hands to mine and touched nothing else in between," Geordie said in a low whisper, as though reading Cat's thoughts.

Of course, he would have been careful. He doted on Evelyn with the same loving affection as Cat's own father always had with her and all her sisters.

Cat shook her head at her own fears. "It is just that everything is so frightening now," she whispered.

Geordie took her hand. "We must speak a moment." He regarded his mother in silent question.

Dowager Lady Strafford tilted her head in understanding. "I'll stay with these beautiful children. Go on and speak."

Geordie cast his mother a grateful look and pulled Cat from the room.

Cat's heart clenched, anticipating the news he would give her. About the land, about its people, about the state of the world they lived in.

She followed with heavy trepidation. "Is it as bad as I thought?"

Geordie's jaw clenched. "Aye. We were prudent to heed Leila's warning. Populated areas have higher levels of sickness. People are dying and their grief is making them mad. Cat, they..."

His hesitation sent a prickle of alarm down her spine. "What is it?"

"They are persecuting healers in some areas, thinking them witches who have brought on the plague."

The fear teasing at Cat's mind took hold with a solid grip.

"Leila," Cat whispered.

Geordie nodded. "We must warn her, so she is prepared. If she spoke of the pestilence to the people of Werrick Castle, she will no doubt be seen as a witch."

Cat clasped her free hand over her heart. Of course, Leila would have mentioned the coming pestilence at Werrick Castle. She would have wanted to see her friends safe.

It was impossible not to think of those at Werrick Castle now. Cat's father, Leila, Nan who had found happiness with the butcher she'd once so despised, Freya and Peter who were now on their fifth year of marriage. Cat had heard Isla was now rumored to be 400 years old and still delighted in tormenting Bernard, who had only become twitchier as time wore on.

Aye, Leila would have sought to protect them, just as any of the sisters would.

"Thanks be to God Leila never leaves Werrick Castle," Cat whispered. "I hope it will ensure her safety."

Geordie pulled Cat into his arms, knowing as he always seemed to that she needed his comfort, his wonderful strength. "We will do everything we can to help keep her safe. All will be well."

Cat nodded against his powerful chest, the tension already draining from her shoulders. For together they were always stronger and could face any challenge life set in their path, even the great pestilence.

"I love you," she whispered, but their hearts were so in harmony that he heard her quiet words.

"As I love you." Geordie lifted her face up and smiled down at her. "My beautiful baroness, mother of my children."

Cat pressed her lips to his, overcome with gratitude to find a life with the man she'd thought lost to her too many times. Even in these trying days, they would make it through, together, and come out stronger in the end. Without hesitation, without fear, without secrets; for love transcended everything and they had love aplenty.

* * *

Thank you for reading CATRIONA'S SECRET! I read all of my reviews and would love to know how you enjoyed the story, so please do leave a review.

Next, check out Leila's story and the exciting series conclusion in LEILA'S LEGACY !

LEILA'S LEGACY

Lady Leila Barrington has always known she was different from her sisters, not only in appearance, but also due to the visions she's been plagued with since childhood.

When her prediction of the great pestilence comes to fruition and the people are looking for someone to blame, she knows she will finally meet the Lion – the man who is destined to kill her, and who she is fated to love.

Keep reading for a first chapter preview of LEILA'S LEGACY

To stay up to date on all my new releases and get your FREE copy of The Highlander's Challenge, please sign up for my newsletter:

https://dl.bookfunnel.com/ff96yjtq8c

LEILA'S LEGACY
Chapter 1 Preview

January 1349
Brampton, England

THE GREAT PESTILENCE HAD COME.

Lady Leila Barrington, youngest daughter to the Earl of Werrick, had seen it in her visions for as long as she could remember. Lingering on the horizon like a patient beast stalking its prey, growing hungrier, stronger, and more desperate.

She'd told no one of the things she'd seen in her mind. Not when the visions were so horrible, not when she'd hoped so fervently that time might cause them to change.

But the future had not altered. It had pressed upon Leila throughout her life until the visions came daily, and she knew the beast was about to pounce upon the unsuspecting people of Christendom.

And it did.

Leila tied the handkerchief filled with herbs around her face. The sage, lavender and mint crinkled as she secured the handkerchief, the dried bits of leaves and stems poking at her cheeks. Once the combination of such scents had reminded her of all things clean; now, the scent recalled illness and death. Isla, the healer at Werrick Castle, had wanted to soak it all in heifer's piss for good measure, but Leila had refused.

The older woman waited for her presently by the entrance to the castle with a similar handkerchief tied to her withered face, and a basket slung over either arm. She handed one to Leila as she approached, her sharp amber eyes narrowing from over the top of her handkerchief.

"Are ye certain ye want to venture out today?" Isla asked.

It was the same question she asked every day.

Leila took the basket and replied as she always did. "There are people in need."

The basket tipped precariously, but Leila quickly steadied it. The flagon of water weighted one side more heavily, but it was by far the most important of the items they carried with them. There was no cure for the great pestilence. Through all of Isla's and Leila's knowledge of healing, neither had found a way to cure the illness.

No one had.

Outside of those people suffering a random injury or non-pestilence illness, Isla and Leila had become little more than easers of suffering.

"Ye're lady of the castle." Even as she offered the protest, Isla turned toward the doorway to lead the way to the village.

"All the more reason to be there for my people." Leila followed her outside where the otherwise sunny sky was hazy with brown gray smoke. It stung at her eyes and its acrid odor penetrated the sweetness of the herbs about her face. Ash floated in the air like light snow and sifted silently to the ground.

The ground was sodden, the dirt churned into a sludge that was as slippery as it was thick. Even with conditions such as these, they left the horses safe in their stalls. It was more than the fear of them falling ill that encouraged the ladies to keep them stabled. It was the very real concern that a villager so eager to flee the grasp of the pestilence would steal their lord's horse and leave their family behind.

And a large number of people did leave their families. Wives were abandoned by husbands, aging parents abandoned by their grown children, mothers fled their sick children. The latter was the most difficult to happen upon. Dirty-faced children whose eyes were bright with fever, screaming in pain and fear, with no one to aid them. Those were the ones that most broke Leila's heart.

Such was the terror of the great pestilence that it overtook even a mother's love for her children. Extreme measures of escape, however, had been for naught, for the great mortality lay its shroud over the whole of Christendom. There was no escape.

They neared the village with smoke rising from within where pyres had been lit to burn the dead and their belongings.

"I dinna like ye doing this," Isla muttered from beneath her mask of herbs.

Many did not like Leila going out into the danger of the pestilence to aid others. They did not understand what it meant to her, how it helped heal the hurt within.

For all of her life, she had felt very much outside her family. It was not only her looks that set her apart from her sisters, her dark hair or the narrowness of her face. The sense of not belonging even went beyond her visions.

She had never felt as though she was worthy of the love her family offered. How could she, when she knew the truth? She was not a child of Lord Werrick's loins, but that of a marauding Graham reiver. The attack had nearly killed Lady Werrick, but it was Leila's birth that had finally snuffed out her life.

It was why Leila had turned to healing. In giving others life, she was repaying the one she had taken. It gave her purpose; an action she could perform in a situation she was otherwise helpless to change. As though her aid toward others might put the violence of her making to peace.

"You put yourself at risk every day too," Leila reminded the old healer.

Isla snorted. "Death wants nothing to do with me, or I'd have been dead several dozen times over."

"Death will not come for me." There was confidence behind Leila's words, the same as there had been when she finally made the declaration of the incoming arrival of the pestilence to her family. "Not until I meet the Lion."

Isla slid her a wary look. The older woman didn't like when Leila brought up her visions of him. For it would not be the pestilence that took Leila's life, but the man with golden hair, bronzed skin and hazel eyes. A man who was as ferocious as he was beautiful. A man who would first steal her heart, then her life.

It was preposterous, the idea that she would love a man she knew would kill her. But was it not equally preposterous that illness would consume the population of the world as readily as a spark set to dry tinder?

Leila shuddered as they stepped into the empty village. Under normal circumstances, it would have been a market day. But now where once there had been the bustle of people, there was emptiness; save for several bodies strewn out for collection. Where once people called out to bring shoppers to their wares, now cries of anguish and mourning pitched through the chilly air.

A woman moved on the ground as they passed, lifting her hand to them. "Water," she groaned.

It was not an uncommon sight, seeing those who dragged themselves to the filthy streets in search of water just before death claimed them. Before Leila could bring the flagon to her, Isla was at her side crouching with knees that popped in protest.

The woman's breath huffed in white puffs in the icy air. Her skeletal fingers clutched the flagon to her lips, and she drank greedily before finally releasing it with a gasping breath.

"Thank you." The woman struggled to sit up. "My neighbors. We must go to them."

Isla assisted her so that her back rested against the wall of the hut they stood near. "Is it the swelling?"

From what Leila and Isla had gleaned from tales of travelers, there were two sorts of pestilence. One which caused swelling in the form of knobs of darkened skin that rose at the neck, armpit or groin, and one which covered the sufferer in a rash and made them vomit blood. Of the two, the latter was almost always fatal.

"'Tis the swelling." The woman brushed aside her tangled red hair and touched the side of her neck where the skin remained flushed with infection beneath a bump that appeared to be diminishing.

Leila breathed a sigh of relief. Thus far, they had only seen the swelling in the village. At least it was possible to survive, even if the chances were higher for death.

"Ye shouldna be outside," Isla chastised gently. "'Tis colder than a witch's soul."

Rosiness colored the woman's cheeks, and her pale blue eyes were bright with the effects of her fever. It was obvious she had not been outside long. If she had been, she would not have survived. Not in the bitterness of the winter.

"There are children nearby." The woman pushed up as though she intended to walk. "I could hear them crying." She gazed out desperately to the small home beside hers. "I was trying to go to them."

That was all Leila needed to hear. She left Isla and the woman behind and hastened into the small cottage. The putrid odor of sickness within was like a slap, even with the facecloth of herbs covering her nose. Two skinny children lay side-by-side on the cot, their hands clasped together. Their wails did not cease as she entered, but instead continued even as they stared up at her with large, dry eyes.

They were emaciated, filthy, and doubtless gone too long without water, if they were devoid of even tears. Leila rushed to them with her flagon of water. Fleas darted over the bedding, but she ignored them as she settled beside the children.

She called out to Isla and bent to offer the children water. They parted dry lips and drank with a thirst that hurt Leila's heart.

Isla appeared immediately and together they were able to get the woman, a widow named Rose, as well as the children to the large hut that had been erected to assist those who had fallen ill with the plague. It was a way of containing the illness, not that it had done much good. But also, a means of having all assembled to offer the most care.

While the swelling pestilence had some survivors, there was an alarming number of people who entered the structure and did not emerge alive. Rose, who had insisted walking herself, would doubtless be one of the survivors.

Once she and the children were tucked into pallets near one another within the pestilence hut, Leila and Isla returned to the village in search of more souls to aid. Every day it seemed there were more in need. As well as more stacks of dead.

An old woman scurried by them, her haste indicative of good health. "They're here," she hissed. "Hide yourselves."

Leila met Isla's eye, but the old healer merely shrugged with equal confusion. The villager stopped and glared irritably at them. "The reivers." And with that, she was gone.

A hot wind of anger blasted through Leila. In this time of death and suffering, when all were losing so many souls, the marauders still thought only to take what belonged to others. She handed her basket to Isla and slid a pair of daggers from her belt. This was why she wore trews instead of a kirtle when she attended the ill, and why she was never without her weapons.

Whoever sought to take advantage of those within the village would not leave unscathed.

NIALL DOUGLAS CURSED THE DAY THE KEEPER OF LIDDESDALE made him his deputy. Granted, it was a position Niall had coveted, but he hadn't thought his duties would someday include stomping through a pestilence-ridden village in search of a witch.

And it had been a witch responsible for the illness, of that Niall was certain. There was no better explanation for the disease that had ravaged the debatable lands. He brought only five men with him, men who joined him at the risk of death and disease solely because of his reputation.

The Lion. Fierce and brave, honest and loyal, all things Niall had spent his adult life working toward. And it had led him to this stinking lot of land outside the opulence of Werrick Castle. The massive structure stood safe behind its protective curtain wall where the English West March Border Warden lived without fear of death, with his witch of a daughter who nine years before had cursed the Armstrongs.

Niall put his arm to his nose to prevent the foul-smelling miasmas from transferring contagion to him. He had no dried herbs with him, or even a sponge of vinegar to protect himself from inhaling the illness. He would ensure he had at least that much next time. If there was a next time. If he survived this fool's errand for information.

He pushed his nose into the crook of his gambeson sleeve and breathed in the musty smells of worn leather and dirt. The five men following did likewise. Mayhap it would save them.

He stepped around a body with a painful looking lump thrusting out from the skin of their neck and shuddered. Mayhap it would not.

There was naught within the village but death. Prior to their arrival, he'd been so certain of his purpose, to seek out information on the dark-haired daughter of the Earl of Werrick. There would be many dark-haired lasses in the village. Most of them most likely either ill or dead.

"Water." A croaking voice pulled Niall's attention to an old man sagging on a bench, wavering forward.

Good sense told Niall to keep walking, but there was a deeper part of him, a thread of genuine kindness from his father that ran deeper through him and stilled his steps. He pulled the stopper of his flagon free. "'Tis ale."

The man's thin lips curled into a smile under the wispy strands of his beard. "All the better."

Niall handed the skin to the man who accepted it and downed the flagon in great gulping swallows. The villager sighed in satisfaction and held it out to Niall with a shaking hand.

"Ye can keep it." Niall stepped back from the flagon and the man, both likely contaminated with pestilence now. But he did not leave. Not when the villager might be good for information.

The five reivers with Niall held back, fear passing between them in side glances.

Niall wouldn't be cowed thus. Instead, he regarded the villager. "I hear ye had warning of the plague. Is it true?"

The man's gaze turned suspicious. "Ye want to steal our food stores?" He tightened his grasp on the ale.

Niall shook his head. "Nay, we've plenty of food. We're

searching for the reason why the pestilence has swept upon us." And they did have plenty of food. For the first time in decades, no one complained of an empty belly. There was more food than they could possibly consume, for there were too many people dying.

"Tell me about the warden's daughter," Niall said. "Yer lord."

The villager blinked slowly, as though on the edge of sleep. "He's got several daughters."

"Ye know which one I mean." Niall spoke loudly this time in an effort to wake the villager.

The man's eyes blinked open. "Lady Leila."

"The one with dark hair?"

The villager nodded slowly.

Leila. Such a benign name for one who had sent the pestilence streaming through Scotland. But Niall knew better than to trust benign.

"'Tis rumored that she warned the castle, as well as the rest of her family, of the pestilence before anyone fell ill," Niall said. "'Tis said she knew it all, for she brought it. Is she a witch?"

The man's mouth curled up in a smile, revealing yellow teeth. A low whimper sounded in his chest and grew into a chuckle.

Niall folded his arms over his chest. "Ye think I jest?"

The man tipped the flagon to his mouth and drained the ale as he slowly dipped to the side of the bench.

Niall took a cautious step back, lest the man fall forward and touch him. Something flew in front of Niall's face. Exactly where his head had been. It slammed into the wall at his right with a hollow thunk.

A dagger jutted from the white-washed surface. A *dagger*?

Niall darted behind a cottage and pulled his dagger free. His body acted before his mind fully wrapped around the idea that someone in this death-ridden village was healthy enough to fight them. He peered out in the direction the dagger had come from.

A tingle at the back of his neck alerted him to danger, and he jerked back as the next blade sailed past him.

He nodded to his men, motioning for them to go around the opposite side of the building. They would be a distraction while he moved closer. No villager would throw daggers at his head and live to laugh over it later.

He dashed forward, ducking behind buildings and abandoned carts as his men obeyed his orders. The clash of steel told him his men had arrived. No longer needing to mind his back, he ran toward the hut and charged toward the whoreson seeking to attack.

Except it was no bedraggled man fighting off all five of his warriors.

It was a woman.

A bonny woman at that, with streaming black hair and long, lean legs encased in red leather trews with a belt fastened over a loose leine. She kicked one of those lean legs high into the air and caught Argyle in the side of his head. The man dropped like a sack of grain.

"Enough." Niall spoke the word with booming authority.

Everyone went still. Or rather, his soldiers did. The woman spun around to face him, twin daggers gripped in her hands.

The fierce set to her face dissolved for a moment, letting him glimpse the softened expression beneath. Delicate muscles stood out at her neck and bright blue eyes widened.

"It's you," she whispered.

He lifted his eyebrow. While he wouldn't mind knowing the lass for a bit of bedsport, he'd never met her before.

He stepped closer and her face hardened.

"Be gone from here." There was a huskiness to her proper accent. English, of course.

"We're no' here for theft," he said.

Argyle rolled to his side on the ground and slowly staggered to standing.

She didn't bother looking at Niall's reiver. Instead she dragged her gaze over Niall as though sizing him up. "What are you here for?"

"To find the warden's daughter." He crossed his arms over his chest in an attempt to appear at ease.

The smirk of her rosy lips indicated she saw through the guise. "He has several." She stalked closer to Niall, those daggers poised in her hands. Several more lined her belt; perfect for throwing, no doubt. Her hips swayed in a decidedly female manner as she stepped one foot in front of the other in his direction.

His men tensed, but he shook his head. He would not be intimidated by this woman. "She is called Lady Leila." His gaze remained trained on her to see if she reacted to the name. Mayhap she knew her. Mayhap she *was* her.

After all, he'd heard the warden's daughters were skilled in weaponry. But would the warden really send her to the pestilence-ridden village? And with no guard?

If the woman recognized the name, she did not show it. She came to a stop and stared boldly at him. There was a sweet, fresh scent about her, like herbs. Sage and mint and lavender, mayhap. A kerchief was tied about her neck, no doubt filled with herbs, pulled down when she launched her attack. "Leave."

Niall squared his shoulders. "We want information."

"Are you not afraid?" She slid her daggers into her belt. "The contagion carries on the air. It's breathed in as an odor. Do you not smell it?"

Unbidden, Niall's thoughts wandered to the man he'd left on the bench. The villager had smelled terrible, of illness and rot.

"The man you spoke with is already dead." Her cold stare held his, ice-blue and veiled with thick, long black lashes, slightly tilted at the corners like a cat. "Do you know how the pestilence strikes?"

Niall held his ground, as any warrior worth his merit would.

"As it works its way into your humors, it will heat your blood and carry a fever." The woman tilted her head in a pitying manner. "'Tis quite uncomfortable. I wouldn't be surprised if you were already growing warm..."

Niall gritted his back teeth against her words. His body had begun to heat after speaking with the man. His pulse raced with intensity.

"Your heart will bang in your chest like a drum." She curled her hand into a small fist and bumped it over her own heart. "*Dum*," she intoned. "*Dum. Dum. Dum.*"

The pounding was in his head now, thrumming an unmistakable rhythm of fear.

"An aching head comes next." She kept her ice-blue stare on him and pressed her slender fingers to her temples. "Roaring in your ears until you can scarcely hear."

He said nothing as her husky voice wound around him like a spell, saying aloud every symptom as he felt them.

"If you leave, you might still be safe." She turned on her heel and Niall's men's eyes went wide. "Otherwise, you will all soon be dead. Go." She tossed a glance over her shoulder at Niall. "Now."

He jerked his head toward the direction they'd come from, and his men immediately scrambled to obey his silent order to retreat.

"How do ye know me?" Niall asked. The woman said nothing.

"Do I know ye?" he demanded.

She smirked at him. "Stay, then." She turned, putting her well-formed backside toward him, and strode casually away. "'Tis your death."

Damn her. And damn the whole bloody mission he'd had to accept in coming to the village.

He spat out a curse and went after his men. If they weren't on English soil right then, he would have hauled the woman off with him. For he knew without a shadow of a doubt in his mind that the woman was Lady Leila. Just as he knew with certainty that she was indeed a witch.

AUTHOR'S NOTE

Catriona's story presented me with a tricky scenario I didn't expect when I outlined the idea for this book: alcohol and pregnancy. Firstly, I'd like to clarify that the idea that no one drank water during the medieval days is a myth. People did drink water, though it was more common among the peasants than it was among those of wealth. Additionally, wine during the medieval days did not have the potency of the wine we drink today. My research indicates that not only did women drink wine during Cat's time, it was encouraged as a means of balancing the woman's humors and fortifying her body. Even juice was instructed to be diluted with wine for pregnant women as a means of minimizing the acidity. I guess they had heartburn woes then too – ladies, I feel ya!

The idea that alcohol was bad to drink during pregnancy was never a though that crossed anyone's mind. In fact, there was nothing even documented about the potential hazards until the late 19th century. Even then, it wasn't until the 1970's that serious research ensued. In the 1980's, the surgeon general put warnings on wine and that is when people really became aware of the true dangers of drinking while pregnant.

That said, it can sometimes be difficult to separate what we know in our modern world from what they did not know in the medieval world. I did not want to write Cat drinking wine, because the mother in me couldn't stop worrying about her baby. However, the historian in me could not simply have her not drinking wine when it would have been frankly odd for her to no longer drink it all of a sudden. In my research on drinks in the medieval days, I discovered that ale was consumed not only by men and woman, but also by children. And for breakfast no less! Ale then was not like you think of as ale today. In the medieval days, it was a nutritious drink that had similar ingredients to bread and had a light fermentation to it. Essentially, it was like drinking bread that sated hunger and thirst in one fell swoop. I can't attest for the taste, but accounts have indicated it was healthy and, well, a little gritty. As I did not want Cat to drink wine, I knew I could have her drink ale and not only keep with historical accuracy, but also be true to my mother's soul in having her consume something that would be healthy for her baby and not at all harmful.

Want to learn a little more about each of the characters and the history of the Borderland Ladies? I have a history of the Borderland Ladies, character bios and free short stories on the supporting characters on my website:

http://www.madelinemartin.com/borderland-ladies/

Outside of historical facts, there is something else I want to bring up in my author's note for Cat's story and that is her rape. What she experienced with Gawain has been happening to women since the dawn of time and continues to happen today. It is far too common for protests to be dissuaded, for hesitations to be worked around, for pushing when one should back down. And it's far too often that the victim accepts the blame.

Cat's story is a sensitive subject, I know. It is a painful one that can tear open scars. However, it was an important story for me to tell due to its poignancy. For every woman who has endured what Cat went through, who has had the blame pushed on her, who bore the burden of a guilt that should never have belonged to her, I want Cat's story to be a message. It doesn't matter how much you drank, it doesn't matter what you wore or what you said or where you went or any other blame that can be thrown at you. The only thing that matters is this: if you did not consent, it was not your fault.

Please note that if you need help or someone to talk to, you can get confidential support from the National Sexual Assault Hotline website https://www.rainn.org/about-national-sexual-assault-telephone-hotline or by calling 800.656.HOPE (4673)

ACKNOWLEDGMENTS

Thank you to my amazing beta readers who helped make this story so much more with their wonderful suggestions: Kacy Stanfield, Monika Page, Janet Barrett, Tracy Emro and Lorrie Cline. You ladies are so amazing and make my books just shine!

Thank you to Janet Kazmirski for the final read-through you always do for me and for catching all the little last minute tweaks.

Thank you to John Somar and my wonderful minions for all the support they give me.

Thank you to Erica Monroe who saves my life time after time for doing an amazing job with edits and is always there for whatever I need. I swear, you add more years back onto my life with all the help and laughter you bring me. And thank you to Teresa Sprecklemeyer (the Midnight Muse) for her incredible work on creating all these gorgeous covers for my Borderland Ladies series.

And a huge thank you so much to my readers for always being so fantastically supportive and eager for my next book.

ABOUT THE AUTHOR

Madeline Martin is a USA TODAY Bestselling author of Scottish set historical romance novels filled with twists and turns, adventure, steamy romance, empowered heroines and the men who are strong enough to love them.

She lives a glitter-filled life in Jacksonville, Florida with her two daughters (known collectively as the minions) and a man so wonderful he's been dubbed Mr. Awesome. She loves Disney, Nutella, wine and could easily lose hours watching cat videos.

Find out more about Madeline at her website:

http://www.madelinemartin.com

facebook.com/MadelineMartinAuthor
twitter.com/MadelineMMartin
instagram.com/madelinemmartin
bookbub.com/profile/madeline-martin

ALSO BY MADELINE MARTIN

BORDERLAND LADIES

Marin's Promise

Anice's Bargain

Ella's Desire

Catriona's Secret

Leila's Legacy

HIGHLAND PASSIONS

A Ghostly Tale of Forbidden Love

The Madam's Highlander

The Highlander's Untamed Lady

Her Highland Destiny

Highland Passions Box Set Volume 1

HEART OF THE HIGHLANDS

Deception of a Highlander

Possession of a Highlander

Enchantment of a Highlander

THE MERCENARY MAIDENS

Highland Spy

Highland Ruse

Highland Wrath

REGENCY NOVELLAS

Earl of Benton
Earl of Oakhurst
Mesmerizing the Marquis

Printed in Poland
by Amazon Fulfillment
Poland Sp. z o.o., Wrocław